Gaelian felt herself e...
delicate merging of r... power. She felt the
air currents under her wings, knew the pressure of
the updrafts carrying her far from the ground. She
pointed her nose upward, driving for the colder,
thinner air.

And then she felt it. It started as a quaver in the
wings, an uncertainty in the fuselage. A hint of a
question mark, no more. She pulled hard around,
felt the entire craft resist and groan. The turn had
been too hard, nose down, and the spin came, spin
and spiral high above the world, and the darkness
began to form behind her eyes.

Ace Books by S. N. Lewitt

S.N. LEWITT

ANGEL AT APOGEE

ACE BOOKS, NEW YORK

For J.M.I.,
who always believed

ANGEL AT APOGEE

An Ace Book / published by arrangement with
the author

PRINTING HISTORY
Berkley edition / March 1987
Ace edition / July 1991

ISBN: 0-441-02279-0

10 9 8 7 6 5 4 3 2 1

IF SHE PUSHED the jitter any faster, the g-force would kill her, Gaelian knew. She tried to focus on the numbers that flashed across her screen, ignoring the familiar darkening of her vision. Close, very close to the line, and pull. The little Macama fighter responded with the speed of thought, sweeping out of the antilaser spin and whipping back to scissor against the pirates with lethal accuracy.

Pirates of the Adedri system usually had no more than ancient lasers and class-four scan. She held her breath and eased the tiny fighter carefully behind the large, atmosphere-capable Adedri ship, praying that the Macama's experimental ion shielding worked. They would never look for her here.

The pirates banked abruptly and began to dive, aiming for the red-pink-green planet that filled her screen. For less than half a moment, she knew terror. The Macama had no atmospheric capability. She could outrun them, but they were closing quickly to the haven of ionosphere.

Time expanded. She touched the firing key with great deliberation.

"Gaelian YnTourne, get out of there. We're due to report for the game in twenty minutes."

Sighing softly, Gaelian touched the panel behind her head. As the lights came on around her, the Macama and the pirates resolved into the familiar Academy sim-range. It had been good of Iesin to call down here and remind her of the time. Reluctantly, she rose from the simulation couch and queried

the main test for the results. Her score, flickering yellow on
black glass for nearly a full second before dissolving, made her
smile. The reputation of the Angel was safe.

No one was killed in nerris anymore. They were civilized
now: the barbed edge of the nerris stick would draw blood and
maybe scar, but no one died. It was only sport. Failure alone
was distressing enough in the test of speed, strategy, and
ruthlessness that nerris had been—that nerris still was.

The field filled with midshipmen in precise ranks. Gaelian
listened for the commands shouted down from company to
company with only half her mind. She repeated an order, and
her company turned to salute the Academy stands as her eyes
flickered over the crowd. In the center of the dramatic curve
of glistening white steel, her family sat with the rest of the nobility. That was reason enough not to have come. On top of
that, her fiancé was the star of the Academy team, and she had
seen Teazerin play. She hated to watch him, unscarred, domi-
nating the court with his cold smile. There was nerris candidate in him still, the old kind, the kind that had been outlawed
six hundred years ago.

She almost missed the barking voice of the commander of
the corps of midshipmen dismissing them to the stands to
watch the game.

There were traditions about nerris, older than any records
of the game. Gealian found her place in the stands, one of the
better spots in the midshipmen's section, and sat gratefully
next to her roommate, Iesin YnOestal. She was just in time to
see the four ultralight, superstrong walls of the court erected.
The clear plastic was tinted in the four colors, and the stands
were high enough to enable the spectators to see over the
three-meter structure into the square enclosure. The four
four-man teams entered, their faces painted with narrow
bands of the nerris colors, wearing shorts that matched the
wall they were defending. Navy was playing in blue today, and
despite the painted stripes, Teazerin's unmarked body was
easy to spot.

Even at her nerris test at age sixteen, she and her opponents
bore sharp-end scars. She shivered in the warm stands, remembering that particular rite of passage, essential for accep-
tance among the Ot-tan. She had defended a wall alone
against three competitors of her choice. One had been Iesin,

who had passed her nerris test only weeks before but held her skill in check. The other two were her father and one of his classmates. The Board had accepted her victory, and she had been named eldest of the eldest of the household, a throwback to the days when people died playing nerris and the Ot-tan were the priests of the courts.

The brilliant white ball was thrown into the court, and Teazerin leapt gracefully, swinging the blunt end of the long nerris stick at the ball, trying for a score and rebound on the red wall. A player in red speared the ball onto the pointed end of the stick and flung it to score against yellow plastic. The wall flickered as the point was made and recorded as a negative in the yellow quadrant.

A player in black had the ball now, batting the rebound with the blunt end of the stick to a teammate across the court. They were trying to score against Navy, Gaelian saw. Teazerin moved. Twirling the stick in an elegant parabola, he brought the barb against the shoulder of the black player who had made the pass. A brilliant stream of crimson showed against the pale skin—first blood had been drawn. Negative points were recorded in the depths of the black wall as the Navy bleachers rose in a cheer.

Blue had wrestled the ball from yellow to score once against the red wall and wound one of the red players for a total of six points. Now the game was becoming exciting. Another black player was eliminated, and it seemed that the game was really between blue and yellow. The walls were glittering with negative points now. Only the blue wall was still quiescent.

The ball was moving quickly, a white speck creating monochromatic fireworks inside the court's scoring mechanism. The last black player had left the court limping from a thrust in the thigh, and the glittering wall went opaque.

Gaelian looked away from the game. Homecoming games were stupid. She might admire Teazerin's ability, but it didn't mean that she wanted to watch. Even with her family there, she could have made up some excuse. Exams were useful, and there were always exams firstie year. Even Dobrin, her cousin, could understand that. But somewhere in the maze of uniforms in the stands was Golran Vontreidi, and she wanted to talk to him before he shipped out to Adedri. His presence was the only reason she had stayed for the game, for the inevitable encounter with the YnTourne family. He would be sitting

down and over to the side with the lesser nobility who were recent graduates. There was no place for commoners here, and
Golran was one of the very few in the officer corps. Not
merely an officer, she thought, but a pilot. Unconsciously, she
fingered the twin starbursts neatly clipped to either side of the
collar of her own uniform jacket. She scanned the crowd
again, but she couldn't spot Vontreidi.

Not so her family. Right down there in the best seats, with
the Ot-tan class, the nerris-tested, they all sat together. Her
father's face was veined and red, and she knew it was from
drink, not from sun. She didn't know how much he drank,
and she didn't want to. He'd collapsed twice in the past year,
and there were rumors throughout the Ot-tan households.
Her grandmother, the head of the YnTourne household, sat
stiff-backed with all her attention focused on the game, ignoring Gaelian's father. As she watched her grandmother,
another face turned around in the box and met her eyes. It was
her cousin Dobrin, and the look on his face made her shudder.
It was the same expression he had worn when she was newly
arrived in the household and he had caught her breaking one
of her grandmother's rules yet again. Then the expression
changed, as it had then when he had decided whether to tell
their grandmother or to use the knowledge for personal lev-
erage.

Dobrin wore the copper uniform of Admiralty, but without
the starburst marks of a pilot. She made herself meet his gaze
steadily. As usual, it took more effort than she liked to admit.

Iesin nudged her. "Look, you don't have to go with them.
My parents invited both of us to dinner tonight."

Gaelian smiled warmly. She was glad of the invitation, glad
that her firstie privilege of a night's liberty was not going to
be wasted. And it would be fun to be with the YnOestal clan.
Ever since she and Iesin had been roommates that first year in
normal school, the YnOestals had stood firm guard between
her and her family. She would have gone over to them after
the game in any case.

Suddenly Gaelian was swept to her feet in a massive cheer.
The red wall had gone opaque, and there were only three of
the original sixteen players left, two blue and one yellow. One
of the Navy players batted the ball against the red wall, using
an upward spin to propel it against the gentle curve along the
top of the walls. The yellow player went after him, not the

ball, with the barbed end of the stick. Teazerin and the yellow player both struck at the same time, the ball forgotten on the now opaque yellow wall.

Teazerin stood alone in the middle of the court without a single mark on him. He'd won again. He held his stick at his side and bowed properly to all four quarters, a grim, tight smile on his face.

As she joined in the nerris anthem, Gaelian tried to look at Teazerin objectively to find the reason she didn't like him. He was tall and well built, with the regular features of the Ottan class, and he was the nerris star of the Academy.

She felt for her starbursts again, fastened securely to her collar. Her pilot's stars had been awarded just before summer leave, an honor only a tenth or fewer of the midshipmen earned. Teazerin wasn't a pilot, hadn't made the cut; and maybe that was it. Her family was Navy enough to know that it was an insult to betroth her to a nonflier, a washout.

The victory ritual over, the great amorphous crowd began to move. Gaelian searched in earnest now, trying to pick out one face from the mob. A single person, the reason she had come today when she didn't want to face her family or to watch the rituals of Dinoreos acted out as they had been for generations. She studied each officer who passed, watching for the glints that proclaimed pilots.

"You're not going to find him in this crowd," Iesin said. "Come over and talk to my folks. You know they'd take you in a minute. And we're going to that great new place that's almost off limits, only with my brothers along there shouldn't be any trouble."

Gaelian nodded and let herself be dragged off. Perhaps he wasn't here, although the message had said differently. And she needed to talk to someone, to him, about graduation and assignment and Teazerin.

Suddenly, as she walked down the steel-lattice steps to the main gate, she caught a flash of stars on russet with an ensign's bars. There was no mistaking him in the bright sun, the proud stance, and the hair the color of his jacket that marked him a commoner.

"Dammit, Gae, this isn't the time for you to be running off to talk to some commoner you haven't seen in two years," Iesin fumed.

Ignoring her, Gaelian turned and pushed her way through

the mob to the refreshment stand where Golran waited, a pack of dried glucose bars in his hand.

He offered one to Gaelian before he began speaking. "Look, I'm shipping out to Adedri in a couple of weeks. It's one thing now, but I'm not sure about sending messages from there. The passwords aren't completely secure, and the lines are pretty open."

Gaelian laughed. "You mean you're worried about compromising yourself, not me," she retorted. From the shadow that passed over his face, she knew she was right. She shrugged, trying to keep the anger out of her voice. "Well, there isn't any chance of your having any problems on account of me, anyway. At least, not if anyone knows the truth."

"I already have enough to handle with the Ot-tan, without having any rumors about our friendship. They already think I'm trying too hard to make inroads."

"And you aren't?" Gaelian taunted him. He was. She knew it, but not with her. The Ot-tan was too far above his reach, as he had told her on more than one occasion. And Golran Vontreidi wasn't about to ruin his chances.

"Look," he said again, exasperation creeping into his voice. "The Altneri are considering me quite seriously, and I don't want to blow my chances. And I don't really think you want to blow them, either. We've been friends, Gaelian. Let's part that way."

She nodded to him curtly and swallowed her disappointment. Golran looked relieved, and she was glad at least for that. The Altneri were of the most minor noble class, but they were a nerris family. If they accepted Golran, he would have far higher hopes for his career than ending up a midlevel officer on some backwater base. He was too good a flier for that to be allowed to happen.

On the other hand, he must know what it would mean to her. He was registered as were all adults who had passed the candidacy test. On the records, Golran Vontreidi was registered as a client to the YnTourne household under the following of the eldest of the eldest. Clients gave a household additional power with the Board, and members within a single household were ranked in part by the number of clients they could attract.

"Last of sixteen," she said carefully. It was a nerris wish, from the time when the game was still a test, a luck wish used only by the nobility. But that was what Golran aspired to. Marrying into the Altneri would assure him of that.

He turned away, and Gaelian watched as he melted into the crowd. Fury rose in her, which she pushed down, fury at Golran's pride that made the Altneri marriage more important to him than her friendship, than herself. The sun blazed across the white cement of the apron surrounding the stadium, and Gaelian squeezed her eyes shut against the glare, against her tears. Then she made her way over the landing circle reserved for the Ot-tan, hoping that Iesin had waited.

The Ot-tan aircars rested together nearer the entrance than the other vehicles and were protectively cordoned. She submitted gracefully to the retinal scan and the slightly suspicious scowls of the occupants of the nearest car. Gaelian hoped to find Iesin before her family found her, but the area was almost as crowded as the stadium had been, with people meandering gracefully from car to car sharing iced drinks and greetings. Outside of Board meetings and homecoming games, it was rare for so many of the Ot-tan of all generations to gather. The opportunity for gossip, and a little informal business, was too good to pass up. Still searching for Iesin, Gaelian noticed a tall midshipman with unusually pale hair standing over a pale silver-blue aircar and ducked out of his line of sight. Even without seeing his features, she could recognize Teazerin YnSetti and had no wish to be forced to congratulate him on today's game.

"So you finally found time for us," a silky voice came from behind her. She whirled around and found herself face to face with Dobrin. "Your little tête-à-tête with that commoner kept you awhile. Grandmother has been worried."

"Pilot talk," she replied evenly. Dobrin coughed politely, and Gaelian resisted the urge to sneer. He reached out and fingered the starbursts on her collar, and she wanted to slap his hand away. She *was* senior to him in the household, even if he were older and ranked her in the service. But she dared not. His liberty could be interpreted in several ways; her reaction could carry only one meaning. That would be poor strategy.

"Maybe if flying is so very important to you, you might like to relieve yourself of less interesting duties. In the household, of course."

"I'm sure Grandmother would be very disappointed," Gaelian replied. "And while we all adore nerris, I'm sure a family competition would be very difficult to fit into her schedule."

Dobrin chuckled almost pleasantly. "Come, cousin, we're civilized folk. Do you really think your father could stand up to a real competition?"

Gaelian cursed herself by all of Anoni's hells. She had been stupid to open the subject. Dobrin could outdo her in ruthlessness, but they were evenly matched in wits, and she had speed on him. She should have known he would find some way out, and she had just about run out of options.

"Actually, I had wanted to speak to you privately about a matter that concerns all of us," Dobrin continued, his face no longer mocking. "Grandmother is ill. And they don't think they can do anything this time."

"What do you mean?" Gaelian demanded.

"I mean she won't sign the release," Dobrin said.

Gaelian gasped and nodded sharply. She understood only too well. No matter what techniques the hospital had available, if there was no release then the doctors could do nothing. And it would be perfectly like Grandmother to die just to spite them all because she couldn't stand her son or his heir, or maybe out of pique at the Board.

"She's used this one before," Gaelian said slowly. "Is it to stop my father from drinking, or is it because of something in the company? I mean, it's possible that she'll come around. She did last time."

Last time had been close. She had refused the transplant until the doctors thought that the heart tissue was too stressed to enable adequate replication. Of course, once the Board had agreed to lift the ban on mineral exploration, it was discovered that the RNA hadn't deteriorated at all.

It occurred to her that Dobrin must have some reason of his own for telling her. After all, he had been groomed to take over as head of the household, and the company, at her grandmother's death. That had been superseded when Renan, Gaelian's father, had turned up alive and with a child after eight years out of contact on a primitive world. He had been presumed dead, even legally delcared such. His return had been a blow to Dobrin, one that he tried to swallow gracefully. It wasn't easy, and Dobrin had never quite forgiven her for it.

Gaelian had no doubt that when the time came he would do whatever he could to block her appointment as the head of the company as well as the household. The YnTourne were too important, carried too much weight in the Protectorate and the Admiralty to be headed by someone about whom there were suspicions. Dobrin allowed those suspicions; and for the same reason, he remained in the Navy, despite his other interests.

Dobrin was not really suited to the military, Gaelian thought. He was too much the typical Li-tan administrator, of a class only one rank lower than the Ot-tan. His father had been Li-tan, she remembered, and so it was necessary that he follow every tradition and meet every expectation anyone ever had for the head of an Ot-tan household. The Academy and at least some hint of a Naval career before taking over famiy interests was almost required for anyone with Dobrin's ambitions.

For a moment, it occurred to her to feel a little sorry for him. Dobrin had played the game with every angle and every move he had ever learned, but he had never cheated. And it must have been difficult to remain in the Admiralty when he had no particular gift for Naval affairs. Perhaps, she mused, it felt to him as it would feel to her if anyone ever threatened to keep her from flying.

"Shall we consider the second test?" he asked softly.

Gaelian shrugged. Consider didn't mean play. Nerris was only the first of the tests, the second was clients. And with Golran gone, she realized, she had just lost one of her strongest claims. Which was why Golran was gone. He couldn't afford to be a YnTourne client and aspire to the Altneri marriage at the same time.

"I think we'd better concern ourselves with Grandmother first. Find out what she wants before we do anything, don't you think?"

Dobrin smiled thinly as they walked over to the YnTourne aircar. "I may not tell anyone about you and that commoner," he said carefully, "but I think you should know that the Board will never permit you to be named eldest if you persist in running around with the likes of him."

"Client business," Gaelian said abruptly.

"I hope so," Dobrin replied. "You get very close to the edge too often, Gae. I can't say that I'd mind terribly if the

Board found me more acceptable to be the Head of the household than you. I'm happy to admit it. But Renan's drinking and Grandmother's illnesses are starting to make the Board wonder if we're all unstable. There's been talk in the Admiralty that several of the new contracts should be awarded . . . elsewhere." He turned to face her, leaning lightly against the glistening hull of the car. "I will take YnTourne if I can. But when I do, I want there to be something to take, Gaelian. Ottan, Li-tan, Sonna-tan—we've all been bred and tested since the beginning. Who knows what or who people like that Vontreidi are? You'd better go in and behave."

Gaelian shook her head and gently fingered the lock panel. There was nothing she could say to Dobrin, not when he was right. The ruling classes of Dinoreos had bred true, displaying the traits that had gained them mastery over the entire Protectorate. She clenched her teeth and entered the dark interior of the family car.

Her grandmother and father were already inside, resting on the luxurious foam couches that only the rich could afford. The interior of the car was small but built to maximize space, the deep couches low to the floor and the interior lined with dark mylar.

"Grandmother," Gaelian said formally.

Her grandmother didn't spare her a glance. The woman didn't look at all old, barely half the hundred and twenty she admitted to. Her back was rigid and her cheeks faintly flushed, healthy looking, Gaelian decided. Whatever it was this time, her grandmother wasn't ready yet to make any demands.

Gaelian glanced at her father, who blinked at her groggily. He couldn't speak until the head of the household acknowledged her, and from what Gaelian could see, that wasn't going to happen today. Typical. Besides, it would be just as well not to have to listen to his drunken muddling. She could see the red, broken capillaries in his face reflected in the curved mylar walls, the almost-gesture of a hand that he was too weak to complete.

"My respects to the household," Gaelian said before she stepped back out onto the blazing apron. She stood aside and watched the car lift gently, frustrated and relieved at the same time.

It was only a test, she reminded herself. She was eldest of

the eldest, heir to the household and the company share, but there was more than one test she would have to pass before the Board would confirm her position. Perhaps it was only luck that her father had been confirmed before he left on the survey to Cahaute. Once confirmation came it was never withdrawn, not in the history of the Protectorate. The Board did not make mistakes. The tests were always valid.

She watched the steel-colored car veer off twenty degrees north and cleared the remaining anger from her mind. Tests. They were all there for her benefit, no doubt. It was only to be expected. Anger was her enemy, she told herself. Her grandmother had warned her more than once that she let anger get in her way, making her primitive, not permitting her to think with the clear, necessary ruthlessness that was required of the Ot-tan. When emotion did not choke her, Gaelian knew she excelled in the long-range strategic planning, the balancing of subtle and bold moves, and the technical expertise that had kept them the ruling class for all the history of Dinoreos.

She forced the anger from her thoughts and pivoted quickly, searching again for the YnOestal clan. Their car was somewhere around and should be easy to spot now that most had left. She focused on the pleasure of seeing Iesin's family and enjoying her night's liberty. Firstie privileges were not something she was going to give up.

The YnOestal airboat was larger than any of the other vehicles in the Ot-tan enclosure, and she recognized it by the screaming green paint job. It had been red last time, and a hideous purple before that, but it was always the brightest thing on any lot.

"Gaelian, we've been waiting forever!" Iesin called out. She was perched on the low rail, obviously searching. Other members of the clan were scattered around talking to friends, and friends of friends, and others who perhaps knew somebody who knew somebody. They were always picking up people. Iesin's four Navy brothers were there in uniform, and Gaelian saluted gaily as she approached.

"You're the last we've been waiting for. Everyone else has been here for hours," Iesin said, shoving her into the large vehicle.

Someone started singing "Play for Victory," and they all joined in in at least three different keys while the youngest daughter of the household giggled and punched out the lift

commands from her father's lap. The car jolted up, lurched to
one side, and rolled three passengers from their seats before
Iesin's father got control of the console. Righted and in the
hands of an adult, they drifted smoothly in the upper lanes
away from the stadium and headed toward the city.

"Isn't Tarris a little young to be driving?" one of the
bounced-around friends asked.

"How else is she going to learn?" one of the YnOestals
answered without evident concern.

The commercial district was a maze of light and girders,
bleached whites and greys merging on the clean-lined structures to tease the eye with jagged patterns that were almost
imperceptible. They landed on the roof of a building that
boasted thrusting blanched stone tossed at precarious angles,
beautiful and threatening, which made Gaelian think of a pile
of bones and teeth. An autovalet took the car, and they were
ushered into a private room by a human attendant.

The place was Ot-tan territory clearly. Human servitors led
them through discreet, dark mylar-lined corridors to an enclave of tasteful elegance. Two walls were rough-textured concrete poured around natural stone set in rondelle patterns,
while the other two were dull brushed brass. They settled in
around the antique, dark wood table, which had been polished
to reflect as clearly as the mylar in the halls. The YnOestal
might sometimes act a little rowdy, be a little free among
friends, but they had taste.

She found herself seated at the end of the table next to Iesin,
who couldn't help being inquisitive.

"What did Golran want with you, Gae?" she asked. "And
Dobrin? You spent a long time paying your respects. I could
never understand why you like the company of a commoner so
much. I mean, I know Golran is talented, and it's good that
people like him are being used to their capacities, but I really
never did understand what you had to talk about off duty."

Gaelian smiled. "Pilot stuff, mostly. Equipment, flying,
you know."

Iesin shook her head. "You know, Gae, you can get really
boring sometimes. Did it ever occur to you that there are
people who couldn't care less about any of your infernal machines? You should cultivate something else to talk about.
And aren't there enough of your cohorts in our class, anyway?"

One of Iesin's middle brothers shot Iesin a freezing look. "You aren't eldest of the eldest," he reminded her curtly.

Gaelian relaxed. Iesin might not understand that even with the class barrier, she had something in common with Golran. But Iesin did know that the heir to a household was responsible for client support. Not that she had any clients, she reflected bitterly, not with Golran cutting all communication.

"I see," Iesin said carefully. "But you do have a pretty good following among the younger fliers around the Academy. And that's pure ability, not because you've gone out and made any deals. It'll count in your favor, more than some of the followings other eldest of eldests have built. Besides, what's up with Dobrin? He's a worm."

Gaelian had to smile. "How did you know we were talking?"

"I have my sources," Iesin muttered. Suddenly, exasperation came into her expression. "Honestly, Gae, I don't know why you let him bother you. You passed nerris when you were sixteen. Okay, it wasn't a brilliant game, but you passed. And you've got a real following with the younger fliers and with the Serians, and they count more than lower nobles or commoners. Hells, even I'm registered, and I count for a good two or three, don't you think?"

"Four at least," Gaelian replied, surprised. She had thought that Iesin would of course register in her own family's following. But then, the YnOestal were so overrun that maybe Iesin wasn't needed, and it would be like that clan to support her. The YnOestal eldest of eldest and Dobrin hated each other.

"So far as I can figure, if you don't go and lose your temper, you've got it all over Dobrin. There's nothing to worry about, and he isn't stupid enough to challenge you. Unless there's something I don't know," she added archly.

Gaelian tried to smile. There was very, very little that Iesin didn't know. She seemed to catch information out of the air. It wouldn't surprise her in the least if Iesin knew more about her grandmother's illness and refusal to be treated than Gaelian herself did. Just to test Iesin, she mentioned only the barest facts.

Iesin tried not to laugh. "How many times has she played out that one?" Iesin said. "And they can hold off a bone marrow transplant right up to the zero point, so there isn't any

real risk. I don't know what your grandmother wants, but
Dobrin is trying to push you into playing for position pre-
maturely.''

"I know," Gaelian agreed. "The problem is, he's suc-
ceeding.''

"Only if you let him," Iesin replied firmly. "Personally, I'd
enjoy the game. I don't see why it bothers you so much."

Several large platters of food arrived then, thin-sliced meats
marinated in spices and tart yellow fruit imported from Adedri. As they turned to enjoy the repast, Gaelian thought about
what Iesin had said. It was true, it was only another game. It
shouldn't bother her at all; she should even enjoy her advantages. Only there were things that Iesin, for all her sources,
still didn't know.

"You challenged him in nerris, didn't you?" Iesin asked
when she had swallowed the last of her first course.

Gaelian nodded, still trying to taste the subtle spicing and
relish a dinner far better than the usual Academy fare.

"Then you're going to have to use it to cover yourself. He
made you mad, and you pushed back. You know, Gae, if you
lose on anything, it's going to be your temper. I just don't
know why you let him worry you so much. It isn't like there's
anything there that's different from any other household."

"Let's enjoy being out while we can, all right?" she
pleaded. "I don't want to think about Dobrin or my grandmother or the family at all, and I don't want to miss the next
course because we're too busy to taste it."

Iesin smiled broadly, and they started in on a delicate cream
soup. Gaelian tried to concentrate on the conversation, as it
replayed the day's competition against other games, past and
possible. She drank the wine, sparkling pale green with the
second course, rich purple with the stuffed roast, and dry
ivory with the salad. She complimented the food lavishly,
which was no more than it deserved, listened to Iesin's brothers' astute comments about judging wine properly, followed
them all solemnly, and then forgot them.

Soon they were being crammed back into the car again and
dropped off at the front gates of the Academy. Even firsties
couldn't be chauffeured up to the front door.

Giggling from too much wine, they entered Phkaiden Hall,
the firstie dorm. Their voices echoed off the brushed-steel
walls, and in the greenish half-light suited to the hour the

shadows took on personalities. Or maybe it was only the quantity of wine they had consumed. Down the sweeping central arcade, they saw no one. It was a liberty night. Most firsties in would be those who were in danger of failing or those on punishment detail. It seemed unnaturally quiet without the underhum of escalators and seeker-speakers.

It was Iesin who noticed it first, the heavy, silent reverberations of marching. They vibrated through the decorative girders and into the slab concrete floor and up through the vault of the formal central hallway.

"Wait," Iesin said groggily. "I thought they discontinued midnight diaper drills years ago." She glanced up at the shimmering red chrono over the door.

"Uh huh," Gaelian agreed. She remembered those nights of their first year, the company lieutenant taking them out on the roof to practice marching. But it had been ordered stopped two years ago when the mess hall roof was being repaired. Too many rooftop drills, the Commandant had said. Since then, no one had resumed the midnight rooftop marches.

Gaelian stiffened, and they moved silently down the corridor and up the unmoving escalator that brought them to the great formal observation terrace. Here, two stories up, they had a panoramic view of the entire center hallway they had just crossed, designed for the reception of important dignitaries and parents on graduation day and for the presentation of the new pilots at the Starburst Ceremony. From the terrace to the ceiling high above soared a magnificent mural of chrome, steel, and brass wire inlaid in the rippling black and grey plexiglas depicting the starburst. Carefully concealed in the mural wall were sliding doors leading out onto the mess hall roof.

Here the sound of the marching was clearer. Memories of her first months at the Academy engulfed Gaelian, the six dorms of the six years arranged in a rectangle to make a courtyard two stories high. She remembered the cold night and the steady beat around the perimeter of that courtyard, the bottom of which was the mess hall roof. Through her tipsy haze, she could almost hear the orders echoing from all four sides of the plexi and concrete enclosure. It was something like a nerris court, she had thought then, but over the years the effect lessened. Certainly it impressed the visitors who watched the corps of midshipmen assemble before lunch from these doors.

"I can't think of any reason for it," Iesin said foggily. "I would have heard something. I always hear something."

Gaelian edged up against the door and began to pull it open very slowly, silently thanking any entity she could think of and a few she couldn't that the sliprod was well lubricated. When she had nudged the door open just barely a centimeter, both young women pressed their eyes to the crack.

. Out on the low roof, four full companies were formed, but the uniforms weren't those of the undistinguished diaper class. Pilots' starbursts glittered from the collars of several of those assembled in the ranks, clear in the brilliant illumination of the net that had been turned on for the display. From this distance, they couldn't really make out any faces, but they could hear perfectly well, what little there was to hear. While the high hard walls echoed with even the slightest sound, this was the silent drill.

No orders were shouted, though the ranks moved in perfect unity. Not just feet and arms, but heads, eyes all focused on the same point. It looked like an army of robots, mechanical, uncommunicating, forming and reforming in a series of complex patterns. The walls glittered ash-white in the harsh netlight. Then the companies wheeled, broke, lined, and re-formed precisely in the center of the area, and still without a whisper, they stopped and froze at attention.

Far out across the marching roof, all the way down by the diaper dorm, Gaelian could see the glittering collar bars of a midshipman captain.

"Honor court," Iesin whispered.

Gaelian blanched. Either of them could have easily been members of the court, they both knew. They had been approached in the traditional method by that shadowy organization and had declined. It was a power that Gaelian didn't want and Iesin didn't need, a power recognized from the time when nerris still meant death. The honor court was too silent for their preference, too unknown, keeping its own law. No one knew who the members were. They were never identified, even years after graduation. They had the right to punish or expel and were beholden to none. There were rumors that there was an officer advisor, once a member of the court himself, but those who knew weren't talking.

"Deception and dishonor to the corps," they heard a voice say to a midshipman who stood in front of the assembly.

"Who is it?" Gaelian asked, all trace of her earlier inebriation wiped away.

Iesin shot her a look that meant keep quiet. Already they were in violation of the honor code for witnessing this event. There was a perfectly good precedent that, if found, they could both be expelled simply for watching.

Out on the rooftop, the voice continued. "When the word of an officer is no longer sacred, the honor of all Dinoreos is denied. You claim Ot-tan status, yet it has been satisfactorily proved that your father was a commoner. Do you deny this now, in front of the sacred four of companies?"

The midshipman remained silent.

"You will not speak for yourself. Will anyone speak for you?"

Again silence thundered through the assembly, the hushed waiting silence that denotes some occasion, a moment of great importance.

A gesture. In the glare, two midshipmen lieutenants stepped forward, and even from this distance with his back to her, Gaelian recognized Teazerin YnSetti. He turned to face the still nameless accused, and the light glinted off his hard smile that was not a smile. Across his face still were painted the nerris-bands, yellow, red, black, blue, neat and precise. She remembered the first time they had been painted on her own face, the time that her grandmother had been forced to acknowledge her on the nerris court. On Teazerin, in this strange light, they glittered like the ancient god-masks on display at the National History Museum.

The two lieutenants moved rapidly, each ripping something from a side of the accused's uniform, and then Gaelian saw what they were. Pilot starbursts. Whoever was being disciplined by the honor court was a flier. It didn't matter that he may well have done what he was accused of doing, or even that she might barely know him. He was a pilot, one of her people, and these nonfliers were judging him. They had taken his starbursts.

They stripped off his jacket, leaving him in the plain white jumpsuit that constituted the basic uniform garment. Teazerin dropped the jacket in a heap in front of the captain.

"We do not dispute blood," the captain said. "It is concealment we abhor. Anyone who has counterinformation and is withholding it is as guilty as you who stand accused. Under penalty of expulsion, I order anyone who can clear this person to come forward and speak."

No one came forward. Yet even in the pain of that silence, he did not flinch. Somehow Gaelian was proud.

"Be gone by sunrise," the voice said, and the lights were doused suddenly.

Gaelian was trembling and cold as Iesin dragged her back to their room. She couldn't have moved under her own power, not after that grotesque scene. The silence of the ancient drill and the traditions of the honor court, the traditions of nerris, prevented it. Finality resounded in the slab floor as the four companies marched in the dark into the dorms again. Iesin barely got her out of the central hall before the first member of the honor court arrived.

When they returned to the room Iesin flung her a wash-cloth. "Colors, Gae, you're whiter than stone. Here, wash up, get into your nights. Move."

Gaelian did as she was told, moving like an automaton. Iesin guided her down to the washroom and back again, for once saying nothing about the fuzzy yellow nonregulation slippers that Gaelian used whenever she could.

"Who was it?" Gaelian whispered. "Why? I mean, I know the rules, but so quietly in the night like that. When almost everyone would be gone. It's terrible. And why didn't anyone say anything?"

"I don't know, Gae, really I don't. I mean, you know how the honor court is. Try to get some sleep. We'll hear in the morning, and I for one really need a few hours of sleep."

2

SHE KNEW IT was a dream, the same dream again. Cahaute, she was back on the planet Cahaute where she had been born. Most of the time she managed to forget it, but she couldn't run from the dream of the dark night with the bonfire. There was the smell, the smell of the bonfire with the corpses piled high, and she was so tiny then. Don't cry. She saw a hand in the pile, in the flames, and felt a sickness in her stomach. A great white beast came to her, something she remembered was called a nistora, and it dissolved leaving a necklace. Mother, Mother. . . . There was a hand on her shoulder and soft eyes that looked at her. Her friend, the boy who had made the necklace, had come. She knew he was her friend, but he frightened her. If they found out, it was all over. She awakened herself with a muffled cry.

It was still dark out, but after this dream there would be no more sleep. The wicked red light of the chrono blinked out oh three-thirty from the corner of her screen. How many nights had she lain and watched the red numbers flicker one after the other? Iesin said she should turn it off, but Gaelian liked having it there watching, ready and reassuring, whenever she chanced to open her eyes.

She had thought she was rid of the nightmare, hadn't had one for almost a year, but the strange ceremony on the rooftop mixed with too much to drink had brought it back. They'd find her, Gaelian knew. One day they would find out. It couldn't be kept secret forever.

She groaned and turned, pretending to herself that she would sleep, but knew it was a useless gesture. Iesin was still sleeping, Gaelian knew from her steady breathing. After all that wine, there was no way Ie would wake until the alarm shrieked half an hour before first formation, if then. She didn't want to lie in the darkness alone with her fear and Iesin's breathing.

Softly, she slipped out of bed and began to dress in the dark. The dream was probably only a result of the previous evening's excess, but even so some cool air and movement would feel good. She was still on liberty until the morning muster. No one could stop her, and no one would challenge. She picked up her shoes and crept out in stocking feet, the better not to disturb Iesin. Iesin needed the sleep, seemed to need it more than Gaelian ever did.

At the end of the corridor, she laced up her running shoes and headed quickly down the unmoving escalator in the central hall. It was still deserted. The members of the night's business were probably asleep now, and those still on liberty would be either too drunk to notice anything or waiting it out until morning to appear, groggy but cold sober, at the dawn formation.

There were stars out tonight, billions of them illuminating the 'drangle, the white walkways scoured against the plush grass. The two steel and plexi ziggurats glowed softly, their massive solidity merely wavering shadows at this hour. Gaelian thought they were like twin ships, straining and waiting for the signal to lift. Down a small grade and across from the 'drangle, the gym squatted, guarding the athletic field like a leprous concrete monster. Gaelian skirted it, going down through the break in the bushes that only firsties were allowed to use, the shortcut to the athletic field. She walked carefully, aware that anyone who saw her running would think something amiss—she didn't want to be questioned, even if she was innocent. She wasn't quite sure that she was innocent. There was something wrong, after all, in having witnessed the proceedings of the honor court. And there was something else, something she tried to erase from her mind.

She did not know what drew her to the woods. True, she ran cross-country for the varsity team and felt comfortable on the trail, but that wasn't really it. There was something else that had been part of the dream. There had been woods there, and whenever she awoke from those nightmares she felt the urge to return to the forest. Return? She shook herself. If she weren't very careful, she'd have to report to sick bay for psych evaluation, and there was no way she was going to do that. By the Colors, no way at all.

Quietly she darted into the woods, picking out the cross-country trail before her as if by some instinct. She began to run. Running was almost as good as flying to still the uneasiness in her. Running was control. Not the magnificent control of a flight craft, the freedom of vacuum or the challenge of atmosphere, the tensile strength of her artificial body hurling itself through eternity, but it was enough. There was freedom in the stretching of her legs, the engorged arteries pulsing in her throat. She let her legs take her, not consciously watching the trail but letting her eyes rest on it. She was good at cross-country, dodging the branches and brambles before others even knew they were there. She ran the course, shedding all thought, aware only of her body flying through the foliage, of the yielding moss and the heavy smell of decaying things.

Then another smell came, the smell of the new-dead, of dark blood and excrement, something remembered from another life. Prey, she thought, and kept on running. There was nothing big enough to take her down here. It must be some large rodent that a night bird fed on, or a pup left to wander. She knew it, and yet she didn't know how she knew, and it worried her. The knowledge came from some different place, not from here.

A shadow swung before her, blocking out her view of the path, of the stars. It swung neatly and twisted on itself, the death-smell overwhelming. Gaelian stopped. She had no wish to go on, but there was a compulsion, one so strong she could not possibly disobey. She moved forward carefully, keeping to the bushes, aware that she left a clear mark for the enemy. An enemy surely must have done this. It was no small game.

She caught herself suddenly. She was on the Academy campus. There were no enemies here, yet the reaction had been sure. She shook herself, squinted, and tried to see through the foliage back to the gym or further out to the reactor. The small wooded section was carefully kept only for cross-country meets and for visiting parents to wander and picnic in. If it were light, she reminded herself sternly, she would be able to see through the trees to the rest of the campus, civilization, not this horribly physical extension of her dream.

In starlight frozen by an eternity of space, there glittered a shining white form, resolving from shadow into ghost into a uniform jumpsuit. Twirling lazily on a branch, the rope glittered with copper braid. Even without getting any closer, she was almost overpowered by the stench, although the body had not yet begun to decay.

She crept closer, sure of what she would find. The only question now was who. She had no doubt as to why. It must be the one they had condemned on the rooftop, a suicide out here in the woods. Better than facing the family with their own failure, she thought grimly. She could almost feel the noose around her own neck. And what they would never forgive is that one was paying for another's deeds. *She* hadn't asked to be born to her parents. Then she stepped forward to see the face.

Gaelian screamed, a curdling war cry remembered from some other time, perhaps from her blood before she was born. It was Tembri YnEste, a pilot from her own flight class. No wonder suicide. It was better than not flying. She had laughed with Tembri over the almost-mistakes they had made and pulled out of while others, not so lucky, not so skilled, had not managed. No, not YnEste, he had no right to that name. As she . . .

She began to breathe deeply. She knew she should tell someone about it, report to the officer of the watch, but she couldn't move. Her feet were rooted to the ground in front of the corpse, as she stared wide-eyed with horror. She should at least cut him down. It was the only decent thing to do. But she could not bear to touch the copper midshipman officer's cord and the warm-cold flesh. He had been Tembri so recently. Perhaps they hadn't been friends, but they were classmates and comrades and fellow fliers.

Suddenly, the terror took over again, and she turned and raced back to the track, the nice safe track where nothing could possibly go wrong. She ran as if her own death pursued her, lying back there with the figure swinging on the end of its officer's cord bleached by the starlight. Around and around the track, legs meeting yielding synthetic, guarded by the calm, squat gym, Gaelian ran trying to exhaust herself. She continued until there were knives piercing her side and her knee, only recently healed from a minor track injury, throbbed with pain.

There was some light now, the whispering promise of a sunrise still hours off, but close enough to make it safe. Wearily she trudged back to the dorm and fell on her bed without removing her sweat-soaked athletic uniform.

If she was bleary-eyed at morning muster, she was only like most of the firstie class. Three companies over, there was someone else standing in Tembri's place, and at breakfast there was no sign of his absence. It was as if he had never existed.

Half an hour's sleep was not really enough to get through the day on, although it seemed as if no one noticed that she barely picked through her dinner. One of the third-year students managed a sly remark about the aftereffects of a night's liberty, and Gaelian, managed a weak smile. She just wanted to get back to the room, to Iesin. If anyone had heard rumors, had more information, it would be Ie.

Iesin wasn't in when she arrived after dinner. For a moment, Gaelian sagged on her bed. She wanted to stretch out and go to sleep, but the nightmares would come again. Almost unconsciously her hand found its way under the pillow, and she drew out a soft leather bag. It was old, and the leather was cracked, but there were still traces of the once brightly painted designs. Long ago there had been quill work, too, but most of that had been rubbed off by constant handling.

She didn't open the bag. She didn't need to. Through the soft leather, she could feel the outlines of the tooth and claw necklace it held. Tyakral, her foster mother, had said it was her power, her luck, and Tyakral was hasute, a shaman who understood the circle and the whole and knew these things. But at the moment, it was something dangerous. How many times had she been tempted to throw it away, leave it buried someplace? But she couldn't part with it, couldn't bear even now to think of the face of its maker.

Firmly shutting her mind, she shoved the pouch back under the pillow and flipped on her screen. The quiet in the room oppressed her, and she found she couldn't concentrate on even the simplest astrogation problems. The silence chipped away at her nerves, and finally she switched the screen off and headed down to the study center. It would be bright and full of

people with a background noise of aimless chatter that would
do her good. It was better than going to the gym, avoiding
proximity to the tree bough that haunted her.

She had just settled into a comp carrel and cued her physics
assignment when Teazerin sauntered by. Gaelian leaned forward and cupped her hands around her face, hoping he
wouldn't notice her. She had first met him in normal school,
one of the fancy schools where only the Ot-tan and Li-tan
studied. On the first day in history class, he had stood up,
uncoupled her keyboard, and asked what a commoner was
doing in class.

After dinner, he had gone over to where she was sitting with
Iesin and several others and coolly asked why a half-breed was
permitted in their exclusive enclave. When she explained quite
clearly that she was YnTourne, he had scrutinized her, then
mentioned her father's drinking and long absence on Cahaute.
"You are a half-breed then," he had sneered. "Lower than a
commoner even." And he had twirled the nerris stick, which
even then was never out of his hands, and touched her lightly
with the blunt end.

She had screamed and jumped on him, torn at his hair and
tried to bite his ear before a teacher came over and hauled
them both off to be disciplined. It was the insult above all that
she could not endure. A nerris stick drew blood only from the
tested classes—to point the blunt end was to indicate that
someone was beyond contempt.

On the risk of both being expelled, they avoided each other
cautiously until her family decided that an arrangement with
the YnSetti was expedient.

"You look a little pale, Angel," he said, standing over her
shoulder. "Can't have my future wife coming down with some
bug, can I?"

"Shove it, YnSetti." Teazerin YnSetti was the last person
she wanted to see at that moment, the last in the entire Universe.

But he had reminded her of something. She was on display
here, not Gaelian and private, but the Angel.

They called her Angel, the top pilot in her class. As a matter
of fact, she knew with perfect clarity that she was the top pilot
in the Academy, since Golran had graduated, and it had been
very close between them. It was Golran who had given her the

name. The same Golran who had told her yesterday that they were no longer in communication. Only yesterday? It seemed like some part of the other life, so very long ago that she could scarcely remember any of it, and only what she didn't want to when she did.

It had been the third time she went up, plebe year, in those creaky old shuttle things, the ones left over from the very beginning of interplanetary flight, or so rumor had it. They were still working on basic atmosphere drills, takeoffs and landings.

"Doesn't matter how well you can do in a vacuum," Golran had told them, "if you can't take off and land in atmosphere, you're not going to get anywhere close to trying. And remember, coming into a carrier landing bay is almost as hard as landing on a dit."

They'd all laughed at that. How many times had Golran used that expression, saying only an angel born with wings could land deadstick on a coin. She hadn't thought about it then, only about the tricks of atmosphere, wind velocity, and air pressure.

She'd been up twice before, but it was that third time that it had all come together. Suddenly, aerodynamics wasn't words cycling through her brain, but a surge in her body. She could feel the hull straining around her, holding her. There was no reason to think about it. Like running, it was in her. And for the first time, she knew what it meant to be really free. High, higher she raised the craft, pushing out toward where the blue thinned out, a fledgling whose flight instinct was suddenly engaged. Energy tingled up her spine, and it was only some vague memory that kept her from breaking through into the black canopy that beckoned only a few thousand meters up. A voice entered her private world, ordering her to return.

She did not let them see her reluctance as she came down, carefully losing altitude as the parched grey clay of the field came into detailed relief.

"Put a dit on the field," she had said. And when she swooped in on her final approach she saw it, a pinpoint of copper glistening in the sun. Later she heard that everyone in the shack had thought it was terribly funny. Until she landed dead on.

The name Angel stuck. So did the dit. It had been a tradition ever since, and she had a jar full of them. After all, if she

could land on the things, she'd earned them. She figured another five hundred hours and she might have collected enough
to really let loose. A glass of beer, maybe.

Firmly, she pulled herself from the reverie and forced her
attention back to the screen. Plasma physics was not her fa-
vorite subject. She groaned and made her way through the
first problem, calculating necessary shielding from different
degrees of electromagnetic stress. It wasn't until she had completed two more problems that she noted the due date on the
format line. Not until next week. Stupid, stupid, stupid. Curs-
ing herself, she keyed the problems "save and password" and
logged off. Maybe Ie would be back, and she would be able to
get some sleep.

Luckily, Iesin *was* back when she returned to the room.
"You look like all four of the absolute hells," Ie said, studying her critically. "Tembri get to you?"

"How did you know what happened?" Gaelian gasped.

Iesin shrugged. "I've got sources." She did. The entire
firstie class admired the way she seemed to pick up information out of the air. "So it's got you bothered. How?"

Gaelian pulled off her shoes and sat cross-legged on the bed.
Iesin studied her carefully. Gaelian only sat that way when it
was something important.

"It's Cahaute, Ie. That's all, Cahaute."

"Don't say any more," Iesin said carefully. "I don't want
to know any more. Gaelian YnSerianis is registered as your
mother, and she died on Survey. Your father can't say anything, he's too scared and too drunk. And besides, he's ambitious as yellow for you."

"What do you mean by that?" Gaelian asked carefully.

"You know perfectly well. I can put two and two together,
and we've only been roommates for twelve years."

"So you put it together," Gaelian said, staring at her toes.
She didn't dare look Iesin in the face. "What did you come up
with?"

"Four," Iesin replied coldly. "You've dropped enough
hints." Gaelian swallowed. Most of the time Iesin was, well,
Iesin. But then there was the steel, the cold in her, the nerris
test coming out. Gaelian grasped for it, for the Ot-tan in herself, the nerris candidate who had proved herself to her grandmother six years ago. But somewhere deep inside she could

touch only laughter, sparkling, and a vague pity for the nerris players.

"You're exhausted, Gae," Iesin said gently. "You haven't had any sleep, and you saw Tembri on that tree, didn't you? But you aren't like Tembri. It was his place to die there. It was his place for you. Although I can't understand why he'd do anything so *primitive* as hang himself."

"If it were for me, like you said, it would have to be primitive, wouldn't it?" Gaelian asked bitterly.

"Nerris has four quadrants," Iesin replied slowly. "You've played black for a long time, and yellow. Start to play red, Gae. Play red."

Gaelian managed a weak smile. Iesin was right. She was just too tired. And there was only nerris—in the whole world everything was nerris. And it was time to change quarters.

3

AT OH FIVE HUNDRED HOURS, the world was still, complete, resting in itself. Gaelian felt herself another mote in this pristine universe, as clean as it was, surrounded only by the dull silver array of D-49s that stood to the line, almost part of the grey, cracked clay they rested on. Great white plumes emerged from fuel couplings, cutting the steel haze and shrouding the clay-colored hose lines in acrid mist.

Even the flight shack had taken on the character of the flight line. It was built of concrete, weathered and stained by generations of clay, dingy and squat against the flats. Inside, bright artificial light shone, and there was the sound of chatter, the radio, the sloshing of tea in cups, and the clicking of spoons.

This was real. This was home. Not the innumerable dorms she had lived in since normal school, or, Colors forbid, the YnTourne household, or even the strange, haunting setting of her nightmares. This place was her self. Here she was the Angel.

She stood in the shack, checking the duty board, her assignment for the morning, her artificial anatomy. No, not quite artificial. Here on the ground she was an amputee. In that great zirconium and ceramic hulk, she was whole again.

No one said much in the shack. She smiled and nodded, saying nothing at all, which wasn't unusual, drank two cups of tea, and checked the large chrono readout flickering on the wall. Outside, the ground crews were doing their final check-downs, and Angel waited until they had cleared the field before she went out to Number Nineteen, which was in its usual spot.

The checklist was firmly clenched in her hand, although she glanced at it only periodically, more from habit than from need. The list was graven into her mind, yet she held the clipboard earnestly and carefully marked and noted. It was important. She went over the air hoses, the gauges, the indicators, the fuel. It was never the craft's fault, not now, and the thought sent a shiver of delight up her spine.

Not now, not yet. But someday, the checklist would have something different on it, something new, and the controls would respond slightly differently under her hands. Her fingers almost ached for it, but she held herself back. Distractions made for mistakes, and mistakes made for death. She had seen them die from stupid mistakes, a not too careful check through the list by pilots impatient for the sky. She had seen explosions from improper fuel adjustment, an uncontrolled crash where the pilot had lost his sense when he could have still pulled out; twice there had been flamedowns. She kept the images fresh as she went through her routine. She was not impatient. She savored the minutes of exquisite anticipation, knowing that release, power, thrust, and speed would be hers soon enough.

One button closed the pit, two fingers attached the clipmitt to the collar of her flightsuit. All around the dry clay, the monsters were waking. She waited, poised, until she heard the magic words, "Nineteen, lift position, prepare to lift."

And then dawn broke.

Far below her, the land was seeped in carmine as the lumbering old craft climbed higher and higher into the yellow-red-blue sky, outward. Gaelian felt herself expanding into the machine, no longer merely mechanically, but a delicate merging of mind and unlimited power. Flight. She felt the air currents under her wings, knew the pressure of the updrafts carrying her far from the ground. She was the Angel. She was home.

She pointed her nose upward, driving for the darker colors, the colder, thinner air before there was none at all. Freedom came, and the thrusters cut, and now there was only the infinite privacy of space.

Carefully, she checked her readings and the stars around

her, checked her pulse and bearings, and then flipped on the comp. It was an easy run, a routine monitoring of communications satellite signals, working in a tight inside-outside maneuver called scissoring. Not particularly fascinating, but even a lack of fascination didn't bother her here. Familiarity was friendly, and she watched the graphics plotted on the screen with one eye while she watched out the window with the other.

She was out of atmosphere now, firmly embedded in the unending hunger of forever. Handfuls of careless stars were tossed across the expanse, their sparkles merely hinting at red or yellow or blue-white.

Brighter specks appeared around her, no longer the stars, moving quickly. They were the alternate group, the ones she would have to weave between. Gaelian laughed freely, letting her fingers play over the controls, caressing the unit gently. Coordinates came over her clipmitt, and she registered them duly. They swerved right, brightly dancing one around the other, computers chattering out signal codes from the bright, blind sphere in the center.

Angel danced. She spun and swung through the motions, a quadrille of gleaming white notes dictated by the comp and the order of the dance. First orbit complete and drop one hundred meters to second intercept. Lower, the three rings of the minuet, the third in atmosphere and the most difficult.

Again they danced, and the second ring was complete. She was sorry. All too soon was the most demanding, the true flying part, and then it would be down. The world was not right from downside, and she would disengage and no longer vibrate with thrust.

They came down another five hundred meters, and the sky around her brightened, the color softly filtering through the atmosphere that resisted the cut of the unfurled delta wings. The others came again, but no longer quite so glitter-bright and less defined, glaring, too harsh under the gentle refraction of pale, early blue. Around on the inside, twist on the outside. And then she felt it. It started as a quaver in the wings, an uncertainty in the fuselage. A hint of a question mark, no more. Before her came the brilliant glowing stream of her partners, this one coming on a little too straight, the turn not quite wide enough. She pulled hard around, felt the entire craft resist and groan against the atmospheric drag and stress, and yet her partner still had not veered. She caught the number twenty-two tiled on the tail and winced. It was Tembri's craft. Tembri was never that stupid. They'd flown this together before.

Turn, damn you, she thought.

Only it was not Tembri. He was dead, hanging from a tree out on the cross-country track. Not a bright flameout, one last flight from the heights of the comp building. There was nothing to be lost, only despair, and it invaded her. The gleaming ceramic body was a lie, and her hands faltered, perilously, for the fraction of a heartbeat.

It was all that was necessary. The turn had been too hard, nose down, and the spin came, spin and spiral high above the world. She watched it flip under her, so quickly that it was unreal, and the darkness began to form behind her eyes. Darkness, like the night and the cross-country course. The smell was fresh, very fresh and cool. How did they do smell here? Was it dying? It seemed too plain.

"YnTourne, what the hell are you doing?" the clipmitt screamed in her ear. Suddenly she was alert again. There had been something strange about this, something wrong. Her head was too light, but clear enough now.

Her nose was down, and the spiral was becoming tighter and faster. Plummeting downward, seeking prey, diving. And then it felt natural, suddenly. She flicked the comp off and pulled the clipmitt from her collar. There was something more feral here, in the freshness of the air. Still, there was enough time.

Very gently she pulled the nose up—not too fast, that would strain the structure—but it was her body that felt it, the slight increase in gs. No, pull up gently and try with the wing controls to control the spin. Very carefully; too carefully and be dead; not enough and shatter from the strain.

She felt the wind rushing past, the resistance, the gears and mechanicals and microcircuits screaming and straining under the light touch of fingertips caressing the console. Keys and others, running lights distorting her screen to a flame portrait, a gallery display. It was battle conditions, the pit dark, the lights exploding where they would. She ignored them, opening her hands, her feet, her skin to the pressure. And slowly the nose pulled up, ever so slightly, catching the hint of a current to ride.

*Ride the current, glide on it, on the water of River, the
Power Clan's hair, the hasute of the Mikke. Ride the current,
the soft voice of Breath, friend of the people. Steady, steady
now.*

All of the Power Clan were with her now, and she hummed
a tuneless paean in her throat, a song older than the earth, old
as Rock, the father of Mountain who had made it. *Clan, hear
me. Breath be my friend, cradle of my spirit . . .*

The Angel flew. The sky steadied around her, and she rode
the airwaves, the currents of the clouds, home of the Fire clan.
Home, ever home. The circle was complete. Cahaute.

Below her the patterns of earth and sea, of land cultivated
and wild and tamed, flashed by. She breathed out heavily and
slowly, replaced her mitt, and flipped the comp back on. Her
hands and back felt like lead, her feet were weighted by a million aeons of history.

The mitt chattered to her, "What happened? What the hell
were you doing?"

"Minor malfunction," she managed to say. "Clearance to
land?"

"Clearance granted. You want your dit?"

She smiled, the heaviness all over her now. "The Angel
lands on a dit, or she doesn't land," Gaelian answered calmly.

It was her old answer, the one that let them know she was
still the Angel, and they needed to know that. She had to be
the Angel, the eldest of the eldest of the YnTourne. She
brought the craft down slowly, timidly, not touching the metal
that was as exhausted as she was. Below her the grey clay ran,
flashing past with its interminable crack design, a single glint
far in the distance. Her dit. The aerie. Rest.

Her roll-tipped claws barely flickered over the surface before they came to rest in the smooth glide, the sudden jolt as
the thrust cut. The wings furled modestly and, deadstick, she
brought the front wheel into position just before the small
coin.

The powerdown took its full half-hour, although there
should be a more careful check later. She'd mitted the malfunction, although how it could have escaped her she didn't
know. The oxygen had been too pure and too meager, that
was where the cool freshness had come from. No wonder it
had reminded her of Tembri.

Or had he called her from the grave?

On the ground again, there was none of the magic. It was now near noon, and the strange colorlessness had resolved into definition, a harshness that pointed to comps and mechanical failure and human error. Hers and others. It didn't matter. She had pulled out, done it, and without damage.

The powerdown complete, she hopped out of the pit, jumped to the ground, and pocketed her dit. One more for the jar.

"Angel, I thought you had bought it for sure," someone called out in the flight shack.

She didn't disabuse him of the notion, simply slumped in one of the rickety chairs after signing in. The heavy exhaustion kept her from trembling, but she dared not try to lift a mug. She wanted only to go back to the dorm, take a long, long shower, and go to sleep for a million years.

"Are you sure you don't need to report to sick bay?" Iesin asked as Gaelian stumbled off the transport from the flight field.

"I'm playing red," Gaelian muttered and tried to pull her friend away from the others who were staring. She thought she caught Iesin making silent contact with someone, laying down her source for what had happened out on the line, but Gaelian didn't care. She trudged wordlessly up the corridor and into the very long shower she had promised herself, which didn't feel quite so good as she'd anticipated.

When she returned to the room, Iesin was sitting on the bunk. Definitely nonreg.

"Gae, you don't make mistakes like that," Iesin said. "Not that I've heard. Some people are saying that you're washed up. That the famous Angel touch is gone."

"It was a malfunction," Gaelian replied flatly. "It could have happened to anyone. Why? Who have you been talking to?"

Iesin just shrugged. Gaelian knew better than to push it. Iesin had the information she did because she never revealed a source. As far as Gaelian was concerned, she could as well be reading minds, and probably was.

Further inquiry was useless. Gaelian pulled the worn pouch from under her pillow and handed it wordlessly to Iesin. The other dropped it like an ember.

"You know who saved me up there today?" Gaelian asked

seductively. "Breath and River and Rock, the Power Clan of Cahaute, they saved me. Breath made a cradle for me and held my hand."

"You don't believe that any more than I do," Iesin countered firmly.

Gaelian shrugged. "I'm playing red," she reminded her roommate softly. "And I mean to play with both ends of the stick. Isn't that part of the test?"

"Not like that, Gae," Iesin pleaded. "Okay, you were born on Cahaute and lived there till you were seven. But it's not as if you're a savage. You are the eldest of the eldest of the Yn-Tourne, a pilot, a midshipman. You're not some illiterate, superstitious colonial. And you play nerris. Playing red doesn't mean being half primitive."

"But maybe I am half primitive," Gaelian said, her tongue flicking over her lips. "You know, they say that you are basically formed in the first six years, and after that you can't be changed. Tyakral would have said it was my takka hasuoone that helped."

Iesin glared at her. "That's a new one on me. Okay, what did you say?"

Gaelian smiled. "A spirit helper. Literally, relative-by-choice-power-spirit. Good enough?"

"You're taunting me, Gaelian," Iesin said very deliberately. "If I didn't think you were half out of your mind, I'd report you and challenge you, but as it is, I don't know."

"Just a game, Ie," Gaelian replied. "Just gaming, that's all. Practicing ruthlessness. Really, I'm just tired. The past few days have been more than a little eventful, don't you think?"

Iesin considered this for a minute. "Yes, very likely stress fatigue. What you really need is a weekend liberty. I think I can arrange it. I'll mitt my mother when the rates go down."

Gaelian nodded, carefully keeping the trepidation off her face. A rest probably would do her a lot of good, but things weren't just what Iesin thought. Iesin should know, and she kept that knowledge firmly shut in the back of her mind. There had been a time a few years ago when she had been very tempted to tell Iesin things better left unsaid. Gaelian didn't want to think about that now. Getting away would probably help her mask the anxiety well enough to continue the game, and that was all she needed.

"And now, I've got some really shocking news for you," Iesin said. "You won't believe it. You won't want to. YnSetti has been asked to preside at Tembri's funeral."

It struck Gaelian like a blow. For the first time since she'd found the corpse, she wanted to be sick. "I wouldn't think they'd make it public like that. And Teazerin. It should have been anybody else. You or I could have done it."

"That's not all," Iesin interrupted. "Teazerin refused."

"He can't refuse!" Gaelian screamed. "*Everybody* has the right to a funeral. *I'll* do it."

"I heard they're going to ask one of the YnEste, which is what they should have done in the first place," Iesin said lazily.

"That's not the point. Teazerin is lower than a worm. It's . . . it's despicable to refuse."

Iesin nodded. "And he claims that what Tembri did was worse. I don't understand why. After all, commoners do sometimes get into the Academy. Look at your friend Golran."

"You know as well as I do that it wasn't that that was the problem." Gaelian said warily. "It was the fact that he lied and claimed Ot-tan privileges. I wonder if I could call Teazerin on his refusal, though. I'd like to beat his face in."

Iesin laughed. "Since when did you need an excuse for that? You haven't lost your nerve, that's for sure. Same old Angel. Only one thing, Gae. If you've got to pulp Teazerin, do it when you're both on leave, or you'll get yourself quite honorably expelled."

Gaelian joined Ie's laughter. As usual, Iesin was right. Being Ot-tan did give one a good many privileges, but while in uniform, Navy discipline had to be observed. One of the reasons, her grandmother had said, that all heads of households had to have service experience.

"Hells and Colors, Ie, I'm not that stupid," Gaelian protested. "Besides, I don't have the time right now. I've got an exam tomorrow."

Iesin chortled happily and threw a sock at Gaelian before she turned to her own studies. Gaelian took the seat next to her and prepared to go over another set of physics problems in preparation for the exam, but when she activated the password, her message signal appeared instead of her classwork. Well, anything would do for procrastination when it came to a physics exam. She may as well just give in to it. She cued the message and chewed her nails while the notoriously slow system plodded into action.

> Grandmother requests no further survey on class C primitive planets. Board will overrule. Zirconium, nickel, lithium crit. Renan drinking more. Will not see doctor. Be prepared for worst case.
>
> —Dobrin

She cursed under her breath and then immediately amended it to tag on an honor specific to Dobrin. He hadn't had to inform her, unless he was playing yellow, and very, very carefully too. She couldn't see through to the meaning if he were. After all, Dobrin had given her every reason to distrust him and then other reasons not to. Or to confuse her, like this message.

She couldn't fault him. He'd always expected the household to go to him. He'd worked for it, trained for it, played Grandmother's stooge too many times. After all, every member of that first Survey mission on Cahaute was presumed dead. And then her father, the eldest, had to show up with an heir in tow. She couldn't honor Dobrin at all if he had given up too easily.

But Dobrin was not responsible for her father's drinking, although how anyone could survive as eldest under her grandmother . . . No, Dobrin had done quite well. If her father's habits were a scandal in the Ot-tan households, it was his own fault and a gift to Dobrin.

She couldn't be so sure that Dobrin had had nothing to do with her betrothal to Teazerin, though. It was almost a certainty that her grandmother had consulted him before the contract was signed. Thank the Colors that the agreement didn't call for a marriage until two years after graduation. As Iesin had said so many times, a lot of things could happen in two years. There were moments when Gaelian truly regretted that Teazerin wasn't a pilot. If he were, she could wish with some reasonable chance of success that he would buy it. Or maybe she would. On average, pilots didn't have the longest life expectancy. Except she wouldn't like to give him the satisfaction.

There had been a lot of good reasons for the arrangement. She could not marry another eldest of the eldest because she was responsible to the YnTourne, and Teazerin was second-born in a household as old as hers. Besides, the YnSetti owned the mineral franchise of the Craft Company where the Yn-Tourne held a controlling block of shares. It was to the advantage of both to have more pledges of good faith than could be formalized in the boardroom. Teazerin should be as furious as she was, but he seemed merely uninterested. They saw each other on formal occasions only, and when they passed on campus. Only, besides her old grudge, there was something about Teazerin she didn't trust.

Perhaps it was the way he played nerris. Not a mark on him, although he'd been playing all his life, and that was odd. And there was a coldness in the way he played, an inhumanity and a drive she had never encountered elsewhere.

When they had first been engaged, she had slipped off from the elders after the proper pledging had been done and came across Teazerin near the nerris court. He had challenged her to an informal game, one on one, two walls each, the way they had played as children. She had dragged the sticks and ball from the shack that leaned on the outer wall and entered the court.

He had chosen to play blue and yellow, and she was well pleased to take black and red. Her walls were bolder, more open, but it occurred to her to wonder. After all, the usual division was red and yellow against black and blue, one subtle and one bold quality each. She thought Teazerin was trying to tell her something.

He had taken the stick and blown lightly on both ends. "I hope you have a proper sense of ritual," he said.

She had merely shrugged. She too had been properly educated and knew that nerris was as old as Dinoreos itself, stretching back into the time before recorded history. And she knew that it was fluid, changing, but always the crystallization of who and what they were. From personality to manipulation in the boardroom, all could be described in terms of nerris. There was the choice between the mercy of the blunt end and the ruthlessness of the barb, the opportunity to play on a team as a leader or a follower or to defend the wall alone. Even in the oldest epics, nerris was layered with symbols.

He spun the ball into the center of the court, and they played. They played harder than she had ever played before, even on the team at normal school. He had been a blur of action, driving, the ball secondary to his guard. His eyes had never left her.

She had played well—even for the Ot-tan she had played well. She had been darting and scoring on the walls that gave her points, the ball leaving white smudges against the blue and yellow painted walls of the ancient household court. And the better she played, the more she had felt his breath on her, the slipping of his stick close to her skin. she had meant to show him who she was, and that she had no interest in anything more than a formal contract.

They had played. He had taken the ball with the blunt end of the stick and batted it lazily, not looking for points. It had angered her. His stick twirled almost lethargically, ending sharp barb toward her every time, taunting.

She had understood all too well. It didn't matter how many points she had if he took her from the game. He was not playing toward an objective, but against her. The message was more than clear.

She had had the ball, tossing it from the stick point in a long arc across the court and turning the blunt side to bat the rebound. Only, again, he hadn't gone for the ball at all. In a single movement, he had had the sharp barb against her shoulder and had batted the ball with the blunt end into a different trajectory. It had bounded off one of her walls.

She remembered smiling, shrugging, conceding the match. It was over. But he had not removed the thin point from its guard near her shoulder. He scored her lightly, tearing the fabric of her blouse and the skin underneath it. There had been a smile on his face then too, the thin lips drawn in some grimace that read cool pleasure, his pale eyes narrow and unreadable.

It was not competition. In a friendly game, a guard was enough, a touch more than was necessary. Yet he had made it a competition without her agreement or consent. Another message. She had been furious, and the angrier she had become, the colder his face had grown.

"I had conceded," she said harshly.

He had only shrugged. "It is necessary to draw blood in nerris," he said. "And, besides, I had to see if yours was right. Colors know that the rest of you isn't." He had thrown his stick to the ground and walked out, never turning back.

She had seethed, and what was even more infuriating was

the knowledge that he had meant her to. It was an insult she should not have to bear, but she forced herself to look, to use it. After all, he had revealed himself, disdaining the mercy end for the barb, not out of need but by choice. Something else filtered through the anger, and she recognized it as fear. Reasonable fear. The nerris stick was balanced, both ends with their functions, both necessary, both part of the same whole. Yet he had chosen one end without thought of the other. It was not nerris. It was not true Dinorean.

She had left her own stick and the ball in the court and had run toward the house not wanting to be seen with a ripped and bloody shirt. Even with the best planning, it would not have been possible to foresee that Dobrin would choose that time to take a walk on the grounds. Maybe it was only because there was some business between her grandmother and father and the YnSetti elders that he was not privy to. Maybe he had come looking for her and Teazerin. In any case, he saw her and called. She hadn't stopped, and Dobrin had trotted toward her. There had been no way to hide it. He needed only to look at the bloodstained tear at her shoulder.

They probably suspected because she did look different. Dark hair and honey eyes were not typical of the Ot-tan, but there were throwbacks. Iesin's second brother had brown hair, although not quite so dark as her own, and his eyes were darker than hers. Classmates had called her "amber eyes" in normal school. Once one of the girls had even asked if she wore lenses simply to look exotic.

But if she was too dark, Teazerin was too pale, his hair near silver and his skin a color that resembled stone more than flesh. Perhaps he didn't have any blood. Colors knew no one had ever seen him shed any on the nerris court.

Sometimes she wondered why they didn't all see it clearly on her, how her face was too pointed and her cheekbones too wide set, her fingers too long, all the proportions just a bit off for a Dinorean. Teazerin suspected, she was sure. That was what the nerris game had been about. Iesin had often said that she was beautiful, but what she wouldn't give to look as purely Ot-tan as Iesin. Tembri YnEste had been too close.

Well, genetics was not mathematics. Every once in a while something erupted from the genotype into the observable world, alleles recombined and formed new patterns, old patterns that hadn't been seen for generations. Biology was at best unpredictable. Even her grandmother hadn't said anything aloud. Dobrin, with all his questions, hadn't dared ask anything in public. He might look all he wanted, but his suspicions wouldn't hold up in a court of law, not without a DNA scan. And she was as Ot-tan as he; no court would question her refusing a scan. Indeed, it would be far worse for Dobrin to request it than for her to refuse.

But Tembri was dead for a lesser lie. Now Iesin would be the only one who didn't look at her as if she were somehow a changeling. There were only Iesin, and Golran gone to Adedri and the Altneri, and her father who was drunk most of the time against Dobrin and her grandmother and Teazerin and the honor court and the whole of the Dinorean aristocracy and the entire Protectorate. The odds were not in her favor.

"The economic issues are clear," Dobrin said again. "We know the place is rich, the Survey tapes that survive show that. And if we don't open Cahaute, we're in serious trouble. The current reserves of lithium and zirconium won't last more than ten, fifteen years at most. And the new designs use more, not less. If we don't find new sources, we're going to have trouble with the Adedri, too, and between them and the commoners, they outnumber us."

The Head of the YnTourne household snorted. "I expected you to do your research, Dobrin," she said. "I expect no less. And you will act as my surrogate on the Board for this. But no Cahaute. I hope that's clear enough."

Dobrin sighed and leaned back in his chair. He didn't like the way she looked. This time she really had waited too long, had played for just a little too much time, he was sure. And at the moment, he was not sorry. He searched himself for other feelings, memories of this woman he called "Grandmother," although she was really his aunt, and he could find nothing except a distant respect for her brilliant manipulation in the past. Either she was way beyond carrying out her responsibilities, or she was playing at something more dangerous than Dobrin cared to contemplate.

"Can you at least give me some of your reasons for standing against this?" he asked, shaking his head.

The old woman laughed unpleasantly. "You won't believe me," she stated flatly. "I've read Renan's notes."

"So?" Dobrin could feel her peering at him, inspecting him

as if he were some experimental product found flawed.

"The rest of the Board doesn't have access to the data," she snapped. "I do. That's the important thing to remember. You should find out more about the use of hallucinogens among the tribes of Cahaute. That's one thing."

"And the others?" he asked reasonably.

She closed her eyes, and Dobrin thought that she might have fallen asleep. Then she began to speak so quietly that he had to move forward to hear. "Cahaute is a place no Dinorean should ever go, Dobrin. It holds some key to us, from before the nerris sanctions. It would be better to watch the smugglers on Adedri more carefully. Put together everything you can find out on the third inhabited planet in that system, and we may find some reserves yet. The Adedri always have something to hide, and it's always to their advantage and our loss. That's the way they are. But Cahaute is dangerous."

Dobrin shook his head. There were times when he wondered whether all the painkillers, all the medications of the past seven years had muddled her thinking. "We're sure to lose on this. You've decided to die for something we can't win, and I'm not even convinced we should. I don't even know why I say we when I mean you."

She smiled softly. "Because, Dobrin, I don't want Renan's daughter to take YnTourne. That's the bottom line."

Dobrin chewed his lip. He knew he should leave, shouldn't listen to any more of this, and yet it thrilled him. He studied the elderly Head of the household carefully. Her blue eyes were pale and watery with age, but there was a demonic quality to the force of her gaze. And the sardonic smile she wore hinted at plans, more plans behind others, layers of masks that he wanted to penetrate.

"Is that why you've made things so difficult for her?" he asked slowly. "Teazerin YnSetti?"

The old woman smiled. "Not for her, for you. You will understand how to use it all."

"Do you know what YnSetti did?" Dobrin demanded. "Did you know that on the day they signed the agreement, he blooded her in a nerris game?"

The fury of that discovery was still fresh in his mind. He should have come in and confronted the entire YnSetti clan then and there with their dishonor. Only he hadn't had the courage. The Head of the YnTourne had decided, and he needed her support. Besides, the YnSetti could make difficulties for him on the Board if he ever decided to challenge Gaelian. At least this way they wouldn't feel it was a personal grudge. He had been caught between possible moves.

There were times when he understood Renan perfectly. There was no way to live with this woman, with her plans and schemes that she confided in no one, using them all as her pawns in a game where no one but she even knew where all the players were, let alone anything of the strategy. It had taken him years of constant observation even to begin to untangle the intricate labyrinth she had created.

"Good," she said.

Good! Dobrin wanted to explode. Good! The YnSetti get away with a serious insult to the household, and her only reaction was "good." He forced his face to express only blandness and relaxed his clenched hands.

"I'm tired now. Please send for Missili on your way out," the Head of YnTourne dismissed him.

Dobrin was just as glad. Out of her presence he could think clearly, could use that special Li-tan ability to assemble details and trivia. He suspected that the old woman disliked Gaelian for some personal reason, although he had no evidence for a cause. He himself did not in the least dislike his cousin. The fact that he tried to keep her unsteady and defensive was purely a political move, and if she didn't understand that, it was her own inability, not his malice.

And then he wondered just how much they had all been manipulated. Perhaps Renan's drinking was the result of some other plot. And now that the old woman was dying, Dobrin wondered if she had laid her foundations so deeply, they would continue to play out her scenarios without even being aware of it.

He had gotten to the library before remembering to call the housekeeper, and when that was done he settled himself with a liberal drink. If he accepted the premise that Grandmother had planned for more than just mineral concessions, he would follow her instructions at tomorrow's Board meeting, but he would be watching the undercurrents of the play as the patterns emerged.

4

IT DIDN'T LOOK like a place of power, nor did the people there look like those who did extraordinary things. That was always the first thought that hit Dobrin when he entered the Board chambers. No matter how often he came, it always hit him again. The hard wooden chairs were scarred and blackened, matching the table and each other only in their extreme old age. But there was history in that age—the deep gash where a YnOestal in some earlier time had driven a cheese knife through a proposal and pinned it before the Board, the dark stain on an edge where a YnEste had died suddenly, blood foaming out of his mouth and into the wood. Once the chairs had been painted, but there was no trace of the colors history recorded in that room. It was only a room, a bare and uncivilized one at that, from an uncivilized time.

Dobrin felt extremely satisfied when he entered these precincts, this unchanged vestige of the past. Civilization, like duty, was a necessity to be borne and a pride to be relished. Like duty, one did not have to enjoy it.

He took the YnTourne chair and sat, waiting. Others drifted in, took snacks from the sideboard where fruit and cheese and thin, flat bread had been laid out, already cut. It was an amusing anachronism to forbid knives now when the deep concrete recesses of the wall had been liberally seeded with trigger eyes monitored by security machines, whose memories were wiped after every meeting.

Dobrin glanced at the food. He would have liked something

to eat, a small slice of sharp cheese on sugar-ripe fruit, but he could not in the presence of the Board. He was only a surrogate. He knew his place and kept it.

One by one, they drifted from the sideboard and to the time-honored protocols of place, of inquiries. On the outside, they looked like any members of the Ot-tan class, or even of the lower classes perhaps. Some were fat, and some were anxious. Most wore the same simple, dark unisuits with drab jackets that their underlings in any office on Dinoreos wore. The brilliant colors, the jewels, the face paint, the soft shoes, and the intricately draped scarves, these were for parading among commoners; here they were among their own.

Dobrin looked down at the table in front of him. He could hear the scrape of chair legs on the concrete floor, smell the warm flesh as people surrounded him. And then the sharp slam of a hand against the scarred wooden surface brought his attention back to the moment.

"Are the guards of the four colors present?" demanded Kaes YnArretl, current presiding member.

"Black is present," YnEste answered, rising.

"Blue is present," YnOestal responded.

"Red is present."

"Yellow is present."

"Anoni is present."

YnArretl nodded, and the five ceremonial guards resumed their seats.

"For the sufficient good of all Dinoreos, commoners, and others under her protection, the Presiding Board of Protectorate Manufacturing and Commerce is hereby convened to resolve the issue of opening mining operations on the primitive-restricted class-four planet Cahaute," YnArretl intoned formally. "The proposal to open operations comes from the YnSetti household, majority shareholders of the Mineral Conglomerate, and it is opposed by the YnTourne household, majority shareholders in the Craft Company. Both hold facilities fully operated by client-employees along with minor facilities on Adedri overseen by client Dinoreans. Does anyone question the right of these households to speak?"

Dobrin tensed slightly. Not that he thought his credentials would be challenged seriously. He had spoken as surrogate several times in the past. But someone playing a very careful game might just call questions to waste time and drive members to boredom. That had been done before according to the Head of the YnTourne. She should know. She had done it.

There was silence. No reason to play for time then.

"Since the YnSetti have proposed this undertaking, it is for them to make a summary of the situation and of their reasons for this proposal."

Lyken YnSetti rose and slammed his flat palm against the table once. "Perhaps this seems to concern my household more directly than it does your own," he began smoothly. "Still, it is a major concern for all of us gathered here, the Protectorate as a whole. We are all well aware of the shortages that we face. Lithium, used in ceramics, zirconium, and even simple nickel have been nearly mined out to the best of our knowledge. Where will our new ships come from, if we don't have these things? Ships? I know the Craft Company is against this move, and certainly we can only hope they're verging on some revolutionary breakthrough. I do hope so. Yet that would not change this in the least. There are more than ships to consider now."

Dobrin could feel the blood pounding in his throat. YnSetti went around the matter, approached always from the oblique angle. There was an elegance to it that matched the elegance of the ancient, stained table and the bare concrete walls.

"Far more than this," YnSetti continued. "Although it is usual in this assembly to think of ceramics in terms of such things as lightweight, high-energy machinery, we must not forget simple things. Building materials. Cooking utensils. Why think of cook pots when one is accustomed to considering the stars? The commoners think of cook pots and of public housing projects. They think of the factories that produce those things because they work there. And they think of their jobs. Let us remember that, although there has never been even a whisper of unrest, they are more numerous than we."

"Crap, YnSetti," came a firm voice from the head of the table. YnArretl had abandoned his ceremonial position as presiding member and was now simply responding in his usual manner. "If you're threatening us with a revolution, you've got your head in a black hole."

YnSetti merely raised his eyebrows, conveying such disbelief and disdain that there was no need for more. He was a master of the blue play, perfect in composure and attitude.

"I think we have forgotten something," YnSetti continued,

his voice heavy as if talking to recalcitrant children. "When we say there is no whisper, we mean among our own folk, our own clients. And we know our own can be trusted. Don't they carry the same history, the same heritage? But Dinoreos is one. One single planet with one population. There are three planets full of Adedri. Can anyone here claim to understand the Adedri? Do any of us know what they really think, feel, plan?

"But we *do* know they do not appreciate what we have done for them. Yes, they send their children to our schools, but they learn their own language at night; yes, they will try to get work in our factories since the pay is better, but all of us who have hired Adedri know they grumble about the conditions, when we have done everything to insure that conditions are most humane. Do any of us have one single answer to that?"

"Adedri don't have ships, and they can't get here, so I don't see what the problem is," Esrin YnOestal said softly, her tone as honeyed as her hair. "And you know, I've always thought that odd, that the Adedri don't have interstellar capability on their own. They had basic interplanetary ships long before we did."

"The Adedri have nothing to do with this Board or the decisions of this Board," YnArretl reminded them pointedly.

"But they do," the Head of the YnSetti household said softly, his serpentine whisper slipping into the silence. "They have everything to do with this. If we open Cahaute to exploration, there will be more work for the Adedri, away from their home system. It can be made very attractive."

He didn't need to say more. Dobrin was filled with awe. It was a perfect play, the gambit and the strategy combined to score with both ends of the stick in a single stroke. He was almost compelled to agree, as much from the beauty of the argument as the substance. It was the game in all its perfection, the reason they played and were tested in play.

"Well said," YnOestal agreed softly, her eyes focused on some place on the blank wall. She looked soft, otherworldly, and Dobrin knew it for the ruse he had seen in yellow, the intention to mislead so perfectly executed that even the player was completely absorbed in the deception. "Yes, we can be far more sure of the Adedri than we are, and they pose some kind of problem. Their piracy is troublesome. Troublesome."

"Is the opposition ready to present its case?" YnArretl asked.

Dobrin spread his hands before him as he stood. He had waited and listened, and he agreed in secret. But agreement and secrets were nothing to the act of play itself. He took one deep breath to narrow his mind. Focus was important in the game. Focus could win or lose. Dobrin did not like to lose.

"As you know," he began slowly, without knocking on the table. Only a properly installed member of the Board would do that. "The Head of the YnTourne household is not here because she is gravely ill. Of her own free will. It is to this extent that she opposes the opening of Cahaute to our people and by this measure wishes to express the depth of her feeling to the Board." Dobrin hesitated artistically. "And surely, we of the YnTourne know more of Cahaute than anyone else here. You all know that Renan, the eldest of the household, spent almost nine years there as a member of the original observation team and was the only member of the team who survived. And you know the horror of it left him less than the explorer who started out."

He paused carefully, to let them think of the Renan they had known, he had known, the brilliant student with the courage to defy the Head of the household, the strategy to move around her and the speed to overcome her to obtain what he wanted. And now, there wasn't a person in the room who didn't know about Renan, about his drinking and his inability to focus. For once, and only this once Dobrin supposed, that blot on the family name could be used to advantage.

"The YnTourne do not oppose exploration or the exploitation of important resources. Indeed, we have encouraged them at every chance. There are other possibilities besides Cahaute, some of which might even be better suited to the Head of YnSetti's strategy. The third planet in the Adedri system is one of these. Why Cahaute? Yes, it seems possible that what we need is there. But there are other things, too. People who are barely more civilized than animals, who are unable to understand, let alone accept, the advantages we can offer them. People who might very well incite the Adedri."

"Oh, I rather think not," YnOestal said in her carefully cultivated fuzzy manner. "After all, the Adedri have some pretensions to civilization. They're not about to be influenced by a pack of two-legged herd animals."

Dobrin nodded at her, half conceding, before he continued. "It seems they are savages. We could use the material wealth they have no use for and teach them besides, a mutually beneficial solution. There is one thing, though, something that has not been made very public, simply because Renan has never been able to do the work to present the information in a coherent manner. But it is clear from what notes we have been able to decipher that the people there have unusual skills and that the contamination of food and water is part of the problem. Hallucinogens are a major part of life on Cahaute, and they are present in abundance. In fact, it is quite reasonable to suppose that the contamination is more widespread than we can reasonably guard against. I ask you to think, why would there be only one survivor from the entire party that went down in the first place, and that one survivor ruined for life? Can you imagine Adedri influenced by drugs, hallucinogens that might make their less pleasant qualities more pronounced?"

He had lost. He knew it. Around the table they were looking down at the grained surface, at their fingernails, but not at him. Dobrin could feel the chill around him, as if he had done something unspeakable, and in a way he had. He had lost. He had not defended well. And the life of the Head of his household was at stake.

Yet, he wondered if that alone had been a factor against him. Had Grandmother not pulled one of her crazy stunts, he would have been free to side with YnSetti instead of arguing for something he felt he could not properly understand. Unless there was something he didn't know. Probably there was, and that was unfortunate. Had he known, perhaps he could have won. Grandmother knew that, and knowing it, was choosing suicide.

All of them there, he thought, might be playing both ends of the stick. Perhaps they wanted Grandmother out of the way. Renan could not possibly last long. Renan would be worth less than nothing as the Head of the household. Their only hope really was that he could not live long, not with the drinking and the stress, not without extreme medical measures that would lose him as much status as the problem in the first place. They could not afford that. So Renan would not last.

Then it would be Gaelian or himself, both of them inexperienced by the standards of the Board. It would make Yn-Tourne vulnerable.

The room was dead silent. Dobrin shook himself from his figuring to concentrate on the silence and the meaning of the silence. He glanced at the table and saw, startled, that the only hands resting on the wood were his own. He felt the eyes on his hands, on the carefully manicured fingernails and the heavy Academy ring. Slowly, so slowly that he could barely feel the pull of the old wood against his palms, he slid them over the edge. It was almost as if he had not moved, but that the collective will of the room had forced him bodily. All the decisions of the Board must be unanimous, finally.

And then he understood the final test and didn't want to know it. He had not failed, not truly. In the test of will there can be failure, but this was not it in truth. This was something else. His duty to his household and to the Protectorate had themselves combined with that will, his own desire to use the wealth the geologists had so convincingly displayed in previous sessions. It burned in his marrow.

With a single, even movement of his head, he met the eyes of YnSetti. The elderly Head of the household smiled. They all understood. He could feel it, just as he had played the game with his vote.

There was other, minor business to discuss, but Dobrin rose. "With your leave," he said, "it is important that my household know the outcome of this decision immediately."

They nodded in unison, and Dobrin left.

He did not head directly for the mitts, however, private as they were, but to a small office he had commandeered on another occasion. Here he was alone and could be relatively sure that no one was watching. The building was kept as free of devices as possible, with the exception of trigger eyes liberally peppered in the ceilings, and no one would think of violating the sanctity of those privacy circuits. Or, no one would be willing to be caught doing it, which was more to the point.

Seated in the semilight, Dobrin felt he was burning hot and cold, starving and uninterested in food all at the same time. He knew. His grandmother had sent him, set him up. That last moment had made the game clear. The Board had given him their approval. Gaelian had never spoken before them, but

Dobrin had been set in place. It was the final test, no, not test of will, but meeting of will. The Board had approved him as their candidate.

Grandmother had cleared the field for him while Gaelian was still weak enough to be defeated. She had never intended to win, to recover. There was still something he did not know, of that he was sure, but that something had little to do with the opening of Cahaute. No, it was something darker, for his exclusive use. It was the only way the entire thing made sense.

Calm settled through Dobrin. The game had been very carefully conceived. Grandmother was a good player, he had to admit, but he was going to be just as good. He would have to be. Even with the Board silently behind him, there was still Gaelian herself. She was a worthy opponent, and Dobrin tried to remind himself not to underestimate her, even if she were young and had not yet built up the background and client support she would need in an all-out struggle. He could not afford to let it come to that, which was to her advantage. She was still legally the heir to the household, to the voting shares, and to the company.

Dobrin had played nerris with her since she was young, and he knew that she was no mean adversary. This would be no minor fight, and he relished it. It was good to have a worthy opponent. His goals were simple, and there was no doubt that it would work out for the best.

When they had played nerris for the gods, he might have thought that the gods were very close just now, but he could not believe in the nerris gods any more than he believed in any unforeseen danger on Cahaute. The only god was the play. Everything else was mere preparation.

Gaelian sat in the early spring sunshine pretending it was warm. It wasn't. There was still time before the scorching breath of summer came, but the cold she felt wasn't the chill in the air.

The browns and greys of the scene mirrored her own state. It was too late for snow, or even frost, and too early for any vegetation to venture out. Even the sky was the color of steel, heroically producing a momentary attempt at wan blue before it abandoned the struggle. She sat on one of the benches that ringed the 'drangle, comforted by the solidity of the Academy around her. It shielded her, stately, unchanging. Soon, very soon, she would graduate and leave, but it would remain always itself and always a part of her, as the YnTourne household had never been.

The words lay like scattered ice in her head, the last message she had received from Dobrin just that afternoon. Grandmother was in the final stages of her illness. She would not live long, a month or two at the most, not without the treatment she refused. Now, altogether it was becoming real, very real, and she needed to draw strength from the monuments around her, from the history of the land, and from the dirt itself. It was Dinoreos as the earth of Cahaute had never been, full of history and meaning in its own right. She was connected to them, to the countless generations back, the YnTourne and the others who had passed through this Academy since before the first interplanetary ships had been built. Then Dinoreos had had many groups, nations, languages, until the need to grow had left one dominant. The others were part of the dust, part of the air, their ghosts as well molding the final form of the conquerer. It was the end of the nerris sacrifice, the beginning of civilization. It had formed her, body and blood, shaped her with that need to overcome, to win. Not to win was to die. That was the point of nerris.

She shook herself and stood, trying to rid her mind of useless rumination. If she should remember anything from those lessons, it was to take action when action was called for, and now was one of those times. Trying not to consider any course, only the immediate alternatives, she started to make her way across the brown field up to the firstie dorm.

"Gae, *where* have you been?" Iesin exclaimed. "Come here, look! They've come, they've come!"

Gaelian's confusion was immediately cleared as Iesin pulled a thick sheaf of formal-looking, heavy paper from behind her back and slammed it into Gaelian's hand. It was her orders, her posting after graduation and summer leave. She shook, torn with the need to open the packet and the thrill of holding it still closed. Another part of the ancient traditions, this use of formal vellum instead of the CRT, something to touch and hold and caress and pass from hand to hand as everyone admired or groaned together.

"Well, *open* it. Anoni's hells, I don't think I've ever seen anyone so slow," Iesin burst out impatiently.

Gaelian tore the thick seal and pulled the heavy paper apart.

Then she began to laugh, her head flung back and her eyes wide.

"Well, what is it?" Iesin demanded.

"Adedri, Ie," Gaelian said breathlessly. "I pulled Adedri, first time out. And there's more."

"I know, I know, tell me the details," Iesin prompted her.

"I've been assigned to the shakedown of Tanistin, the new pirate runner. The very classified pirate runner. I mean, it's been in testing for over a year now, and no one's talked about anything else, and now it's got a name, and it's going on a cruise, and I'm assigned. Can you believe it? Golran would kill for this. *Anyone* would kill for this. But what about you, Ie?" she asked.

Iesin glowed. "Junior liaison on the project. Admin, of course, but we do have our uses."

Gaelian threw herself on her back on the bed and whooped. "We'll be together then," she shouted. "We'll have Adedri, in the city of Adedri on the planet called Adedri, and Tanistin too."

"But Gae," Iesin said softly, "what about your grandmother and the household? What about the Craft Company?"

Gaelian felt as if she had been turned into stone. "The household's my father's, thank gracious Anoni and all the devils with him. I've got to tell Golran. And I can't wait to see Dobrin's face. Talk about scoring."

"Somehow," Iesin muttered. "I'm not so sure you and Dobrin are playing the same game."

Gaelian shot Iesin a quizzical look, but the other refused to acknowledge it. "And YnSetti?" she asked carefully.

"What makes you think I know anything about YnSetti?" Iesin asked, her face all innocence before the mask cracked. "Oh, all right. He's on the first outpost mission. To Cahaute."

"Cahaute?" Gaelian choked on the word. The room reeled around her, and she closed her eyes. The idea of Teazerin on Cahaute made her very close to violently ill. She lay back on the bunk and rested her head on the clean-smelling pillow, and almost without conscious awareness her hand reached under her head to the little bag that was her link with Cahaute.

She opened her eyes and turned to the wall. She could almost feel Iesin's eyes on her, and she curled her body protectively around the bag before she opened it. Slowly she drew the necklace out and gazed at it intently.

She had forgotten, it had been so very long since she had looked at it, that it was such a thing of beauty. The ivory teeth had been carefully polished and the claws rubbed, giving the whole a soft luster. It was four layers high, and not one piece of the precious nistora had been stinted in the making of it. The thongs that tied it were as soft and supple as they had been the day it had been given to her. Everything was of the very best, nothing held back, nothing grudged. But that was the way it was supposed to be—cahaute, complete.

She thought about the boy who had given it to her. He had been her only friend, she remembered, the only one who had accepted her when the Keti, her clan, had died. He had been solemn and stern, even then. He would have changed his name by now, so it didn't matter that she didn't remember his childhood name. She wondered if he had become a shaman. Tyakral, her foster mother, had certainly thought that he would have a shaman vision, and Tyakral was a shaman and hasute herself.

She remembered how the boy had become her friend. She had attracted a timid-eyed hopper, those small ones that usually fear people. It was said that those they chose had been born in the center of the circle. Anyway, she usually kept the animal close by, but one day it had wandered in the camp, following her to where the children played.

A boy who did not like her, who called her "chaluda," or "evil shaman," had picked up the small one by its neck and swung it in a circle. Her friend, smaller than the bully, had stopped him. Then he had lectured her, telling her that she must have courage to face those who did evil to the small ones and to the others that were protected in the dance and the circle that was all things. All living beings, the four-legged and the no-legs and the standing peoples and the sitting, all, he had reminded her sternly, were the responsibility of every member of the clans. They kept cahaute.

Surely, she mused, he must be hasute now. Even then he had spoken like an elder of the tribe, one of the wise ones who talked to the Power Clan.

There had been a time when she had translated hasute as shaman for Iesin, during Ie's foreign language period, but that wasn't really correct. A hasute was one who recognized the whole, the circle; and a b'hasute was one who recognized the center of the circle. There weren't really any proper words in Dinorean for it all, she reflected. Strange that she had begun thinking in the language again at times, words and concepts that didn't exist in Dinorean society drifting across her consciousness.

How strange it was that the Dinoreans had taken the word for completeness of spirit, and something more—cahaute— and given it to the whole planet and its people. It was as good as any other, Gaelian thought. She even approved. But no matter how many times she had tried to explain to Iesin that cahaute meant the circle-and-its-center and the moving dance and all things, Iesin had look confused. She had stopped trying to explain, and the fact that she couldn't talk anymore made it harder.

"Gae," Iesin's voice brought her back to the present. "Hey, I know Teazerin isn't great people, but Cahaute is a whole planet, Gae. It isn't your personal property. You've got Tanistin."

Gaelian stuffed the necklace back into the pouch and replaced it under her pillow before she turned toward Iesin with a small smile. "Yes. I've got Tanistin. And as for Teazerin, well, two years is a long time. He could do a lot of damage, Ie. But Cahaute could destroy him. It could completely destroy him."

5

SHE DREAMED OF Cahaute again. The Mikke clan were at the river, swimming. In the water there was the bright reflection of a silver fish. It was a great fat fish, and it would taste very good. She was playing with them, the children in the river, playing and running on the slippery bright grass on the bank.

Suddenly the day darkened, and there was a flash, a loud Sky voice, and wetness all around. The Mikke clan ran for shelter. They were not friends of the Sky clan who sent the great flash-and-noise.

She was Keti. She had stayed out, exhilarated by the storm battering her, playing with the Sky children and the Fire children. Yes, that was right, she was Keti, the Fire-friends, the clan that sang and danced the storm in the drug visions. She was Keti, and her mother had been Keti, of the tribes, but she lived with the Mikke now. The Mikke were friends of River. River and Fire were not friends. She had no friends except one.

The others ran inside, and she danced with the Fire children, danced to their music, to their loud singing voices. How she danced.

A great ball of light flashed through the sky and rolled by her, and she laughed. It was a ball thrown by the Fire children who wanted a friend to come out and play. The Mikke didn't understand. Like their very ancient great clans, the Fire children played with the children of mortals, became their friends, and even gave them gifts of power. She knew this because

Tyakral, her foster mother, had explained it in the winter lodge.

She danced. She danced her joy and her sorrow, her story for the Fire children who came when the others ran away. No, that was not quite right. There was one on the edge of the clearing, a serious one, watching. He was not Mikke. She tried to dance better then, for her friend who talked like Tyakral and would one day have a hasute vision and become a shaman. Tyakral had said so.

The dancing became faster, and they danced with her. Near her leg, a great fallen log was struck by a bolt of flame and exploded. She laughed. The Fire clan enjoyed jokes. It was the way the Keti and the Mikke joked, a big splash with big laughter.

It was bright and clear, and she was happy. She had played with the friends of her people, played games and joked, as was right for a young relative. She was a clan-friend, a visitor in the winter lodge, since her mother was dead and her father had not returned from the early winter hunt. But one came across the clearing, holding a legbone. She heard this one say the word "chaluda," and she knew what it meant. It meant evil shaman.

Her friend, the serious boy who had watched, came over and waved his hands, but the Mikke children ignored him. "Chaluda, chaluda, chaluda," they all chanted.

Gaelian awoke with that word echoing in her head. It was one she had wanted to forget, and now it was part of her again, in her fiber. It seemed the more she tried to suppress Cahaute from her waking life, the more it haunted her dreams.

A young man climbed a hill. He wore nothing and carried only a flute to call the clans. He did not even have a name, for he had given that away the day before he had started through the woods. As he had given away everything else.

It was a good time of year to go hunting, late in the spring when everything was still bright and the sun was not too hot. There was cold water flowing and food bursting through the undergrowth. The standing food was ready for harvest, and the sitting food waited full of sweetness for a person or a notail. But he did not touch the food. Not now, not at this time.

The Dead Hill was not an easy climb. He had many memories of this place, many things he wanted to fix secure before he hunted what consumed him. The man who climbed back down the hill would be different from the one who climbed up.

Like the River, he thought, remembering Tyakral, the hasute of the Mikke and foster mother to the small friend he had left on this hill so very many seasons ago. They were children then, but children are very little different from adults, only more newly come from the place of the spirit. Cahaute.

He grasped for handholds among the rocks and found them with some difficulty. It was not easy to climb here, but there was no reason for anything here to be easy. Easy and hard were the same. Cahaute. All things came together in the center. So the b'hasute had told him, so his heart knew. There was nothing growing on the hill, although the forest around was lush and dense and full with the ripening season.

The top was completely flat and polished a beautiful black. It was as fine as obsidian, which made the best knives and the best arrowtips, but it could not be chipped off here. This place was as old as the legends. When the great clans, convinced by Anoni the Trickster, had divided the people and sent them to different places, it was here that they had left their children, here on the Dead Hill where the Great Lodge had rested before it returned to the heavens.

He held the flute in his teeth as he negotiated the last few feet of the hill and pulled himself over the ledge. Now he had only to call Mountain and wait. For what he was waiting he did not know, but it would be given or withheld, and then there would be understanding.

As he settled himself on the smooth black rock, baking in the warm afternoon sunlight, he reflected on the strangeness that had brought him, as the b'hasute had instructed. It was important to give things structure before letting them loose, as it was important that the bow be pulled taut before the arrow flies.

It had not started in him. He had never desired the spirit power of this place, or of the hasute, but there was no help for it. There was only the movement. He had felt sorry for the small girl, smaller than himself and without friends. He remembered. The Keti clan had all died, all but one. He remembered the battles and the news sayers from other places. The Keti had died except for one who must keep the balance, who belonged to all the people, cahaute.

She had been taken by the Mikke hasute, a good healer—
that was when he had met the child, although he doubted that
either of them had truly been children then. It did not matter,
for they had not met as children but as hasute. The older ones
had told him so, and that was why he climbed the hill today,
hungry, thirsty, waiting to play music for those who would
listen.

They had met, and he had seen a white nistora on his first
hunt. He had made a necklace for her with the teeth and claws
of the nistora, for it had been a hasute thing that had come in
his path, giving him the ornaments. He had used all of them,
leaving none out, for the nistora was not a thing to be taken
lightly. He had given it to her, and then he had walked with
her and her father to this place. He had climbed this hill and
watched and waited when the great flying lodge, as in the time
of the ancestors, came from the sky and took them away.

That was right. The last of the Keti must go to the great
clans and the spirits beyond to learn and grow before she
could come and care for her people. She had to go to her
father's people, the brothers-in-the-sky. All that he knew, although he did not know his own name.

But all this had led him to the hasute place, the place where
people walked the spirit world. Now it was time to gather a
spirit helper of his own. In the stillness that surrounded him he
knew that, and he wanted to cry. He wanted to be home in his
mother's lodge with soup bubbling over the fire and his
brothers and sisters around. He did not want to be here, away
from them, cut off from the world. Only the spirits would
speak to him here—or not speak, and that was frightening for
then he could not return.

He lifted the flute to his mouth, the flute that was the gift of
truth, the gift of calling to the spirits. He began to play as the
sun began to sink.

Around him the shadows began to move, throwing great
streams of flaming light onto the top of the hill. Still he
played. His stomach twisted in knots and protested, the breath
came dry from his lips, and his mouth craved sweet water, but
he did not move. The melody of the flute was high and beckoning, cutting through the night.

"Be patient," Hinacen, the old b'hasute, had said. "Watch
carefully. Everything on the Dead Hill is important, every-

thing that sits or crawls or breathes. This is the place where the forces balance. The forces balance everyplace. There is movement in a stone. Every place and every time is the center of the circle. This place and this time is the center of the circle."

He had nodded, had understood. Three days and three nights to spend here, that was all. The thunder and thirst assailed him again, and he forced himself not to think about it. He had been hungry and thirsty before. These were old enemies that he had defeated many times.

The b'hasute said that he must play and continue to play the flute, letting nothing stop him. The flute kept the mind awake and ready, cutting through illusions. Only the real could exist within the sacred sound of the flute, only the real was important here on the Dead Hill, waiting to become part of cahaute, the center and the edge, the circle. Deliberately, he closed himself to everything but the music, keeping himself motionless except for the drifting of his fingers and the evenness of his breath.

The sun sank in an array of colors, and the stars came out, a star for every tree, spreading a second forest overhead. The temperature dropped sharply, and the wind picked up, buffeting his torso and slowing his music. There was no shelter on the Dead Hill, no windbreak. His legs were cramped from the long sitting, and still he ignored it. Better to sit still and play, keep playing as instructed, playing so the stars could dance and call their elders. Somewhere in that beyond people lived, as they lived here with earth and water.

His arms began to ache, and his hands were tingling, numb, the blood drained from the extremities. Above him the sky began to change, and the chill deepened. He watched the shadows resolve into clouds, great clouds that drifted low and rumbled. The Fire clan had come to look, and he played for them, remembering his young friend, their friend. The flash-and-noise danced across the expanse of woods, the trees joining them in the wind, the tips swaying and waving to the rhythm of his flute. The clouds passed overhead, and they bowed to each other, two lines of dancers across the sky.

His throat was dry and his mouth parched. He wanted a small pebble to suck to bring the water, but the b'hasute had said that nothing might pass his lips. Besides, there were no pebbles on the top of this hill. It had been cut flat and polished and then swept daily by the wind. Nothing at all remained but the place itself, throbbing not only with his music but with time.

He reached back into time, deep into the rock below him. He felt the warmth still living under the surface of the hill, the movement of it, the life within. He was Roneedee, of the Mountain-friends' clan, and all things that came from the earth were his. The trees and the foods, sitting and standing, the small animals and the larger ones not marked by the other clans, they were all his familiars.

He thought of a small hopper, a gift of the Keti girl, and blew a mournful note. The small one had died long ago, for they never lived long. He had skinned it and kept the skin unused, a remembrance of the thing that had chosen him. A thing, a friend, and a power that had left this world.

He saw the hopper quite clearly before him, but the eyes were changed. No longer a stupid no-tail, this one had intelligence. It came up and licked his knee, then backed off, waiting. The soft warmth of its tongue reminded him of when he was a child and the other no-tail had lived with him and licked him. He kept playing and nodded to this one, a messenger.

Regarding him intently, the hopper came up to him again, urgently, indicating with his head that the man must follow. The flute came away from his mouth, not by his own volition, and he stood, following the small one across the flat hilltop. He felt light, so light that the wind lifted him several fingers above the hard surface.

He was led around in a circle and then to the far side of the cliff, where the no-tail waited anxiously for him. Over the side of the cliff, he saw three warrior-birds carrying a fish together. The hopper hadn't moved, but now it began to jump up and down anxiously in place. As he knelt to calm the timid furred one, he noticed a circle of four markings cut into the ice-smooth surface of the stone.

He ran his hands over the markings to know them, and they lit with the fire of the four Colors. The cutting had been smoothed with age and was not visible, but as the brilliant fire ran into the scratches, they came alive, all of the Colors, a hasute marking.

The warrior-birds were silent. They wheeled and flew overhead, circled and dropped the fish behind him.

He turned, and there was no fish but a lance, with stripes of color moving through it, glimmering, like one of the society dance lances. It lay still and quiet, unmoved by the harsh wind, and he reached for it. As his fingers brushed it, it came alive and began to sway and swerve, the vivid painting undulating over its back. He turned to see to the no-tail, because the small ones feared snakes, but it was gone.

Three times he yelled sharply, making sound to break any illusion, but the snake remained a snake, now rearing up its head, which had been the tip of the lance. Its head was green and its tongue and fangs bright red. It was a pretty thing, he thought. It wove in and out around his arm, the tongue flickering over his skin, smelling him. He watched, fascinated.

The snake struck without warning, burying his fangs deep in his wrist. Heat, like liquid fire, poured into him and spread quickly through his arm and into his body. He no longer felt the chill of the wind. Red lines ran up his arm and turned black, and he knew he was dying. It was very warm.

His voice opened to the sky, and he began to sing a dying song, the song he had been given in a dream before his first raid. Without the song he would not go, and the song came through him now, but he did not feel himself singing. He wasn't singing. The song was around him; he heard it from the outside, as if the sky were singing for him. As he listened carefully, the words began to change, and he strove to remember them.

He did not know why he must remember. He would die, and the song was not a song for a man. He sat again and relaxed, watching the changing scene around him, listening to the great singing and waiting for death to come.

The clouds were singing the song now, singing loud and low, grunting and rumbling in their own language, but he understood. He tried to greet them, but his mouth was too dry. For a moment, he had forgotten that he was dead.

A great arrow of sky-fire jumped out from the clouds and buried itself in the hill on his right. He thanked the clouds for their gift. It wasn't bad to die on the hill, but the b'hasute and his parents would never know that the clouds had given him their gift. They would never know the wonderful song repeating itself in his ears.

He looked down and saw that the lines of color had extended over his whole body, painting him brightly. If he were alive, he would return and paint this way. But he knew he was dead.

He looked for the snake, but it was gone. He understood that both it and the no-tail were sent from Mountain to guide his dying. Across the flatness of the hilltop, illuminated in the sky, he saw a great star falling, the size of a winter lodge. He smiled, wondering if it were the Great Lodge of the clans, come again to their children.

There must be a gift in return. He saw the flute lying on the other side of the barren hill where he had abandoned it. Slowly, achingly, he got to his feet and crossed the smooth stone. He played a new tune this time, a gift tune. He had seen. He had understood.

The man opened his eyes with a start. His body was racked with cold, and his stomach contracted with hunger. He couldn't be dead any longer. He had been dead, and he was alive again. The stone beneath his feet was smooth. He tried to find the marked place that the hopper had shown him, but there was not a single scratch on the polished expanse. He had learned something when he was dead, a new song and the power of the snake and the small ones. He had been the friend of Fire, and he had seen the Great Lodge of the ancestors.

In his head he heard a word repeated over and over again. Nyapetin. Nyapetin. Suddenly he understood and laughed brightly. He had a name now. He hooted with pleasure, pleasure in feeling the heat of the sun and the hearing his own name.

He had lost track of the days, but it must be time to go home. He had achieved what he had wanted, a vision and a name, and he had been dead and played the flute in the spirit places. He felt giddy and a littly dizzy, but there was no one to say how a person should feel after having died. He had to return to his tribe and paint his body with the snake lines and sing the new song he had been given.

Suddenly recalling, he turned his hand over, almost fearing what he would find. He breathed a sigh of relief. Two tiny puncture marks were puckered and white inside his wrist, looking old although they had been made only the night before—if it *had* been the night before, if not the same day, or a long time ago. . . . He had been dead, and there is no time for the dead. Maybe he had been dead for a hundred seasons.

He shook off those thoughts and climbed down to the forest

below, reining in his excitement. The descent was not an easy one, and he was weak from hunger and thirst. But the cool shade of the trees and the moisture of the air refreshed him. Last year's pine needles under his feet made a luxurious carpet, and here below the harsh wind was only the soft whispering scent of sweet blossoms that grew in patches of light between the trees. The air smelled of life, rich and clean, and he reveled in the walk.

The stream came upon him almost too quickly. Nyapetin lay his flute on the bank and laughed again. He stepped into the water and rubbed himself vigorously with sand and his hair with the tappa leaves that grew nearby. Letting the water take him, he swam downstream to a placid pool at the lower end of the stream and lay on the grassy bank to dry. It was only then that the thirst assailed him and he returned to the pool.

As he knelt to lift a handful of water, his breath caught in his throat. He had seen himself reflected in this pool many times, but there was a different person there now. The bones had not changed, nor the copper skin, nor his hair. But the expression was clear now, as if the other he had been had not been defined, hidden in some fog. Everything was thrown into high relief, shorn of age or youth, polished like the Dead Hill. In his own face he saw the center of the circle. Cahaute.

He took a mouthful of water and spat it out, and then another. This one he held in his mouth until it warmed before he swallowed. Cold water on a starving stomach made cramps, and it would be a bad omen if he returned ill. Silently he thanked River for its generosity and pulled out a single strand of hair, offering it to River as a thanks-gift.

The camp was just beyond. He braided his hair neatly, tied the ends with strands of tough yellow grass, and rubbed his teeth with a freshly peeled stick. Then, feeling clean and ready, he fetched the flute and returned home.

At the sound of the flute, his family and the b'hasute went out to greet him, the new one returning. His sister came forward and threw a robe over his shoulders, and his family surrounded him and led him back to the lodge. There Nyapetin ate and slept for a long time, unmoving and without dreams.

When he woke, Hinacen the b'hasute sat and listened with more than his ears. He looked carefully at the scars on Nyapetin's wrist and made small noises in the back of his throat.

"You were given the name that means 'returned guide.' Do you know why?"

Nyapetin shook his head. He had not understood this, only that it was the right name and that it was his own as nothing had ever been his own before.

The old man shook his head slowly. "Well, well, there are things moving. The balance is kept and not kept. The Fire-friends are gone and must return as you have returned, friend of the Fire clan. And you have seen it is so, that you are a spirit helper to others and spirit helpers are given to you. Now go away. I want to sit in the sun."

Nyapetin rose and wandered back to his mother's lodge where the family and Roneedee clan had gathered to make a feast to honor his vision and new name. He reclined to watch the activity and did not notice Hinacen come up behind him.

"Young ears, and you hear nothing," the old b'hasute chided. "Still, deaf as you are, there is something I have remembered."

Nyapetin waited, wondering what Hinacen would say, but the old man said nothing. Instead, the weathered fingers untied the thongs at the back of his neck, unfastening the nistora necklace that had been Hinacen's as long as anyone in the tribe could remember. It was the symbol of the great warrior shaman, one who was b'hasute. He felt like stone, like Mountain, unable to move as the ancient b'hasute tied the necklace around his throat. It fit comfortably, four tiers high, with all the teeth and claws, none left out. Hinacen turned away, and Nyapetin said nothing. There was nothing and everything to say. He had not wanted to be this thing, responsible for the balance, the point within the center that he had seen in the pool. To be the center of the circle was to be responsible for the people, for Mountain and River and the whole of the world. He did not want this at all, but it had been put to him.

Even though the spring sun was warm and Breath had scented the air sweetly, Nyapetin was cold. Around him he noticed his parents and friends watching in amazement. Hinacen did not make mistakes. This thing must be right, but it was terrifying.

The good smell of meat roasting over the open fire no longer attracted Nyapetin. The bright singing of his sisters sounded far away. They lowered their voices and then became

silent as everyone noticed the nistora teeth around his neck.
They all looked at him, but none straight in the eye. He was
changed. He had become hasute.

In a sudden panic, Nyapetin fled down to the pool by the
river. There, in the deep shadows, he curled up in a ball and
mourned for the life that was gone. All of his own life had
been taken by that gesture. He felt no power in him, no revela-
tion, no great mystery.

He could hear voices on the hill, the people having a party in
his honor. He couldn't bear to listen. He played the flute
again, the song he had learned when he was dead. It did not
make him more comfortable, but the playing kept his mind occupied, away from the friends whom he no longer owned and
the family that was no longer family. He was owned by all the
people now. He was kin to all and none.

He thought back to the little girl he had left on the Dead Hill
so very many seasons ago. She was Keti, the one who was like
himself, belonging to all people and to none. With his whole
heart he wished her back, so there would be someone who
would look at him and not be afraid.

As he continued to play, he saw a slow movement in the
grass, of something jewel-like under the soft gold of the late
afternoon sun. It glided toward him and away, a snake
brother, a messenger. He called to it softly, but it did not listen. As he watched, the snake danced in the tough grass, growing longer and longer until its length had doubled. And then it
moved off. Nyapetin saw that it had shed its skin and left it
lying in the yellow grass, a thing of great mystery. He took up
the snake skin and tied it in his hair.

The sun was setting, throwing deep pinks and blazing reds
across the pool. On the hill, he could hear them laughing
loudly now, far away. They were celebrating his vision and his
name. The sorrow drained out of him, fled, and was gone, and
there was only silence and the distant voices. He stood and
then wandered deeper into the woods, to a place where their
singing would not disturb him. Tomorrow he would return, he
knew, and start to learn from Hinacen. Tomorrow. Tonight
he would sleep alone in the woods, away from all people who
now owned his soul.

6

GAELIAN GOT OUT of the cab, waited for what seemed an interminable length of time before her card popped out of the credit slot, and shouldered her bag. From the front gate, the house didn't seem any different than the first time she had seen it, when she was seven and her father had brought her back to this strange and unwelcoming place. It was still bleak. They hadn't sent a car for her, although they should have, and she only prayed that the rest of her luggage would actually arrive as ordered.

For a moment, resentment flickered. The harsh, clean lines of the house against the sweeping grey apron reminded her of YnSetti's face, closed and slightly sneering. Now, back at the Academy, the rest of her class was busy with parties and preparations. The hall of the dorm smelled of cleaning solution and polish. Firsties paraded up and down the halls in their new uniforms, admiring their newly tailored figures, surprised to catch a glimpse of an officer instead of a midshipman. Tomorrow night was the traditional firstie bonfire, when all her class would toss something symbolic—a hat or an athletic uniform or pages of printout—into the flames. Gaelian could see the heavy pile that she had planned to feed to the bonfire, printouts of every single homework assignment from required plasma physics, semesters one through n. Now, Iesin would make the toss for her.

Her grandmother could have held on for two more weeks to permit her to graduate. It wasn't that she wouldn't finish and get her commission and her assignment. But the ceremonies, the traditions, the rewards, after six years of study and what seemed like more than six years of misery, were denied.

The notification had come what seemed an eternity ago, although in reality it had just been two days. Her grandmother, the Head of her household, was in the final dying stage. Gaelian had to return to witness the death and the traditions of installing the new Head. And herself as the new eldest. Iesin had volunteered to come with her, but Gaelian rejected the offer flatly. After all, she had explained to Ie, how would she get every detail of Graduation Week, who had made fools of themselves, who had attended which parties with whom, and what everyone had said, if Ie didn't go to all of them and report everything with complete accuracy. Iesin hadn't volunteered twice, and Gaelian didn't blame her.

Now the household had deprived her of her right, her own graduation as the top flier and fifth from the top overall in her class, and they couldn't even spare a car to meet her at the port. It was typical of her family. Some things would change when her father was Head of the household, she hoped. But it didn't look likely.

She glanced at her chrono. Fifteen minutes spent in self-pity was more than enough. At least it should do for now. She turned to the house and began to walk across the blazing apron, idly wondering if anyone had noticed her approach or if they were all closeted away making plans.

The massive slab doors parted for her after a momentary hesitation. Security was lax. There would be a lot of people coming and going at this time, doctors and nerris priests and the suppliers of funeral goods, and soon friends and other members of the Board and all the rest. There was no reason to set the thing on a serious scan. It would only bottleneck the whole affair, and the death of the Head of the household should be stately and silent. Her grandmother always did everything in the very best of taste, and there was no reason to suppose that dying was very different.

It wasn't actually dark once she got inside, but the opaqued windows and the puddles of artificial light created the impression of gloom. And it was silent. Gaelian cursed softly to herself. Someone should come down to greet her. It was only proper. Defiantly, she threw her soft bag onto the floor, where it lay illuminated by a stray shaft of fluorescence.

"It's good you were able to come."

Gaelian raised her eyes from the bag and found herself staring into Dobrin's face. There was no expression there, even though she could clearly read the weariness around the eyes and mouth.

"Shall we go up?" Gaelian asked pointlessly.

"She's sleeping now. We shouldn't disturb her. The doctor will call if there's any change," Dobrin replied lightly. "Would you like something to drink? There's brandy in the library, if I'm not mistaken."

She recognized the strategy easily enough and had to give Dobrin his due. Perhaps he wasn't a master of the blue yet, but was much better than she remembered. She knew she would have to be very, very wary around him, and she was tired. It had been a long trip, and she didn't even know what she was playing yet. Or, as Iesin had said, if they were even in the same court.

"I'd rather wash up first," she replied. "It was a long trip, and you know how good the amenities are when you catch military transport."

Dobrin smiled grimly and nodded. "When you're done, join us in the library. I think we should be prepared, don't you? And there are a few things I think we need to discuss before Grandmother wakes. Then, of course, we'll have some time with her."

Gaelian only half grunted in acknowledgment and climbed the stairs to the gallery that overlooked the great hall. From here she could see her bag, still lying on the floor, and Dobrin staring at it unmoving. She shrugged and made her way to her own suite.

It had been untouched since the last time she'd been home. Not that Dobrin would think her so stupid as to leave anything useful where he could find it so easily, but it was good to know that there was some space here that was inviolate, hers alone. The warm colors, the brass, and the pale yellow rug reminded her of the sunlight on Cahaute; the modern wood sculpture, the Adredri hanging of raw and dyed yarns reminded her of Tyakral's lodge, of trees and the smell of the new-green time, the time of new life. It had been her enclave, and even now, in this house where she felt more like an intruder than a welcome guest, let alone a member of the family, this place was a sanctuary.

She washed slowly, enjoying the luxury of the hot water and the scented soap, letting the water take the tension of the long ride from her. She knew what she really needed was a couple of hours of sleep, but there was no time for that. And she would need all her wits to deal with whatever Dobrin had in mind. There was no question that he wanted to get at her while she was still too tired to think straight. She dialed for a mild stimulant while she dried her hair and dressed in the loose full pants and tunic that contrasted so sharply with her uniform. She thought for a moment and then took out a long, heavy scarf. The glowing gold and brilliant red pattern went well with the rust brown she wore, and deliberately she draped it over her right shoulder, looping on her left arm. She smiled unpleasantly. Let Dobrin remember who was the eldest now, or very soon to be. He had been in uniform, and there was no doubt that that was to impress her with his superior rank. But here they were family, and she ranked him.

She drank the stimulant, puckering at the slightly sour taste, and sat on a hard, straight chair to wait for the effect. The tingling began very subtly in her limbs, and she inhaled slowly, dropping everything away.

Focus was the way to win in nerris. Focus and awareness, letting go of the self and going with the play. Like flying. When she rose, ready, she had forgotten the nightmares and flying, the household and herself. She had forgotten the parties that she was missing, even the graduation. Now she was ready for Dobrin.

The library was in a different wing of the house. Books lined the walls, although no one ever read them. They were far too fragile to be touched by hands, and the knowledge they held was safe in the computer system. There was no reason to unlock the glass cases that lined the walls, that attested more to the wealth and antiquity of the household than to the good taste and learning of its members. In the center was a table, with a carved replica of their solar system on it. Dobrin stood in uniform on the far side, the table like a barrier between them, offering a glass. Whether it was a peace offering or a challenge, Gaelian couldn't guess, but she accepted. She seated herself in one of the large, overstuffed chairs before Dobrin invited her, insolence from a junior officer and propriety in the household.

"I'm not sure we have anything to discuss," Gaelian began

slowly, savoring the vaguely sweet taste of the fruit brandy. "My father is eldest, and although he isn't in perfect health, he isn't dying, either. He will be the next Head of the household, no matter what we decide. So I rather think this is all immaterial."

Dobrin took his time. A sip of brandy, a cursory glance at the glassed shelves. "There have been a few developments," he said very softly. "You should be aware of them before Grandmother dies and the whole world invades our privacy. It would be better if the Board, among others, stayed out of household business. Anyway, it isn't the Board that I want to talk to you about."

In his left hand, he proffered a heavy sheaf of papers. "Read them very carefully. If you have any doubts as to the legality of the signature, notice the names of the witnesses. There is, of course, a proper record complete with retinal scan, too, but I thought you would find the more traditional declaration convincing."

There was no triumph in his voice, but Gaelian wasn't fooled. Properly, she took the papers with both hands, with a generous respect that was necessary between adversaries. She only had to glance at the heading; it wasn't necessary to read more, but she stared at it blankly, pretending to read.

She had to get her bearings quickly. This was beyond anything she had suspected. She should have been notified immediately—or consulted beforehand, made a witness herself. But here it was, presented to her as accomplished, leaving her with no alternatives.

"I trust you find the legalities in order," Dobrin said smoothly.

"It isn't the legalities that concern me. Why wasn't I notified immediately? Why did you keep this from me? Don't I have a right to know?"

Dobrin merely shrugged. "A right, certainly. And I'm not hiding anything, nor is anyone else. As you will notice from the date, it was done while you were in transit. We did attempt to contact you, but since you had opted for a pickup on whatever you could get, well, there wasn't really any way to trace you properly before your arrival. And I had no wish to send this over open lines. Better that everything's resolved between all of us before the Board and the other Ot-tan catch a word. The very least we can do is present a united front."

She studied him carefully, thinking. He was playing blue. His tone, the whole atmosphere of reasonableness, the care of it all made it obvious. And obvious in blue opens the attack. She had prepared to play red, but something changed.

"Dobrin, I might be a lot of things, but I'm not an idiot. You are forcing a confrontation now because I will only get stronger in time, and you don't mean to give me that time. Fair enough."

He smiled, and this time there was a shadow of delight. He sat back comfortably and began to savor his drink. Now, only now that it's finally open, is he able to be comfortable in my presence, she thought. And she knew that the relaxation itself was a calculated move. Yet not calculated at the same time. He was playing so perfectly that the correct action and the true one were single. She gave him credit for that.

"Was there anything else you thought we should discuss in private?" Gaelian asked, rising.

"I only wanted you to know about this," Dobrin said, his eyes half lowered, the image of contentment.

"Then, if you don't mind, I'd like to rest. It was a long trip, and you know just how pleasant military transport is." She placed her half-consumed glass on the table and glided out.

She went up the stairs and crossed the gallery but did not turn toward her own suite. Instead, she went on, past the closed-off rooms that were used for guests and the nursery where she had lived before she had been sent away to normal school. At the very end of the corridor, she found the door and knocked.

There was no answer, and she knocked again, harder. Finally, she tried the door and found it open.

"Why, Papa?" she asked in Cahaute.

Renan YnTourne was lying on a glossy grey sofa, one arm flung over his eyes as if trying to escape the world. He could have been drunk, asleep, or dead, and in the low light, any of the three was possible.

Gaelian crossed the space and curled up on the soft carpet beside the couch. She touched his forehead gently. Her father lowered his arm and brushed his hand lightly over her hair. "Your grandmother, Dobrin, and the Board. They couldn't force me openly, but there was nothing I could do at this point. She almost made it public, and we couldn't risk that, or your chances would have gone too."

Gaelian took his hand. He was drunk, but then he was very often drunk since they had returned. She thought that he should have stayed, but he had been ambitious. Not for himself, but for her. She hardly remembered the father she had known on Cahaute.

"Gae, they knew I didn't want the Headship of the house. I never have. And when your grandmother threatened to expose us both, well, I could only protect one of us."

Gaelian shook her head. "I'm not sure Grandmother would really go public. She wouldn't want the scandal. And I think Dobrin's of the same mind. You should have thought of it. They'd never hurt the household. Papa, you look terrible. You should at least go to sleep, or something." Thinking of the household, she didn't realize that she had spoken in Dinorean.

"Speak Cahaute, Gae," he said. "Tell me about school, about all the things you've done. Tell me about the people you know, about your plans for next year. Is Iesin going to get the admin post she wants? I'd heard something about getting some very special posting. Tell me about it."

She shook her head and began to speak softly, sometimes dredging her memory for words. It was their ritual every year and the only chance she got to speak the language she knew as her mother tongue. She drifted into their ritual, letting the dark and the difficulty of explaining in a language not structured to the demands of her life take over her thoughts and observations. Suddenly the reverie broke, and she saw only the drunk Renan, the one the Ot-tan talked about, lying with his feet on the arm of a sofa, his eyes too sensitive for full light.

"Papa, you threw me out!" she shouted like a small child. "You let them take it from you. Mama would have been ashamed. All the Keti would have been ashamed. You were to be chief, and you walked away. You said, here, take it, go. And you left me with nothing, nothing to fight with, nothing at all. You gave away your place in the tribe."

"The hasute gives away everything," her father reminded her softly.

"You are not hasute," she retorted. "You did not have a hill vision, you did not look into tomorrow, and the people do not own your soul."

She jerked her hand from his and wrapped her arms around herself. It was cold. In the white time, it was always cold. A storm blew through her, and she shuddered like a small child, trying very hard not to cry. Children of the Keti were strong and did not cry.

She let out a long wail. It was not for herself, but for the storm in her. He was right. It was not the thing he drank that made him do this, but the truth. It was uraka to walk away from things, to give them over. The word startled her. Uraka. Her father had it, more than she who was born to it but had forgotten.

"I walked away once before," her father continued. "When your mother died. My takka brother told me. I was alone, tracking. I burned everything. Everything. And then when you found me again, I left even more. I left with you, everything remained there. Since then, I have had nothing, only hope."

He spoke like someone she remembered, from some time far away. It was the language of Cahaute, but it was also the being, the need, the freedom. He had left Cahaute, the only home he had ever acknowledged. And now he was leaving the Headship of a household, which meant nothing to him and never had.

"But you should go and sleep," he said to her. "It's late, and you've traveled far, and you've found more unhappy news. Sleep. Tomorrow will be itself."

He turned slightly toward the back of the sofa and tossed his arm over his face again.

She returned to her own room. The stimulant was wearing off and her head felt fuzzy. Too much was happening all at once, and she couldn't make sense of any of it, although bits of sense somehow flickered around the edges of her thoughts. She was too tired to grasp or pursue them. She was almost too tired to undress.

The next morning everything had receded. She remembered what Dobrin had said, what he had shown her, but in the light and with a clear head, it seemed to merge with the dreams of the night. Pulling on a thin robe, she signed in on the small terminal discreetly placed over her delicate antique writing table.

The authorizations and then the words flowed in amber light over the screen. Renan YnTourne, due to ill health as well as his dedication to scholarship, has decided to renounce any rights to the Headship of the YnTourne household and the Board, as well as any active position in the Craft Company.

There were only five sentences, bound on both sides with authorizations, witness codes, and permissions from the Board, her grandmother, and all other necessary and nonessential personnel. Gaelian stared at the message for a long time, permitting the shock to ride through her. It had been the last thing she would have expected, and the circumstances last night had made everything suspect.

Finally, she rose from the intricately carved chair and drew the inlaid screens over the terminal. She washed and dressed in civilian clothes again, though choosing a less formal outfit than she had the night before. She draped a long grey, red, and purple patterned scarf over her shoulders in an informal manner. It was too late for breakfast, and the rules of the house were strict about mealtimes, so she sneaked into the kitchen and dialed herself a light snack. She hadn't realized that she was so hungry, but there hadn't been time for a decent meal the night before, and she had slept for a long time. Then she walked in the garden.

Walking stimulated thinking. Running was for not thinking, but walking was good to turn ideas around. She found herself near the family nerris court and deliberately entered it. She had wanted to avoid this corner, but perhaps it would give her something to work with.

The court was old, older than the house by far, and had been unused for a very long time. The stone walls were covered with verdure on the outside, and the paint was chipped and faded on the interior walls. Weeds were working cracks in what had been a smoothly paved surface, and the whole had the look of something long abandoned, forgotten.

By all the laws and traditions, she should inherit. It might be her father's choice to resign from the family business, but after him she was the heir. Dobrin might have her grandmother's support and more experience than she, but by all they held by right of age, the household and the Company were hers. On the Board, she should be able to count on the support of the YnSetti and the YnOestal at least. They were her own connections. It rather amazed her to think that the engagement to Teazerin might have some redeeming feature. It did bind his family more to her rise and fortunes than to Dobrin's. And the YnOestal she knew well. There was personal loyalty there. She had been counting on a few more years, with her father as Head, to build her own base. Still, the

YnSetti and the YnOestal were nothing to dismiss.

Then there were her shares in the Craft Company. By law, her grandmother's shares would be divided evenly between her, her father and Dobrin. If she could get her father to throw his shares in with hers, either through a proxy or as a free gift, she would have controlling interest in the Company, enough to overrule anything Dobrin tried. And securing controlling shares would prove her ability to the Board. The skeleton of a plan started to come to her, and she smiled alone in the nerris court. Then she left the high, crumbling walls and strolled back to the house. When it was all safely hers, she would keep the court as it was. No modernization. Perhaps a little grooming now and then, but the faded paint and weeds had given her sanctuary.

"Where in all four hells have you been?" Missili, the Adedri housekeeper, asked sharply when Gaelian appeared at the back door. "We've been looking everywhere for you. And just like a little savage, too, running off as soon as you get home and not even asking to see your grandmother once, and her so sick."

"You will kindly remember not to address me in that manner," Gaelian replied coldly. Missili had been with her grandmother since the Head of the YnTourne had been seventeen years old. She was perhaps one of the few human servants left in the entire universe, and an Adedri, but she had become so thoroughly a part of YnTourne life that she had taken on the air of a family member. Surely, she thought herself one. The housekeeper had never accepted her as a real member of the family, not since she first entered the house wearing a cutdown spacer's jacket and speaking Dinorean with a heavy accent. The accent was gone, but the image remained. Missili was the only person who ever dared remind her of it.

"Your grandmother has asked for you and Dobrin together to attend her. I think she has something very important in mind. And not for you to go traipsing out into the garden on a fine morning, when she's waiting to die!"

Gaelian pushed past the irate housekeeper and made her way through the back halls into the foyer and up the stairs.

Dobrin was already there, waiting, when the door opened silently to admit Gaelian. There was so little light in her grandmother's room that whatever colors were present had bleached into tones of grey. Even shrunken and still as she was on the massive bed, Gaelian thought that her grandmother had the aura of command. Her face was drawn but as stern as ever, her eyes startlingly clear and appraising. As Gaelian bent to kiss the old woman's palm, she was sure she caught the hint of a sneer crossing her grandmother's face.

"Well," her grandmother said, smiling harshly, "it's all finally open, isn't it? So good of Renan to do as he's asked, don't you think? I wanted you both here for a reason. Dobrin, there's a packet for you over on the table."

Dobrin rose and crossed over to the dull steel sideboard on the far side of the room. Several packages lay there, and he rifled through them.

"No," the woman on the bed said. "The sealed one. On the left. With your name."

Dobrin recovered the package and returned to his place.

"Gaelian," her grandmother asked, "do you have any idea of what I'm giving Dobrin?"

Gaelian shook her head. She had a pretty good idea, but there were several other possibilities. Even dying, the Head of the YnTourne wasn't above playing the game. The old-fashioned way, that was, the way where a scratch was minor, where the sharp end of the stick was driven deeply into the opponent's body. Coolly, she assessed her position and realized that she hated and respected her grandmother in equal proportion but that the hate was not personal. There was nothing at all personal between them.

"Now, how does the tradition go?" her grandmother asked. "I believe that inheritance has to go to someone of confirmed parentage, fully of Dinorean blood, Li-tan or Sonnatan at the least on the non-Ot-tan side. Although it is better to be Ot-tan on both sides, of course. Isn't that true?"

Gaelian nodded and felt her stomach drop to the level of her feet. She knew what was coming, the one thing she didn't dare try to face down.

"I have had my suspicions," her grandmother continued. "Not only from the way you look, although that honestly does have something to do with it. But also because of the fact that your father has never had anything to do with the YnSerianis. Nor have you. It is strange that you would have nothing to do with your mother's family."

Gaelian smiled tightly. "I don't know what you mean," she said. "You might suspect that my mother wasn't Gaelian

YnSerianis, but there's no way to prove it. And as for . . . that other thing you alluded to . . . You know perfectly well that species can't interbreed. Biological definition of species—but you know all that. Common gene pool. Members of different species can't produce fertile offspring, when they can produce offspring at all.''

"There's no proof that you can have children," Dobrin said, deceptively mild.

"The doctors seem to think I'm perfectly normal, thank you," Gaelian countered, her voice cold. She knew she should keep to the controlled, reasonable tones that Dobrin used, but fury was getting the better of her.

"Well, it wouldn't be any problem to do a chromosome scan. It doesn't take an hour," Dobrin suggested, seemingly at the height of reasonableness.

Gaelian smiled nastily. "You wouldn't demand that, though. You wouldn't dare. Because if I don't check out, you've got a fraud and a scandal on your hands, and I don't think you want that in the household. And if I do, which I would, you'd face charges. From me, for trying to do me out of my inheritance, and from my father and the YnVereanos for libel."

Her grandmother looked very happy, as if she had been waiting for this scene. There was even a tinge of color in her face as she beamed at them, the image of the kindly loving grandparent.

Dobrin seemed taken aback. He wasn't controlled enough to prevent her from seeing that she had surprised him. Good. Let him think that she had come up with all of that on the spot. The fact that her father had drilled her in that little speech ever since she was twelve wasn't relevant.

"The package I gave Dobrin gives complete information on all of my suspicions, the why and wherefore, with background data," her grandmother chirped quite happily. "How you two use it is up to you. Play well."

The old woman closed her eyes, and Gaelian and Dobrin both knew they were dismissed. Gaelian rose and preceded Dobrin from the room. He permitted it, acknowledging if only temporarily her position. Gaelian headed directly for her own room without a word to her cousin. She didn't want to talk to him before lunch.

She washed quickly, made it to the dining room a little before the other members of the household, and took her grandmother's place at the head of the table. If her grandmother could not preside over a meal, it was the place of the eldest to do so. When Dobrin entered the narrow room and saw her in that place of honor, he hesitated momentarily before he took his own seat. Dobrin was canny; he wouldn't be an easy enemy. They ate in silence, her father making his appearance at the last moment as usual. The meal over, she followed her father into the library.

"Let's walk," he said. "Let's go out to the garden."

She followed quietly, not knowing quite why he wanted to leave the cool shelter of the library. Once they were out among the flowers, he turned to her.

"Gaelian, it isn't really safe for us to talk in the house," he said in Cahaute. "It's one thing that we speak in a language they don't understand. I've managed to convince everyone that it is simply an intellectual's preference not to forget a language once learned and to that I refuse to permit you to forget it, either. Which was quite reasonable. You were very young. You know, your grandmother tried to force me to stop speaking to you in anything but Dinorean. 'What use has the child got for another language anyway?' she'd say. Late at night, you understand, after you had gone to bed. I could let it pass. I thought, still think, that some day it will be important for you, that you didn't forget."

"Papa, today Grandmother said a bit too much about who my mother might have been to Dobrin. In front of me, I said what you told me to say," Gaelian informed him. "I think it had an effect." She bent down and pulled a single flowering weed from the ground, twisting the stem in her fingers. "But there's something I don't understand. You always said I'd check out in a scan, that I wasn't infertile, and I don't know how that's possible. I mean, everything I know says that my existence is impossible, or at least pretty improbable."

"I didn't want to talk in the house because I'm pretty sure that Dobrin's got ears everywhere," Renan continued as if he hadn't heard. "I've been pretty sure of that for awhile. Gae, how much do you remember of Cahaute? What are the four sacred colors?"

She looked at him blankly. That was a stupid question. "Red, black, yellow, and blue," she answered, shrugging. "What has that got to do with anything?"

"Do you remember any of the Chants of the People, for example, the ones on the selection or the giving of the gifts?" he asked, ignoring her question.

"Some," she said. This was craziness. No wonder they hadn't wanted him as Head of the household or of the Company. He'd always been a little strange, like this, but she thought it was because he was a scholar. Now he was just avoiding everything, preoccupied with his own passion for Cahaute. And there was surely no reason they couldn't have had this discussion in the library. What had he said that Dobrin couldn't hear, anyway? Besides, Dobrin didn't know a word of Cahaute.

"Maybe we should go back," Renan said. "Dobrin received a gift today, a gift of knowledge. So you should receive one as well. I made copies of my tapes of the Chants of the People, of Hinacen telling all the old legends. I was going to give them to you when I thought you would need them, or maybe as a graduation gift. Yes, let's call it a graduation gift."

Gaelian returned to her room completely bemused. Her father had been no help at all.

She dared not miss dinner, the ritual of taking her place at the head of the table. Only Grandmother was dying, finally and forever, and now the game was for real. She had thought that she would be happy when this time came, and she found that she was not. There was only the sense of vague relief. Gaelian ate without appetite and returned to her sanctuary to find that a stack of tapes had been delivered and waited on the ladylike writing table.

Fingering the thin desk box, rage filled her. She wanted to hurl the tapes across the room, through the window. Instead, she opened the ornate cabinetry and slid a disk into the base of the terminal.

7

In the days before the first people, there were only the Power Ones in their own clan, and of them there were only six, hardly enough to fill a single lodge. There was Rock, the father of Mountain, and Breath, the mother of wind. There was Blaze, the father of fire and of the flashing sky, and there was River, the mother of water and the bringer of tears. And there was Yenhica the War Maiden who made the lance and the arrows, and with them lived Anoni the Trickster. It was a very small band, and there were no children living among them yet, and they were lonely. They longed for others to visit during the white time and to hunt with them in the summer, to share feasts and parties and to exchange gifts. And as they spoke about it, they became more and more lonely.

One day Blaze, the father of all fires, said to Breath, grandmother of Sky, "My sister, if the four of us who are the powers of all the worlds come together, we can make people."

Breath agreed that it was a very good idea. So Rock, the father of Mountain, made them bodies of stone, and River gave them blood and tears. Breath gave them air in their lungs, and Blaze gave each a tiny fire, a little secret flame of thought that made them different from animals.

For a time, everyone was very happy, and there was much visiting and exchanging of presents. There were many fine feasts, for Mountain and Sky and River *yielded up their food, and Blaze gave them fire to cook it. Yenhica taught them to use the bow and lance and to hunt the herds. Anoni told stories and jokes, and life was very good.*

Many seasons passed happily, and those of the Power Clan spent all their time among the people. Then, Anoni became jealous. He went among the Power Clan saying, "Look at these people we have made. They have everything. They are strong because Yenhica gave them good eyes for the lance and bow. They have the voices of the sparkling creek and dance like bright water over the rocks. They hunt and eat all the foods of Mountain, the sitting berries and the standing foods, and they are never hungry. Some day they will think that they are so powerful, they will come and make war on us, on our children, because they are all alike and we are different from them."

The Power Ones listened to Anoni. At first they said, "He is a trickster, always telling jokes. How can we trust him?" But they saw the people make war on each other, raiding to show their bravery. And then they said, "Anoni is a trickster, but he has a quick mind and is clever and often gives good counsel."

"What do you think we must do?" River asked Anoni in the Council Lodge.

"These people are all happy and joyful. They all call each other brother and sister. Even when they make war, they raid to show skill and courage, not to harm. We must split them apart and send them different ways, as different tribes to far places. Then they cannot bind all their power together against us. And we can visit each tribe, because alone they cannot hurt us. Then we can be happy and enjoy their company."

The debate in the Council Lodge was long, but the Power Ones understood what Anoni said. The people they had created had the power of each of them all blended together, and that was greater than any one thing alone. Finally, they all agreed that the people had to be split and sent to far distant places so they could not all come together. But Breath said, "We made these people, and we cannot send them away like enemies. They are relatives. We must give them special gifts before

we make them go." They all agreed with Breath, and
they set a day for a great gifting.

On the morning of the great gifting, all the people
gathered. They divided into four great tribes. One tribe
would stay, and the other three would go to faraway
places.

Yenhica spoke first. She raised her green lance over all
the people gathered and said, "It is not fair to give a gift
to one tribe and not all. I give the gift of courage to all
the people who will use it wisely and well."

Then Rock said, "I give the gift of food to all, too,
because no people can survive without food."

All decided that this was fair. Then Blaze, Breath,
River, and Anoni took sticks and painted them, each
with one of the sacred colors, and they threw these sticks
in the air. Each group of people got a stick.

The group that got the red stick received the gift of
Blaze. He stood over them, and there was a flash of light
in the sky. "To you, who will go to a far place, I give the
gift of mind and understanding, of learning and curiosity
to consume as fire consumes everything around it, leaving nothing untouched. All people I have gifted with
intellect, but to you I give the curiosity to make a conflagration of that tiny spark."

To those who got the yellow stick, River spoke gently.
"You who will stay behind, to you I give the gift of patience and of waiting quietly. I give you the gift of knowing that you will someday visit your friends of the other
tribes again."

Our own people caught the blue stick, and it was
Breath who spoke to us. "People," she said, "I give you
the gift of the sacred flute, which is the presence of the
truth. Wherever you go, you will see the truth and will
tell it again, and you shall remember it always."

The three tribes agreed that these were beautiful and
generous gifts, to be loved and cherished and remembered always. They were very happy with their gifts. But
the fourth tribe was still waiting, the tribe that had
caught Anoni's black stick. So many good and beautiful
things that had been given that Anoni could not think of
what to give his own people, and he felt sorry for them.
He turned his face away in shame. And then he cut a tiny

piece of his own tongue and boiled it and gave it to the fourth tribe to drink the water. "I give you the gift of my quick tongue and clever mind. And I give you my shoes, that you will travel farther than any of the others, with all my tools and sharp knowledge, for that is the only gift I have."

And the people of the fourth tribe were not unhappy with their gift. All four tribes thanked the Power Ones for their gifts, and then the three tribes that had to leave went to their great lodges.

Each of these lodges was as large as five winter lodges all together, and the Power Clan carried the people on their backs through the dark. It was dark for many, many days, many seasons. Children were born in this nighttime, and it was forgotten that the other tribes were traveling too. This, of course, is what Anoni wanted and what the others agreed to.

Finally, each tribe arrived in its own place. The Power Ones come and visit each and are not afraid but are happy and enjoy the company of their people. But after that Anoni, who was always a trickster, could never talk straight because his tongue had been split and the flute was gone.

Gaelian shut off the tape and cursed softly under her breath. It was true, she had forgotten the details of that legend—no, more, she had forgotten most of it, although the basic story she could recall. But why her father had given this to her when there were so many other things she needed, that she could not understand. Anger burned quickly. She was an educated, able woman, not some illiterate to believe in creation myths. And then the rage died silently. She knew that Renan cherished these mementos from his time on Cahaute more than shares in the Company, had given her something that he considered truly valuable.

Someone was shaking her. She fought back. It was one of the Mikke children, relatives of her takka mother Tyakral, the Mikke who hated her. They were shaking and jeering . . .

She fought back, all the way to full consciousness, and the shaking didn't stop.

"Gaelian, get up," Missili half shouted in her ear.

She opened her eyes tentatively.

Missili dove into her closet and tossed some clothes on the chair. "Get dressed. Come down. Now." Then the housekeeper turned and walked out.

Gaelian pulled herself up, splashed her face with cold water, and turned the lights up high. It was the middle of the night. And then she noticed what Missili had thrown out for her to wear. Green, brilliant, startling green, which was worn for only one occasion. As they said on Cahaute, green is the color of life, of growing things, and in the time of death it is life we must remember. She knew. The battle was joined. Her grandmother was finally dead.

When she got downstairs, she found Dobrin and her father in the library. Dobrin was still bleary-eyed, moving heavily with sleep. Her father was already drinking.

"Gentlemen," she said, "I believe that there are people to be notified and a funeral to arrange."

Dobrin turned and looked up from the terminal. "It's all taken care of, Gae. I just sent out word to the Board, the other major families, and the fax services."

She glared at him, but he seemed to take no note of it. It was her place to order these things done. Already the fight was starting. She went over to the screen and studied it. "Any incoming messages?" she asked.

He shrugged and keyed for the queue. Only one message appeared, directed to her attention. Dobrin looked at her coldly and then moved away. She spoke softly, her voice print opening the private message bank, and suddenly amber writing glistened in front of her. It was the record of her commission. Dated early yesterday morning. She had forgotten all about her own graduation, about Tanistin. Somehow, it all seemed very far removed from the household. She blinked, trying to let it hit her, but the impact didn't come. It was only words, after all the years and hopes. Only words, when Dobrin was seated opposite her father on the other side of the room, the Head of the YnTourne just newly dead.

"Missili is taking care of the body," her father said. "She requested that. Everything else is on file. Dobrin's already notified all the proper authorities."

His voice was singsong. He was already drunk, at this cold hour of the night when nothing moved.

8

IESIN ENTERED, CLASPED her ceremonially on the shoulders, and then led her from the hall. The house was full of people. They had been coming all day, all night, for almost two days now, ever since they got the news. There were more families represented than when the Board met, more people than she had seen since she had attended her Starburst Ceremony a year ago.

"Come on, Gae, let's get out of this mob," Iesin said, pulling her up the stairs toward her own room. Iesin had been a guest in the YnTourne house often enough to feel comfortably at home there. "You look like you've got a headache, you know?"

She let Ie lead her, not wondering that her friend was there, only grateful that she was. When they had safely closed the door behind them, Ie pulled Gaelian up on the bed, both of them sitting crosslegged as they had when they were still children in normal school.

"Okay, Gae, what's going on here? I know you're not really upset about that old lady. She made your life miserable. So what are your father and Dobrin up to? I got here as fast as I could."

Gaelian nodded. Ie must have jumped the first shuttle after the graduation ceremonies had ended. "Papa declared himself uninterested in the Headship, which I guess you heard," she began slowly. "Well, so it's me and Dobrin. You knew that. Everyone knew it would come to that." She hesitated. She didn't know if she really wanted to go on, didn't know how much she really dared reveal. It was a family thing, after all.

"Come on, Gae," Iesin prompted. "It doesn't matter, not with me. I can't help you if I don't know all the details."

"I'm not sure you can help," Gaelian said. "It's Dobrin . . . well, and other things. Cahaute. My grandmother, she, well, she suspected that . . . She told Dobrin that . . ."

Iesin sat up and wrapped her arms around her legs, hugging herself. "Let me tell you what I think," she said softly. "Then you don't have to say it yourself. You've hinted around the subject enough. Your grandmother suspected that you are half Cahaute by blood. And that you and Renan are involved in some massive cover-up. But Dobrin doesn't know for sure, and he's afraid that what you've been saying all along might be true. But right now, that's his only hope of getting rid of you, at least as Head of the household, and he wants the household more than anything. Is that right?"

Gaelian nodded, staring at Iesin wide-eyed. A chill went through her, and she realized just how glad she was to have Iesin as a friend. Ie would make a very dangerous enemy.

"Dobrin wants the Headship of the household more than anything," Iesin repeated. "Everyone knows it. The Board knows it. Dobrin's never wanted anything else. But what about you? What do you want, Gae?"

Gaelian started. She had never expected that question from Iesin. It took her aback, and she needed to think. "Well," she said finally, "I want what's mine. I think I want the household. I believe that it is my right."

"I'm not disputing your right," Iesin said softly. "I agree it is. But what do you *want*? Somehow, Angel, I can't seem to picture you here, stuck issuing orders on a screen. Giving up flying for that."

Gaelian gasped for air. "I'd never give up flying. There's no reason to give it up, is there? I mean, that's *mine*. I worked for it, I deserve it, I want it." The conviction that rang in her voice surprised her, even more so because suddenly she realized just how true it was. She had never really thought about what being Head of a household meant. After all, her grandmother was supposed to live for years, and her father would be Head after that. She could well be a grandmother herself, past the age of mandatory retirement, before she had to take up the duties of Head. All that had changed, radically, in the past few days.

But in those days, the Headship had become some prize she

and Dobrin had struggled over. It was the struggle itself that had involved her deeply. So deeply that she hadn't really considered what it was she could very well win.

The Headship of a household and a company was not something that could be taken lightly. It was an entire career, something people trained for their whole lives. Military service, even flying, was seen simply as a segment of that training. On a day-to-day basis, the Head of the YnTourne would have to stay here, in this house or at Craft Company headquarters, handling manufacturing decisions and work schedules, budgets and deals, and approving new designs for development, for craft she would never fly. Her life would be lived in Board meetings and negotiations, twelve to fifteen hours a day behind a desk.

It was unbearable. She could not give up her own life, her own rewards, to sit in a chair all day, give up the fast, high craft that her fingers, her whole body itched to fly. She was the Angel.

Iesin reached out and stroked her arm. "That's what I figured," she said. "I know you too well, Gae, and I've known you too long." Iesin dropped her eyes, trying to hide her face. "And this way, you have what you want. Dobrin has what he wants. And the truth, whatever that truth is, is buried. No one will care."

"What truth?" Gaelian asked.

"The truth you don't ever want to tell me. You can drive a good bargain with Dobrin. You've still got your shares and voting rights. That's good for something. You can insist that the engagement to Teazerin be terminated. The YnSetti won't object. They wanted a Head of household anyway, not some crazy pilot who won't quit. And that's what everyone'll see anyway. You know what they say about people like you and Golran and the rest. You really are a crazy pilot, so it won't look strange. And you won't have to think about Tembri YnEste anymore. Dobrin won't do anything if he's got the position he wants and you don't."

"Whose side are you on?" Gaelian demanded angrily. "I don't believe it, Ie. I mean, I thought you were for me."

"I am," Iesin replied firmly, meeting Gaelian's eyes boldly. "I refuse to see you waste yourself as a pilot in order to fly a desk."

"We'd better get downstairs," Gaelian said dully. "I'll be missed. I'm supposed to be around all those people before the funeral. It's supposed to help.''

Iesin nodded her compliance. She knew that she had said something shocking, her suggestion being stranger than anything she had yet come up with. She didn't even know why she had thought of it, or who or what game she was playing.

Gaelian walked through the throng downstairs, accepting their condolences almost absently. Wryly, she was aware that they saw the perfect image of a good member of the household mourning deeply. It was almost funny. Iesin's idea kept running around her head, refusing to leave her alone. There was no reason she had to fight Dobrin. It wasn't a matter of honor, to fight for something you did not want. Not wanting it made sense. And yet, it was very strange even to consider that she really didn't want to be Head of the YnTourne for the rest of her life.

She refused to think about it. It wasn't fair, opening up an option, a tempting possibility of freedom. Yet, as she went through the rooms, she realized just how much she hated this house. She hated these walls, the dining room where she had kept silent so many years while her grandmother presided at meals. She hated the library where her father drank alone late at night, supposedly working on his great scholarly opus that would never be done and see publication, the nerris court where the bands had first been painted on her face, the sticky, thick stuff unfamiliar, making her eyes water. She especially hated the kitchen, where she had to eat with Missili when she missed a meal or came in even a few minutes late. The realization that there was nothing here she would not be happy to leave startled her and upset her deeply. It was not the way anyone was supposed to think of home.

She didn't realize that time was passing, that dinner started and ended. She didn't notice the thinning of the guests, each of them taking his or her leave, going upstairs if they were staying or out to the apron where their aircars were parked. And then she was alone in the library with Dobrin and did not remember quite how this meeting had come to be. Only now it seemed to be a tradition, five days old, that she and Dobrin meet privately here each night.

Dobrin stood where he always stood at this time, just behind the table, pouring the late-night brandies. On the table, she saw the package, still sealed, that her grandmother had given Dobrin on her second day home. She tried not to stare at it as they took their usual chairs and sipped in silence for a moment, the one moment of calm in the day.

Dobrin watched her steadily through the cut facets of his glass. Tonight it was nerris, and he was going to win. Those who went to the gods in nerris were always the real winners —he remembered that from the time before they were civilized. It was considered an honor. And so, losing was winning and winning losing. He could feel the strength in him, warming him more than the nightcap.

Yes, he played, but he played by the rules. All the rules. Clean combat was the only meaningful kind, and somehow he understood that his grandmother had not always played cleanly. It was the same thing that he had thought of when he had watched Teazerin YnSetti on the nerris court. Correct observance was the entire validity of the game itself. To win with skill, by ruthlessness or subtlety, was the only way to win. Simple cruelty without finesse did not constitute winning, no matter how many matches were on Teazerin's record. Without the values of nerris, they were not Dinoreans. They were nothing.

"Gaelian," he said, "I know you saw that packet on the table." He rose, deliberately, carefully watching her watch him. He went to the table and took it in his hands, both of them to show respect for the gift. "Tomorrow she's buried, and perhaps just to ourselves we can admit, no matter which way it goes, that everyone is better off. But I'm not going to play like a savage." He took the packet, still sealed, and quickly crossed the room and threw it into the disposal chute.

"Don't misunderstand," Dobrin continued. "I still want it, and I'll fight you every second for it. But I'm not playing with my stick sharp at both ends."

He didn't need to say any more. It was done. By now, the packet had been broken down into subatomic particles. Whatever, he was clean. He was nerris itself, the spirit of the old way. He knew he had won.

Suddenly, Gaelian began to laugh. It was a joyful, merry laugh, full of freedom and happiness. Dobrin was confused by the gaiety in her face, the almost miraculous change that had drained all the tension from her.

"You know, Dobrin, I'd have fought you all the way if you hadn't done that," she said, between fits of laughter. "But, well, sit down. I've got a proposal to make. I'm serious. I talked with Iesin today, and she showed me something. I don't and never have wanted the Headship. Only fairness. I'm willing to deal. No marriage to YnSetti, control of my own shares."

"It goes without saying," Dobrin sputtered. "And full rights, of course, the same as if you were a younger sibling. But *why*?"

"Dobrin," Gaelian said, trying to keep the merriment from her expression, "I just got assigned to the hottest new experimental class ship in the fleet. You think I'd give that up? And frankly, the more I think about what the Head does, day to day, the more I just plain don't want the job."

They were both on their feet, laughing raucously. Dobrin picked Gaelian up and swung her around.

"If Grandmother weren't already dead, this'd kill her," Dobrin said lightly. "She always thought we were the worst of enemies."

"Well, we were," Gaelian said. "But that doesn't mean that we can't come to an accommodation. Maybe one of these days we'll even be friends."

Dobrin refilled their glasses, trying to keep the strangeness to himself. He couldn't understand it, and yet it made perfect sense. He had known, really known, that he was going to win. That that one single act of propriety would give him everything. Contentment suffused him, and he found himself looking at Gaelian as if he'd never seen her before. She'd make a good friend, he thought suddenly. Gaelian and he were evenly matched, courage for courage, speed and skill. Only, they had been playing in different courts all along. Together, as a team, what would they win?

"There are a couple of things I want to finalize before you leave," Dobrin said a few nights later as he poured their ceremonial nightcap. "Foremost, we've got to talk about how to vote on Cahaute. You know what the Board has decided. They've already begun the preliminary camp there, but things are at an exploratory stage. We do need the mineral rights, there's no question about that. But, I hate to say it, you know Cahaute."

Gaelian sat back in the large chair, caressing the glass that Dobrin had brought her. Ever since he had burned whatever it was Grandmother had given him three nights ago, there had been a strange closeness between the two of them. She recognized him, in the Cahaute way that had no Dinorean equivalent, as having uraka. He had consulted her before this, about long-term plans for the company, often throwing stacks of blueprints at her for her opinions.

"Most of all," she said slowly, "I guess I believe that Cahaute should be left alone."

He nodded. "I thought you'd say that. But it isn't possible. So, in practical terms, at least give me some information."

"In the first place," she said softly, considering each word separately, "I think the Cahaute might not be terribly different from us. It's strange, when you consider it, that the Adedri, the Cahaute, and ourselves look so similar and speak languages that, while they are very different, are at least learnable. I would think that, given all the variation in the different environments, we would be more different than we are."

"So?" he asked, raising an eyebrow.

"When I was in school, I learned that the whole point of the Protectorate was to provide for the benefit of every citizen through competent administration, regulation of trade, and protection from outlawry," Gaelian recited by rote. "The Board and the Protectorate are really the same thing for all intents and purposes, and the purpose of the Board is to make profits and expand. Which is not a bad thing in itself, but it can create unpleasantness for the people we expand around. Or into. Or over.

"I lived on Cahaute until I was seven. They are illiterate. Except for herbalist shamans, medicine is practically nonexistent. The infant mortality rate would be shocking in the worst slums of Adedri. There's no technology at all. Do you know how they start a fire on Cahaute?"

Dobrin shook his head.

"Well, if I remember correctly, it goes something like this. You get a pile of dead, dry leaves and put a stick in it. Then you take a bow and wrap the bowstring around the stick. Then you saw the bow back and forth, and it turns the stick very fast, something like a rotary or a winch. Uses friction." She paused for a delicate sip. It was a fruit brandy tonight and very sweet.

"The point is, it works. Everything works. Stone knives might not look like much, but they cut pretty well."

"What's the point of this?" Dobrin asked.

She was pleased to see that the question came from curiosity and not contempt. "Really, it's very simple. The technology is very simple but also extremely effective. Just because they don't have power hoists doesn't mean that they don't understand the principle of the lever. And that really is the whole point. On Cahaute, it is the principle that counts. There's more. I'm not sure if I can explain it all."

"Try."

"The word *cahaute* itself means the wholeness, the point in the center of the circle whose perimeter is everywhere. And that is *whose* because the circle itself is living. Anyway, it means that they have this whole way of perceiving the universe, which means that they see that two mutually exclusive events could take place simultaneously."

"That doesn't make any sense," Dobrin protested.

Gaelian grinned. "Course not," she agreed amiably. "But let me give you an example anyway. Say someone dies from an infection. Now, the concept of physical illness is well understood. Anyway, someone dies. He also died because it was his wish to die. And he died because he was being punished, because an infection is very painful. But also, it isn't important because no one, nothing is ever really dead. No, that's not good. I mean, he is alive because he was alive, since there is no time, only now."

"You were making more sense before when you weren't making any sense," Dobrin scoffed.

"That's because you're thinking in a line, Dobrin. On Cahaute, everyone thinks in circles. Anyway, that's not the really important part. The important thing is, for some reason, maybe because they think in circles or maybe because of something else, there's a kind of power on Cahaute. Maybe you'd call it magic—I only know it works. They, they manipulate things. I don't know much about it. But I've seen it work."

Flustered, Gaelian took a mouthful of her drink a little too quickly and started to cough. Dobrin handed her a glass of water and returned to his own chair, not sure of where to look.

"Gae, this isn't getting us anywhere. Just tell me where you stand on status. You vote your own shares, and it would be a lot easier for me to make a proposition to the Board knowing where your vote will go. Just give it to me like that, so I can use it."

Gaelian's mind twisted. Talking to Dobrin, she had been lost in the strange hasute magic of Cahaute. Now she wrenched her thoughts abruptly back to the present necessity. She had thought about the vote earlier, when she had heard the first rumors that the Board might open Cahaute. There were three classes of status that the Board used. Open restrict:on meant that the company would mine out the necessary minerals, leave the people to themselves, and engage in no contact. It seemed the best to her, only she realized it was robbery. Cahaute was a rich place, and taking its riches without giving anything in return was theft. On the other hand, it would mean that the people would be left strictly alone, a very good idea. She had had enough trouble learning Dinorean, what was expected, and how to think in straight lines. Doing that to all Cahaute would destroy them.

Then there was protected status, which was what Adedri had by choice. There was some exchange with the Protectorate. They had trade, and individual Adedri had the right to work on Dinoreos in nonsensitive positions. They were not full citizens and could not aspire to the ruling class, but then they didn't have the same taxes or voting responsibilties either.

"Citizen-state," Gaelian replied very slowly, voicing the third alternative.

"It will destroy them," Dobrin said soberly.

Gaelian shrugged. "That's my shares voting, cousin, whether you like it or not."

Dobrin sighed. Gaelian had learned in the past two weeks since she'd been home that that indicated only the fact that he had gotten the kind of answer he was looking for, not necessarily his opinion. She took it purely at face value. There was no way now to read Dobrin when he didn't want to be read.

"I assume you're going to insist on that military transport tomorrow," he said, changing the subject abruptly. "But would you mind a decently chauffeured lift to the base?"

"Thanks," she said, trying not to betray her pleasure at the offer.

They sat in companionable silence, Gaelian letting her eyes run lightly over the titles under the glass behind Dobrin. The books were ancient, and many of the titles had faded into the leather or cloth of their bindings. A kind of wistfulness came over her as she realized that she was more relaxed than she had ever been in the house, felt more at home now than she had ever expected to feel.

Then she snapped herself out of the nostalgia. It was stupid. She was coming back, after all. It was her home.

9

THERE WERE MORE lodges from the sky today, Nyapetin thought. They were building their camp in a stupid place, out in the center of the plain far from water or standing food. Today they built lodges, ugly things of white mud. He wondered what decoration they would use, what stories they would paint. He hoped he would be able to understand their stories, and so know why they came. Perhaps they were outcasts from their tribe, and that was why they cut all their hair off, to show their grief.

"Are you thinking about the short-hairs again?" Hinacen asked him.

Nyapetin turned suddenly and nodded sharply, once. He wished to learn this skill of Hinacen's, to see into another's head and hear the words there.

"I want to know how they will paint," Nyapetin said. "And I want to know why they are here. I think they are perhaps persons outlawed by their tribe, or else why would one band come so far?"

"Do they seem such an ordinary band to you, then?" Hinacin asked, his eyes gleaming. "Are you more blind than an old man? Are your eyes almost gone?"

Nyapetin thought. "No," he said slowly. "There are no old people and no children. Only those of warrior age and hunters. But I do not know what they track across the night-and-night."

"So. You are not blind. You are not too stupid, either.

94

Sometimes you act stupid, but when you look carefully you do see things," the old man admitted grudgingly.

"And what do you see, takka?" Nyapetin asked politely.

Hinacen sat on his robe and stared at a tree for a long time. "I see nothing," he said quietly. "I wish to see nothing. I will die soon, and I do not wish to see what will happen. When they came before, it was the beginning of changes. I was not young then, and I saw the changes. The Keti are gone. The Keti are important. But I will not see the end of it." He waited a long time, falling into silence.

The silence was something Nyapetin knew. It was a common thing between them. In the two white times and the seasons in between that he had studied with the b'hasute, Hinacen was often silent, and after his silence he would have a new task for Nyapetin, something Nyapetin did not want to do. Always there were these things, pointless things like finding a yellow stone or making water hot and pouring it back into the river. Later, he would understand that it was not the task, but the action itself that was important. Recently, Hinacen had not asked him to do anything that did not make sense, and he was pleased. Now Hinacen was silent again, and Nyapetin was sure that another task was coming.

"I was thinking, uncle, that we must welcome these visitors if they are honest people and not outlaws. Where are our manners that we do not invite them to hunt and feast, to play games? We do not bring them any gifts, and that is a shame to us. They will think us very poor, or very rude, if we don't go visiting with presents."

Hinacen held up one hand, signaling silence. "Go to the river and wash," he ordered brusquely. "Then paint yourself with your serpent paint and come to my fire. And do not eat or drink anything before. Do not touch that stew in your mother's pot! When you eat stew you are a hunter and not hasute."

He said nothing to Hinacen and made his way to the river. He did not go to the place where all the people went to swim, where now the children played splashing games, frightening the fish. He walked far up along the bank until he could not hear the people anymore, until he could not smell the good dinner that waited for others at home. He walked until he passed the place where the women drew water in the morning, past the stand of trees where the flash-and-noise had burned many trees, making a ghost place. The ghost place did not frighten him. There was no one there, only the ghosts of the standing food, who were too silent to worry about being dead. Even dead, they had many bird-friends visiting, which Nyapetin was sure made their ghosts happy.

He came to a place where the river was wide and lazy. He lay in the water, motionless, enjoying the coolness on his skin and the green-smell from the overhanging trees. There was an ending in this moment, in this place. This stillness, which had been here since before the Power Clan had brought the people through the night-and-night, had become perfect. Now it was time for something different. The calm had been stillness for so long that it had died, stagnated and abandoned this place. Now it was empty, waiting for something to happen.

He stayed in the water for a long time, until the sky changed color and the light became sparkling and visible. He did not think about anything at all. Thinking did not help. Only doing or not doing helped, and not doing was doing. (The water taught him this, and he let it pucker his skin.) Then, after painting himself, he returned to Hinacen's lodge.

Hinacen looked old. Nyapetin had never thought to look at Hinacen like that. The b'hasute was himself, not changing, like the seasons or the places where the herds went to water. But Nyapetin saw now that Hinacen looked old, his skin clinging to his skull like a dead one's, his arms withered like the branches of the ghost trees waiting for the winged friends.

"Nyapetin, tonight I give you a gift. The gift of edonys, the drink of the vision."

There was a bowl between them on the robe. Nyapetin looked into it, seeing the pale yellow liquid there. It looked smooth and thick, like the mud after a storm. It did not smell like anything he could name. Hinacen lifted the bowl above his head in both hands and then offered it to Nyapetin.

Nyapetin took it with both hands, to show respect, and lifted it again. He lifted it not because he had to, or because Hinacen had done so, but to make the moment longer. After he tasted edonys, he would never be quite the same again. Already the tribe saw him as hasute. He had had the hasute vision, had become brother to the snake, could so some healing and draw evil spirits from the bodies of those who were ill. He could call the small ones and find the sitting food hidden. But this was not hasute. This was only shaman, something not in itself cahaute. It was only a skill, like using a lance or a bow, like tracking the herds or building a lodge or cooking good stew. Hasute was more, edonys more. So he made the time last, the time between being a person of flesh and becoming something less and something more.

Hinacen began to play the flute. Nyapetin recognized the tune, the same as his own song. He remembered the time he had been dead and the Power Clan gave the song to him. Now Hinacen played, and he raised the bowl to his mouth and sipped carefully.

The stuff was evil-tasting, viscous, and painful on his tongue. It slipped through him like a snake, his brother. He drank it all, knowing that all was required, and then lay back on the soft hide robe and listened to the music.

The seeing came slowly. At first, he drifted in the music, the pleasantness of the tune, and the sacred truth of the flute. Then the music became colors, and then solid things. Everything was clear and bright with light that came from inside of it, as if he could see right into the essence of the thing and not notice the shell that it wore.

He was flying, suddenly, over the night of the camp, seeing the plains and the herds, where they were and where they would be all the same. He saw the Dead Hill, the spirit of it curled inside waiting, and within that the egg of a warrior-bird. And he wondered what bird would be born there and fly in the spirit places.

Truly, everything was alive in the spirit places, everything moved and breathed. Even the place of the ghost trees was full of their spirits, ghosts truly now, the standing people who watched in silence. They watched forever, from before the time of the tribes. He stopped to ask them what stories they remembered, but the music became a great wind and blew him onward, away from these familiar places and to the plain.

The music blew him all the way to the short-hairs' camp, and he looked within it and saw a great fire spirit chained and tormented, weeping heat and brilliance. Around this spirit were others, things that he recognized as people, but different from the people of the tribes, for there was little shining about them.

He saw all but felt nothing, nothing but the wind of the flute. And he saw Nyapetin walk into that camp with robes, a gift from the tribe, and he saw the short-hairs considering seriously. This he saw with one set of eyes, but the edonys eyes saw their spirits laughing, raging, blazoned with war paint.

The short-hairs touched the robes, and his one set of ears heard the kind sounds they made, feeling the robes carefully, as if admiring how very soft and fine they were. He had brought the finest in the camp, a great present for these visitors. But the edonys ears heard more, heard things under the nice-sounding words like the current deep in the river when the surface of the river seemed bright and innocent.

They showed him things, ugly little black marks that looked like insect tracks, praising and making many fine and large gestures to these tracks. But the edonys read the tracks and saw that this was not something that belonged to the people and was not something that was good. He took the thin bark with the black marks and threw it on the ground.

This was not polite, he heard the music tell him, and he felt sorry. It is bad to say a present is not to your liking. But the edonys self knew that this was no present, given freely with uraka. This was something else, a spell like the spell that held the great fire captive in the plain round lodge.

All this he watched carefully, like a scout looking for enemies in the springtime, in the season of raiding. In the edonys senses, there was a strange smell, somewhere off distant, just enough to be a warning. The mountain-self, the body without the spirit, picked up the bark with the black marks and said polite things and smiled. The short-hairs smiled back. The edonys self watched, curious to know what was missing.

Then he saw it, understood somewhere beyond his mind, even beyond the edonys mind. The short-hairs did not *recognize* him. They did not admit to his right of being, any more than they saw the herds or the standing people who made the shade of the forest comfortable, any more than they recognized the sitting food. And the lack of that recognition struck him worse than the blow of a war club.

In the edonys, his mind was very clear. The vision was very strong and swift. He was back in Hinacen's tent, and the old b'hasute was still playing the flute, so Nyapetin knew that what he saw was truth. Outside it was becoming light, and the people were rising for another day. He could hear the women chatting as they went to the river for the day's water. He heard the children as they slipped out and began to play, and their parents' clear requests to fetch wood for the fire. The edonys eyes were gone, and he had only his own eyes now.

"You went to the short-hairs' camp," Hinacen said. "Tell me what you saw and did there."

So Nyapetin told him, and the old man was very still for a long time. "You must tell this to the council. First you must go to the council lodge and tell them. Then you can wash and sleep. The council will decide what the people must do about the short-hairs. But your vision tells true; we cannot pretend that they are not here and that they will go away. If they do not see, then the whole of the world will suffer."

Hinacen looked sad and weary. Nyapetin felt the b'hasute's weariness in his body. Suddenly he felt very old, as if he had lived and seen as Hinacen had. Perhaps the council would decide on war or revenge, and for the first time this did not bother Nyapetin. He was too young for the council, and he would not decide. Besides, he was hasute, and the hasute give advice, but they do not sit in council. The council is a place for elders of the tribe, and the hasute belong to all the people.

Suddenly, Nyapetin hoped that Hinacen would advise the council to organize a raiding party and raid these short-hairs. He hoped that they would shame them so that they would leave. But now he was too tired to think. He must sit in the council lodge and tell the old men, the old women what he had seen. And then he would sleep. Perhaps when he woke he would paint for war and not for magic.

It took all of twenty minutes to sign into Adedri Base, find the single bare room in Temp Quarters, and hang two uniforms on the hook behind the bathroom door. Gaelian wasn't scheduled to report up on Tanistin until oh seven hundred the next morning, and it had never occurred to her that there would be so much time.

Time. It was strange. For the first time in years, in just about forever, Gaelian thought, she was alone. No one was going to call on her, no one knew precisely where she was. She closed her eyes and enjoyed the peace. Then the silence was overwhelming, even worse than her curiosity.

They said there was a corner bar in the Officer's Club that, from four in the afternoon until the dinner hour, was the sole preserve of the pilots. Now, finally, she was one of them, and she wanted to go down, maybe see some people she'd known, and yet she felt a little shy. There would be veterans there who might not think much of some newly minted ensign wandering into their preserve.

Excited, she studied the two uniforms, figured which was fresher, and washed and dressed a little before five, which was correct. Golran had written that only the newest grads arrived before five.

The smaller cocktail lounge was deep blue and invitingly dark, its polished wooden tables and green plants doing nothing to brighten the atmosphere. It had an air of comfort and anticipation, as if even the barstools knew that for the next hour or two there would be only one topic of conversation —flying. Tattered photos of every kind of craft imaginable were tacked up in no particular order. It was something of a jumble, the simplicity, the almost arrogant shunning of luxury somehow reminiscent of a flight shack. No wonder it was popular with pilots and not terribly frequented by anyone else.

She stood in the doorway for a moment, letting her eyes become accustomed to the dim lights. A hand motioned her over, and she squinted. There was a small knot of people squeezed around a back corner table. She couldn't make out any features.

The hand motioned again. Hiding her surprise, she went over to the bar, punched in her drink order, and tried again to make out the members of the little group. Her drink appeared before she had any idea of who sat in the corner waiting for her. She picked up the glass and wandered over.

When Gaelian reached the table, she grinned with delight. The hand that had motioned to her belonged to Golran Vontreidi, sitting with Asteri Sessov and Vi YnHersow, two of the best junior-ranked fliers in the service. With her, it made the full complement among those who knew the pilots to watch.

"Just signed in?" Sessov asked.

Angel nodded and set her drink on the table.

"Hey, we all heard about what went on in your household, Angel. It's a rotten deal. My cousin worked for Dobrin for awhile and said he plays the sharp end just for the fun of it. That was low, what he did to you. Low. But Tanistin should make up for it."

Vontreidi and Sessov looked acutely embarrassed. Vi YnHersow had never been known for tact. Even so, Gaelian was more than a little shocked that she would bring up the in-

ternal matters of a household in front of one of its members.
Gaelian decided that Vi must be a touch drunk, as well as
rude.

"So we're all assigned to Tanistin?" Gaelian asked, changing the topic. Golran and Asteri looked relieved. "I've been a
little out of touch for a bit. What's been going on?"

Golran smiled broadly. "You won't believe it, Angel. You
haven't seen the specs yet, have you? It's too hush-hush to
broadcast over an unsecured line. But you've never seen anything like her, not the equipment, not the design, nothing.
There isn't a single thing, not one bolt, that's ever been used
before."

"Of course," Sessov interrupted dryly, "he's only giving
you the Board line. Sure it's new, it's so new that it may just
fall apart if you blow on it. Some of those bolts look pretty
funny to me. Not that it matters much to any of us, naturally.
We're only the junior complement. And if you don't know
what that means, you'd better get used to the idea that the
brass has not let these boys and girls out of school to have a
good time. No, all the good times belong to the all-holy, high
muckety-mucks. Who should be coming through that door in
exactly seven minutes, twelve point eight seconds."

"What Sessov means is that you haven't seen the roster
yet," Vi said, grinning evilly. "Of course, we haven't seen the
roster yet either. Officially, that is. So officially, we don't
know that our major function will be sitting in the port bays
running simulations, and maybe powering up and powering
down and powering up and powering down. But if you'd
wanted excitement, you'd have opted for Shore Patrol.
They're the only ones who see any action around here."

Gaelian looked from face to face, trying to read some meaning into Vi's comments. She had realized that they were still
too junior for the most important runs, but it didn't dampen
her enthusiasm. There was the chance that later on, further
out, they would get a chance at the new equipment.

But Shore Patrol? That was something she hadn't heard
about. Adedri Base was huge, perhaps the largest installation
not on Dinoreos itself, but there was no reason to suspect any
more unruly behavior here than on any other base. More
numbers, maybe, but how serious could it be—a little drinking, a few enlisted people out on the town, maybe a fight with
the locals every couple of weeks? She shook her head.

"That's two, Vi," Sessov said grimly. "No reason to confuse the kid. And you talk like you learned your manners in a barn."

"So when do we get the grand tour?" Angel asked, trying to break the icy silence after Sessov's rebuke.

"We don't," Golran answered. "At least not for ten, twelve days. Briefings start at oh seven hundred tomorrow. You should have looked at your schedule before you came down here. Engineering briefings. Test briefings. Design briefings. Tactical briefings on piracy in this system. More test briefings. More engineering briefings."

"Stop it," she laughed, gasping. "I thought I'd finished school."

"Innocent and naive," Vi commented.

"Between all these briefings and you and Iesin, it's going to be like I never left the Academy."

"You never do," Sessov said seriously. "There're only so many pilots and so many ships and so many years and so many briefings."

They each sipped their drinks. Gaelian noticed that the place was filling up. Almost exactly on Sessov's schedule, she saw a group of six with faces she barely recognized. Golran whispered the names to her, names she knew well. They were the senior pilots on Tanistin. They spared a glance for their younger colleagues, and then chose a table far away. Angel felt the relief surge around her, and for the first time in her life, she felt herself truly outclassed.

A soft, crystal chime sounded in each room, indicating that dinner was being readied in both the main and auxiliary dining rooms.

"You staying here?" Sessov asked no one in particular.

"I don't have any better place to go," Gaelian answered.

Sessov and Vi rose, shrugging. "Well, we promised to show up at some alumni thing with terrible hors d'oeuvres. Be glad your class wasn't invited," Vi said, as Sessov glared at her.

"You going?" Gaelian asked Golran as the other two prepared to leave.

"No," he said. He was silent for a moment, and Gaelian could read his face clearly, even behind the stony mask. He was accepted for his work, envied for his talent, and never really part of the rest of them socially. Strange, Gaelian reflected, how minor and major nobility could mix easily in the service, but someone like Golran, more gifted than most, was never more than a commoner outside the flight shack.

"How about some dinner?" he asked heartily.

Angel took her drink and followed him into the smaller dining room. She was glad of his choice, since the other was too large, too open, too white and gold for her taste. There had been enough of that at home. The smaller room was far cozier without giving up elegance, and there was less chance of running into classmates. Angel was in no mood to face more condolences than were strictly necessary.

And then she realized that that was the very reason Golran had chosen it. Not consciously, perhaps, but from the habit of being a commoner, almost instinctively knowing that one of the Ot-tan class might not want to be seen with him in public. Not socially at least, and surely not as intimately as a dinner for two might suggest.

Not that Gaelian felt all that intimate. It was strange sitting here across the small table from Golran. It had been different in the lounge, with the others and the avid talk of flying, but now it was uncomfortable. They had not been alone together since Golran's Starburst Ceremony five years ago, and it had been nearly a year since they had spoken at all. At the homecoming game, she remembered suddenly.

They sat in silence while the food was served, tiny gamebirds in a sweet fruit sauce and glazed, minted greens. The food was always exceptional on Adedri Base, and how the club found and managed to keep its chef was a military secret on par with Tanistin's equipment. But Gaelian found it difficult to taste what was set in front of her.

She found it even more difficult to look across the table. Gol's eyes were on her, questioning and trying to comprehend. She didn't know what his questions were, and knew that she didn't want to answer them. It was no longer simply uncomfortable. It was unbearable. She knew that she should not, could not ask. And she knew that she needed to.

"Should I congratulate you?" she said softly, trying to keep her tone light.

Golran turned away from her and looked out the window. The large screens had been drawn out of sight, and the windows overlooked the port. At night it was beautiful, constantly changing, the stars and the brightly colored running lights that were ships and shuttles and even sporty aircars going about their business.

"I know what I am, and I know what you are, and nothing is going to change that," he said tonelessly. "I know I've been lucky, and I knew what I was in for when I first applied. Only the seventh commoner to be accepted. I'll never rank above commander, never have a cruiser. I'll never make it to the Admiralty. And people like Vi act like it shouldn't bother me at all, and in a way they're right. I can fly. I ought to be content."

"The marriage didn't work out," Gaelian whispered.

He turned to her, his eyes flashing fury, and then looked back at the windows again. Then he shrugged and laid down his knife, indicating that he was finished with the meal although he had barely eaten half of it.

"No," he answered. "No, it didn't work out. I was a fool to think it could. Well, it has been done before. Rarely. But I thought . . . That doesn't matter. I shouldn't be too disappointed. But . . . Angel, when I was there, the snubs, the little social things that people like Vi have always done. But that wasn't important. She's an idiot, Angel, I mean she can barely speak properly. Retarded. Mostly, they were interviewing for the position of steward for the family, with some minor inducements added. The worst part was that I was the only possible candidate, or else someone even more unsuitable. I was the absolute dregs, as far as they were concerned, the only person with enough ability to control the finances and desperate enough to put up with them and take her."

"Then you're the one who said no," Gaelian said quietly.

Golran lowered his eyes to the table. He seemed to study the pattern on the dark red cloth, his square fingers moving aimlessly across the edge of the plate.

"Why?" Angel asked. "You wanted it, and you could have done it. Why did you turn them down?"

"I have my pride," Golran said slowly. "Most of the time I can ignore the way most of your class, and those below you, act. I'm a better flier than they are anyway, than all the rest of them combined."

He met her eyes and held her glance, and Gaelian was frightened. There was something else he was trying to say and not say, something else that was part of it all, and she wasn't sure she understood. But to understand she would have to ask, and she'd breached propriety more than once this evening. She couldn't do it again.

Their dessert arrived, and they ate it in silence. No matter that the cake was fine and light, that the fruit sauce was just a bit tart, that the crust was still warm and crisp. Gaelian barely noticed. The bill was placed on the table, and Golran glared at her, challenging and forbidding, and signed for it.

"Shall I walk you back?" he asked stiffly.

"No," she replied. "I can walk back myself."

Gaelian returned to her barren quarters, exhausted and yet not quite ready for sleep. There was something about the way Golran spoke to her, looked at her, that was both challenging and insulting, but also almost pleading. Confusion merged with exhaustion, and her mind became hazed, everything flowing together into a river of images that made no sense. She pulled off her clothes and lay down.

Tyakral would have understood all this, she thought. Tyakral was hasute and would have seen *into* it and told her. She could have *recognized* Golran.

Golran left the club and walked. There was a lake nearby, just a short way beyond the gates. There, in the mornings, he ran, watching the sun rise over the water and enjoying the solitude. Now the lake still offered calm, but of a different kind. It was dark, almost ominous, to match his mood, no stars reflected in the still water. In the morning it seemed placid and tranquil, but at night it was a dark mirror, waiting. His own mythology, private, personal, supplied the rest, the demons that cavorted at the bottom, unable to come up through the stillness and destroy him. The thoughts that must never break the surface had to remain chained below, their fury had to remain the impotent thrashing of things held in check, never, never permitted to betray their existence. That was why the lake looked so calm, why it seemed so inviting.

He slung his jacket over his shoulder and walked, feeling the underlying chill in the air, the hint of moisture. He had not wanted to see her, and he had wanted to very badly. He shook himself. It had not been his choice. They had been assigned together, and he was not about to give up this place, this opportunity. There might even be enough work that he could lose himself in it.

There were options, of course. There were always options. Then he chained himself again. He was Golran Vontreidi, the best flier of his year, destined to great things. She was Yn-Tourne, as far from him as Dinoreos from Adedri in real space. Giving up the household had not changed that.

He remembered that year, her first. He had gone back home on leave during the holidays and talked to his brother. His brother had practically spat.

"You would have done better," he had said, "if you weren't so smart and if you weren't so good."

That was the problem. He would never be acceptable. He and Gaelian would never be equals. Never. The Angel he could joke with, talk flying with, but Gaelian was YnTourne. There was no possibility of anything else unless he sacrificed his pride, and his pride was all he had.

When he had accepted the assignment, he had known that the running was over. There was no possiblity that she, too, would not be called for Tanistin. It was too good a thing for them both. For him, it could mean his career. Do well enough and he could write his own ticket, choose his assignment, as long as they were not above the reach of a commoner.

Anger flashed over him, heating his fingers and shortening his breath. Not simply anger, but fury, intense rage at the mockery. It would all be so simple if he could look at her without desire—without two desires.

He laid his jacket on the grass and slipped out of his jump-suit. It was cold, but the cold was good, feeding on his anger. He jumped into the water and watched the black ripples around him, flustering the smooth surface. Break the quiet seals, let the demons come to the surface, release them as he was released.

He swam hard, venting the energy of his anger, delighting in his own skill. He moved freely, enjoying the sensation of strength that was his own, of his own physical control. As he controlled the machines he flew, the subtle power of them, the freedom that he found in that power, he controlled himself. Freedom comes only with power, he reflected, in his body, in the machine, in the universe. And with so very much power to control, there were powers that controlled him, powers that he could not, dared not ever hope to change.

He swam until he could move no more, unable to breathe or lift an arm. Dragging himself out onto the coarse grass that bordered the lake, he looked back. Its surface showed no sign of his passing. The demons were locked back in their chains.

Tanistin was unlike any vehicle Gaelian had ever dreamed of. It was singular, a work of art in its own right, not some motley collection of pieces from here and there, structured, squeezed, stretched into some new function. There was a proportion that rivaled classical art, every component integral to the whole, with nothing wasted and nothing gratuitous. The sense of completeness permeated her with the subtle, subliminal purr she sensed from the engines, the harmonic configuration of the briefing room, the elegance in each bank of breath-sensitive control boards.

Gaelian was in love. It had taken only a few minutes before that love had engulfed her. At the end of each day, when they were instructed to return to the shuttle bay for the trip back to Adedri Base, she felt bereft for the second or third time in her life. She hardly noticed Iesin at her shoulder when she signed in back on base and turned in the daydisc that permitted her entry to Tanistin.

"Do you want to come or not?" Iesin asked insistently.

"Come where?" Gaelian replied. She could not remember Iesin saying anything before.

"Into the city," Iesin said with exasperation. "There's supposed to be something going on tonight, some kind of festival or other. Anyway, I'll meet you at the gate in an hour. Exactly. If you're not there, I won't wait. And wear civvies. You don't want to be seen in Adedri in uniform."

Gaelian shrugged and returned to her temporary quarters. She was too full of Tanistin to care one way or another about going to some Adedri festival. They always had festivals, so she heard. Strange religious things, things very alien to Dinoreos. Without thinking, she pulled on a plain brown outfit, one of the three sets of civvies she had brought. She took a scarf patterned in red and gold and draped it casually across her shoulders. Then, on impulse, she painted two narrow scarlet bands across her face.

Iesin was waiting at the gate, along with Golran, Asteri Sessov, and Ayas Lograннis, one of the engineers from Golran's year who was also assigned to Tanistin. Lograннis, Ie, and Sessov all wore nerris paint. Golran wore none at all. They all seemed vaguely surprised by her own choice.

"Come on!" Icsin said. "We want to get down near the Temple as soon as possible or we won't find a place at all for the procession."

"It seems like you know a little more than the rest of us about what's going on," Sessov complained. "And where's Vi? Why isn't she here? Or didn't you invite her?"

Iesin turned to him coldly. "I'll tell you what's going on down there, which you would know if you bothered to look at your mail. And you know how Vi is. The last thing we need is an interplanetary incident because she makes some stupid remark."

"What do you mean, if she makes some stupid remark?" Vi said, appearing behind them suddenly. "What do you think I am, some kind of uneducable moron?"

Gaelian saw the worry cross Iesin's face and suddenly started to worry herself. After all, Vi had told her on the night she arrived that all the excitement here was with Shore Patrol, and the last thing she wanted to do was to find out why. Not now, at least. Not when she had found her ship. She hung back slightly, but Iesin herded them out of the gate and into a beat-up, ancient aircar that stood to one side of the parking apron.

"The thing of it is," Iesin started to say as she took the controls of the ancient transport, "is that this has something to do with that Adedri religion. Has it ever occurred to you that no one, no native that is, ever shows any kind of doubt about their Temple and all the rest of it? Anyway, tonight is something called the Festival of Anoni, which we are perfectly free to join in. Actually, no one can figure out whether they got Anoni from us or the other way around. It ought to be fun, as long as we stay nice and friendly with the locals. And don't say anything stupid." Ie took her eyes from the screen and glanced directly at Vi before returning her attention to flying.

Gaelian could barely see their approach to the city. It seemed like all the lights had been doused. Peering over Iesin's shoulder, she could see that Ie was flying on a combination of infrared and radar. There was no way she could make out the buildings or landing areas otherwise. From the screen map, Gaelian knew they were approaching the edge of the Temple area of Adedri, somewhere vaguely near the center of the city, if the mass that was Adedri could be said to have a center.

Iesin brought them down on top of a building that the screen indicated was a public lot.

"From here we walk," Iesin instructed. "They don't permit any vehicles around the Temple during the festival for about a kilometer or so, not that there's any really accurate measurement in this place. More like tradition."

There had been no large lights on, Gaelian noted, but there were flickers coming from the streets. As Iesin led them, they passed groups of people carrying torches and candles. As her eyes became more accustomed to the darkness, the whole scene seemed more like something out of a strange neo-art entertainment tape than a festival, of Anoni or otherwise.

The people were all brightly dressed, so it seemed at least where the feeble torchlight touched their clothes. She could see the brilliant colors, and the forms of face painting were even more complex than those of a Cahaute war party. She felt almost naked with only her two crimson bars. Faces were painted to represent birds, fish, flowers, and a few as skulls. Those who were painted as skulls wore only white, and people made way for them, even when it meant pressing deeply into the solid mass of flesh that the crowd formed. There was a heavy smell in the air, indolent and too sweet, and Gaelian noted that many people carried flowers, full blooms that were almost as large as her hand, which seemed to be the source of the scent.

They pressed on, following the crowd closer to the Temple, being pushed on all sides, hurried, hushed. For so many people, there was little chatter, as if they were all intent on something, one thing, many things. She dared not ask Iesin what it all meant, although Ie undoubtedly knew.

The crowd swarmed around them, carried them with the press of bodies in the thickly scented night air.

Suddenly, a tremendous moan erupted. People started wailing, pulling hair from under hats or confining scarves. Cries that sounded as if they came from victims of torture pierced the low rumbling agony of the festival goers.

"What in all four of Anoni's hells are they doing?" Vi demanded loudly.

Gaelian was silent as Sessov, Golran, and Ie turned and eyed the other woman coldly. Vi seemed to shrink, and Gaelian caught the reference to the Shore Patrol. If too many people talked too much, there could well be more than a few bar brawls with the locals.

"Happy are they who are with the rain," the crowd started to chant. "Happy are they who have gone to water. Happy is the rain."

Over and over again, the beat of it built like a hard, relentless storm, threatening to break and holding back. In the torch light, everything seemed grey and then became almost hideously bright when caught in sudden, uncertain illumination. Gaelian thought she was in one of her nightmares. No, it was worse. In some ways, her nightmares made sense, and this did not.

There were thousands of people around her, some pressed tight against her, their shoulders gouging against her back, elbows invading her ribs, packed in so she could barely move. She could smell the sweat on them and see the tears reflected into lines of glitter by the feeble candles the children held in disposable cups. The tears streaked much of the careful painting she had seen earlier, and now most of the faces had brilliant highlights and rivulets of darker color blending and turning into muddied eddies just before the paint ran down their necks and across the flowers, the white, white collars. It looked like blood, variegated and pulsating and alive. They were bleeding here in the street, screaming chanting.

The chant rose higher, louder, almost distant, as if carried only by the breeze.

"Happy are they who are with the rain, happy are they who are with the rain."

The words themselves became less distinct, and there was another current. Hands clapped out the intonation of the chant, underlined it; the clapping became complicated and asymmetric. It was endemic, beating all around her, and in it she could still hear the chant echoed in her own head, or was there still chanting somewhere in the distance?

The staccato clapping filled her. The rhythm drove her, entered her, became part of her pulse, beat in her temples. She began clapping along, not sure how she knew how to follow the intricate rhythms. Her hands beat time, beat out the chant that she did not understand. Her body swayed, moved to the clapping. The rhythm took her body entirely and drove her through the crowd, gyrating helplessly with the rest of the mob.

She was one of them, another entity moving through this night that did not exist, that did not matter. Once she saw that, all separation was gone, and she knew that nothing that happened this night was real. The night was a mask, like the paint, like the scarf she pulled off her shoulders and started to twirl over her head, like a thousand, a hundred thousand scarves twirled over the multitude. Nothing was impossible. They merged, the crowd together. She was Adedri here as if she had always been, and she knew that since it was not real, then it was not important what happened. If she died in the festival, she would live again in the morning. She merged, melted into the festival itself, the rhythm that resonated off the ancient stone walls, through the streets, through the long bones of her body. She became one with them, cahaute, and *recognized* them.

The recognition made her freeze, and she no longer felt imbued with the festival. Vainly she searched in the flickering light for a glimpse of Iesin or Sessov or Golran or even Vi. She could make out nothing. There were only shapes and colors, rhythms and patterns being woven and broken all at the same time. She couldn't find her friends. She couldn't find anything at all familiar. Fear swept through her like a sharp wind.

This was madness. The entirety of Adedri was insane. They institutionalized their own insanity and put it out in the open for others to catch, raw and primitive. But how did they know, she wondered coldly, logic an easy thing to cling to in the disintegrating mass mind that surrounded her. How did they know the rhythms that would move her just so, the strange juxtapositions of words that would permeate her psyche and make her respond before she even realized she was gone?

Her terror was cold, a fear that had nothing to do with her own safety. It was that she had *recognized*, and it hadn't felt like other evil things she had touched. There was something precise about it, careful and structured, the exact antithesis of the festival she was more than simply witness to.

Gaelian steeled herself, waiting for it to end. She thought it might go on until morning, and that thought worried her. There was no way she could leave now. She couldn't find Iesin or the car. She couldn't even move against the press of bodies fixing her to this spot on the pavement.

A sudden explosion so low it made her thigh bones vibrate

split the rhythm of the festival, and then the sky exploded.

Gaelian tensed and then relaxed almost immediately. It was only fireworks, with the sound effects stepped up. The street seemed slightly wider as people disappeared, only to blossom again suddenly on roofs and strangely shaped outcroppings, the ornate gables the Adedri loved on their old buildings. The masses were now spread on every horizontal surface at every level. It was lovely, and she quieted. The hideous beating had stopped.

A hand clamped on her shoulder, and she jumped, startled.

"Gaelian, thank all the colors of the game! We'd lost you there, when the clapping started. Come on, we'd better get out of here soon, before they start up again and it gets ugly, or else Shore Patrol is going to have one hell of a good time booking us into the brig."

Golran's presence was more than a relief to her. It was like finally being let out of prison, some dream she couldn't wake from. She grabbed his belt and hung on as he started to make his way back.

"You know where the car is?" she asked.

"Come on!" he urged her and pulled her farther down the street, cutting through a narrow alley and twisting around several corners that stood at odd angles to each other.

"I've had a little time to get used to this place," he said softly.

"This is a filthy place," she murmured.

The fireworks still rumbled in the background. She turned once to watch them, brilliant colors exploding across the sky, but Golran threw his arm around her shoulders and pulled her onward. They walked more slowly now, the alleyways and streets silent and deserted, as if the entire population of Adedri was down in the square kilometer or two that was the traditional festival district.

"What was it?" she asked finally, as Golran guided her into what looked like a more modern business district, a place that resembled the area where they had left the car.

He stopped and looked at her. "Adedri," he said carefully, choosing his words, "is like a drug. It touches everyone that way, some more than others. Things happen during these festivals. Fights, murders, everything you don't want to know about. It isn't safe to stay after the fireworks begin. Some people just disappear during these things. They go, and no one ever hears from them again. They never come back. The Shore Patrol has almost given up trying to find them. They're just entered as absent without leave."

"Wait, Gol," Gaelian said. "Tell me more. People just . . . disappear in Adedri? What if they're killed or kidnapped or something?"

"That's probably what happens," Golran agreed with her. "But we don't know. Only they never come back. And the Shore Patrol doesn't think it's kidnapping. I mean, after all, with kidnapping there's usually some reason, like money or something. People get caught up in the festivals. We all get caught, to some degree. Maybe that's why we come, because it's so easy to draw close to the edge and become part of the festival. But then you have to remember to draw back. Some people hardly get caught at all. Vi's like that. The rhythms don't work on her as strongly."

"And you?" Gaelian asked softly.

"They work," Golran replied harshly and then turned abruptly, leading her into a slightly wider street and to the public lot's elevator system.

The others were already waiting at the car when they arrived. There was little conversation on the way back to base, most of it from Vi who didn't seem to understand that no one really wanted to talk. No one really wanted to do anything other than get back to safe territory, Gaelian thought. Home, safety. Anything not Adedri. Somehow, it seemed very unclean to her—the whole festival, the emotionalism, the beating that carried her in its sway, that merged her with the mass mind of the festival.

It was a relief to return to the base. Everyone seemed to relax at least slightly as Iesin touched the aircar down on the apron.

Gaelian went back to her quarters alone. She didn't want to talk to anyone, didn't want to communicate what was still vague inside her head. She had hated the festival, what it did to her. It was worse than being drunk, robbing her of all power and control. But it was also potent, and she acknowledged that she wanted to return. There had been something euphoric, even exalting in becoming part of the festival. Part of her wanted that again, to experience it more fully, not to be pulled away.

Tanistin and the festival, both in the same day, she reflected. One was supremely elegant, the other unquestionably sensual, yet both had touched her. Both were working in her, like the silent knowledge of her Cahaute heritage. Perhaps that was why it had caught her so deeply. The part of her that was primitive, that belonged to Cahaute by blood, language, and upbringing lurked in her, a hidden flaw. She resisted it, but the flaw was still there, an essential weakness in the structure. She could try to overcompensate in other directions, but what Cahaute had given her would not disappear so easily.

An image of her true mother drifted across her vision—Myhinta, a woman of the tribes. Gaelian YnTourne was a half-breed.

She whispered the word in the shadows, whispered them to hear them and make them more real. Half-breed. The secret had lain buried as a part of her for so long that she barely acknowledged it. It had lain buried in her father too, and his own silence and loss had driven him to his destruction. She knew that neither Dobrin nor her grandmother, nor any of the Ot-tan families, understood Renan YnTourne's drinking, his self-imposed isolation or his half-crazy destructive behavior. Only Gaelian knew that it was her father's price to keep up the pretense, to live every moment of his life renouncing all claims to honor.

And what did that make her?

Something twisted inside her. Stress on the flaw would cause an explosion, a collapse of the system. Tembri's death had primed the explosive. The festival had set the fuse. But it was a very long fuse, she told herself. There was still time to run and tamp it out, time to reset the dials and defuse it. There had to be time.

10

"WHAT DID YOU think of that?" Kaesoma AnAserin asked Teazerin YnSetti.

The other shrugged. They were sitting in the reactor control room, the only building that was finished on the site. Not that the power was on line yet, Teazerin thought ruefully. They were only too often reminded of the fact. That savage getting in last night, for instance. If they'd had power for the field fence, there wouldn't have been any problem. As it was, though, they were wide open, and he didn't like it.

Not that he liked anything about this assignment. It was rotten getting stuck in some backwater dump like this, without even the most basic amenities like air conditioning, and it was insufferably hot.

"So what do you think?" AnAserin asked again, almost insistently. "It was pretty strange, coming in with those hides and all. What are we going to do with a bunch of hides? They smell."

"Burn 'em," Teazerin said. "What else would we do? They're probably infested with who knows what kind of miserable insects and bacteria and so on anyway."

He was sick of Kaesoma. He was sick of all the people who were assigned to build this base on Cahaute, and the last thing he needed was some Adedri laborer sitting around making conversation. As if they had anything in common, anyway; as if they had a single thing to talk about.

"But, somehow, I don't think it would be really, well, right, if you understand me, to burn those hides. They seem to be a present of some type. It isn't, well, polite or something, to burn presents. Maybe we should ship them back to some university or something," the Adedri mused.

"Aren't you supposed to be on perimeter guard?" Teazerin asked abruptly.

The Adedri looked down, obviously shamed, and then slowly made his way out into the heat.

Teazerin YnSetti lay back on the single cot in the control room. One day it would be used for the third person on duty here, running the reactor, checking the power feed, but now it was the only civilized place to sleep. At least for an ensign. The superior officers used the bunks on the scout ships. YnSetti cursed the heat that kept him from sleep and the exhaustion that the previous night's watch had left him with.

It had been bad enough to have one of the natives wandering into camp on his watch. Everything about this place was worse than he had imagined. It was practically exile, this far from anything remotely connected to Dinoreos.

He knew why he had been sent. His parents had told him as well, just in case he wasn't astute enough to understand without being told. He didn't disabuse them of their notion of his innocence. He was here both to protect the interests of Dinoreos and to see to the interests of the mining corporation, in which he was personally a major stockholder. In theory, strictly in theory, he understood the necessity for it. Personally, he could think of a lot better ways to push his career than to ride herd on a bunch of half-washed Adedri.

He cursed Cahaute again, the heat and the bugs and the lack of running water. No wonder Gaelian was a little strange. She had lived here, wearing hides, for seven years. He couldn't decide, even now, whether he was furious or relieved about Gaelian. It was two months since her grandmother had died and she had renounced her claim to Headship of the household to run off and play pilot. He hadn't exactly been looking forward to having to marry her, but he had very much been looking forward to what he could do if he were in a position to have influence over the Board. And inside information on the Craft Company. That, plus his own holdings in the mining combine, would have the makings of a dynasty that could have superseded the other Ot-tan families and held the reins on trade. Now there was nothing left. On the other hand, he didn't really want to have to live with her.

It was too hot to sleep. He tossed on the cot, praying for oblivion, but it didn't come. His thigh itched. So did the back of his hand. Grumbling with exasperation, Teazerin stood and fumbled for the jury-rigged portalight. The luminescence it gave was faint; obviously the charge was getting low. But even in the gloom, he could see that his left hand was red and swollen. More bugs.

Suddenly fury grabbed him, as it had the night before. Then he had had to control himself, although every instinct had screamed at him to slap the savage who had come visiting. There was nowhere else he wouldn't go, nothing else he wouldn't do, so long as it didn't concern Cahaute.

The savage represented everything this assignment had started to mean. He could see through it clearly enough. It was punishment. The YnTourne were in it with the YnOestal, and between the two families there was a lot of pull in the Admiralty. They knew he represented a threat, the ancient kind of nerris priest who understood that there was no wrong in the Ot-tan using those lower, who knew his own worth. And they, all those younger members of the Board like Dobrin and Iesin's oldest brother, the eldest of the YnOestal, they scoffed at his old ideas of blood and power and what the Ot-tan really were.

"You still up, Teaz?" someone asked softly.

YnSetti moved into the light. He could see a form outlined in the doorway.

" 'S only me," the figure responded.

Teazerin relaxed. He recognized the voice now, Aberdas YnLodri, from his own class. Another ensign who shuttled between the cargo bay and the cot in the control room. Something flittered across his mind.

"Hey, Abs, have you heard anything about last night?" he asked casually. They were on different shifts, and YnLodri might have heard something. "Am I in any difficulty or something?"

YnLodri seemed to glance away for a moment before he came into the light and sat on the cot.

"No, I wouldn't really call it difficulty. But you've been camped out here, not listening to what the brass has been saying. Don't worry, it's all getting put down to inexperience, nothing's going to come down. But you should still know."

YnSetti studied him. "Know what?" he asked softly.

"They didn't like the way you handled our first contact with the natives, especially given that a local initiated things. We want good relations with the locals, Teaz. You don't know how important it is. I've heard a few things . . . stuff they really don't want us lowly ensigns to know about. But didn't you ever wonder why the Navy was making an official priority out of this place?"

"No," YnSetti answered shortly. He liked Abs, but the YnLodri, while of the Ot-tan class, weren't on the Board, weren't part of one of the major companies. They dealt in small-time affairs, short-haul transportation of foodstuffs, things like that. They weren't considered really major. Abs wouldn't realize what the mineral rights here could mean to Dinoreos in general.

"Well," YnLodri said, "I've been hearing stuff around. I figure I should let you in on it. Well, we've always had trouble with the Adedri, since no one knows why they'd do some things and not others, accept some parts of what we offered them and not others. It never made sense, really. They don't seem to want any contact with us at all. But these folk, these Cahaute, well, they're primitive, but some of those early reports show that they're intelligent. Really intelligent, like the Adedri or even us. I've heard rumors. They might not have to be part of the Protectorate like Adedri. Hells, the Adedri don't even want any part in it, except the economic advantages. But with the Cahaute, once they're cleaned up and educated, well, it would be something all new. New people. A whole different culture. And maybe some fresh ideas. And look at this place. Really underpopulated. I don't understand it really, only that there's a whole lot of excitement out there, and it's like someone really big is behind all of it."

Something about what Abs told him chilled him, even in the heat. There were some on the Board, even some in the Admiralty, who might just talk the way YnLodri said. They were soft, mewling excuses for people, but they had power.

"I guess I'll have to behave better," he said, smiling at YnLodri. He hated saying it, but there had been a lot of things he hated saying. He said them anyway. They were necessary, and Teazerin was a realist enough to bow to necessity. "Now, are you going to catch any trouble being in here when you've got a watch?"

"Just keep in mind that these are people here, right? Who knows? Once we wash 'em up and teach 'em to read, they might be worth even more than those crummy minerals you're so hot on." YnLodri hesitated for a moment and shifted his weight back. "Actually, I was asked to come and get you anyway. We've got to rig the portapower into the fence after last night."

"Thanks," Teazerin grunted. "Can you give me a few minutes at least, splash some cold water on my face? Hells."

He had no doubt that YnLodri had been sent to warn him, unofficially of course, about his attitude. But he had a funny feeling that they were all wrong. One of these days, those natives were going to attack the base, and then he would be vindicated. Let the softies like Abs weave candy-dreams. Those people, if that one who had come last night was any indication, would take generations before they'd ever have anything to offer the Protectorate. If they ever did. And they could be dangerous. That native last night had a knife and a spear, and YnSetti would bet a month's pay that he could use both. He for one was going to feel a lot safer when they had the fence powered, even if rigging the portables was going to deprive him of some sleep.

He made his way to the washroom, dreaming of his vindication. Then he would get what he wanted, off Cahaute, with a citation perhaps. Invigorated by the pleasant fantasies, he made his way out to where Abs's group was already sweating under the hot sun of Cahaute, readying the fence for use that night.

They were all gathered there, the Mikke and the Roneedee, the Haka and the Astanepa. The clans gathered and the moieties responsible for war, for the hunt, for the camp. The young people did not paint, not until they heard the decision of the elders.

Nyapetin sat to the side next to Hinacen on a fine robe. The old b'hasute had another robe wrapped around his shoulders, but it had no pictures on it. Even Hinacen did not know what the elders had decided.

A young child, sucking marrow from a bone, wandered through the crowd and disappeared into a lodge. The wind did not touch the standing people and rustle their heavy leaves, and the winged ones did not call out in the early dark. The

smell of stew from many cook fires wafted over them, and
Nyapetin remembered that he was hungry, but there was no
one to stir the meat, no one to ladle it into bowls.

He could see shadows moving inside the council lodge. They
would emerge soon to tell the people what they would do. In
front of the lodge stood two sturdy posts, the trunks of young
trees planted deep in the ground. One was painted with a green
band, the color of Yenhica the War Maiden, the other with
yellow and blue, red and black.

The flap of the lodge was pushed open from the inside, and
one by one the elders emerged. Their faces were like stone, old
and carved by many rains. The eldest of them, Teawattanee,
wore all twenty of his warrior-bird tail-feathers in his hair.
He had been a great war chief once and a good guide to the
people. Each of the elders carried a short stick, the symbol of
their authority. It was the lance of war and the baton of punishment and the stick of herding.

One by one the elders stepped to the pole with the green
band and struck it with the stick of authority.

Loud trilling broke the silence. Excitement danced like
water, like fire through the camp. Nyapetin found himself
trilling with the rest, his voice expanding into the night calling
on all the Power Ones to hear him, to the clans and the small
friends.

The young men leapt forward to strike the war pole. The
young women began to sing, and the elders shouted encour-
agement. Nyapetin also leapt up from his robe and danced to
the war pole. He touched it lightly and joined the other
dancers. He saw others dancing of how many they would kill
the next day, of how bravely they would enter the camp of the
enemy and how many shoes and how many shields they would
take. And of how they would burn down the strange white
lodges.

Nyapetin did not dance any of these things. He danced only
as his brother the snake had showed him, the dance of danger,
of waiting, of power. He danced his power as the warriors
danced theirs, as the children danced hope to remember this
raid forever and to tell it to their grandchildren.

Then Hinacen stepped forward, his arms raised to the sky.
"Tomorrow is a good day to die," he said loudly.

The dancing stopped, and the elders and warriors, Mikke

and Roneedee, turned to the old man who spoke louder than one of his years usually did.

"It will be a good day to die," the b'hasute repeated. "I wish to make a gift. If I should not live, I give my power to this young person."

The old man's bony hand fell hard on Nyapetin's shoulder, and he shivered.

"Grandfather, raiding is for young people," someone shouted out of the dark.

Hinacen's face darkened. "We do not war on others of our people. We do not raid the hiding-in-the-tall-grass or the ones-who-follow-red-wings," he said. "There is magic in these people. I do not understand their magic, so maybe they do not know ours. But we will need more than strong arms and good lances. We will need Rock and Breath and River and Flame. So. Go back to your dancing and eat your dinner before it is cold. You will need your strength tomorrow."

Nyapetin joined several of the Roneedee warriors, he who had been Roneedee before all the tribes had claimed him. They passed around bowls of fresh water, not talking. Several boys and girls who were old enough to be there and too young to raid ran between the river and the small groups, refilling the bowls quickly. Nyapetin drank four, five drinks of water, enough to force him to rise well before dawn. They had a long trail before they came to the strangers' camp, and dawn was the traditional time for a raid, when the inhabitants were just starting to rise and were too sleepy to be ready. Then he rolled up in a light, soft robe and drifted to sleep with the Roneedee warriors, humming a happy song to himself.

The water worked well, and he rose with the rest of them in the coldest part of the night, when the late-flying ones sang mournfully. Paint pots were passed around, and he painted as he had been taught by the snake brother, painted his own death in red and yellow and blue lines weaving on his arms, his chest, his face. But he did not secure a green painted lance to his breechcloth, nor did he take a bow or sling a full sack of arrows across his back as the others did. Instead, he took his flute in his hand and tied a rattle to his thigh. Even in this black time with very few stars above, the white of the hasute necklace shone brightly.

Finally, their small band of six joined the others, all of

whom had made the same preparations. Hinacen came out to
join them, and the old b'hasute daubed a smudge of green on
each of their foreheads and on his own. Nyapetin could almost
feel it cool, burning, against his skull, the mark of the warrior
who knows that any day is good to die.

Silently, they went in single file out of the camp. The Mikke
warrior, who was the war leader for this raid, moved swiftly,
following the two scouts who had gone ahead long before the
others had risen. Nyapetin could read the scout signs in the
high parts of the trees. The elders and children, the mothers
and those others who were staying behind watched them leave.
There was no singing, no trilling to break the stillness of the
night.

They trotted briskly over the trail. Nyapetin relaxed and let
his legs stretch, enjoying the cool air on his skin. They went
around the place of the ghost trees, because it was not good to
invite even benign ghosts on a raiding party. He let go of himself, of Hinacen's promise, and of the raid itself. There was
only the running in the forest that smelled of almost-morning,
the soft sounds of night dwellers or others on the trail. The air
became dank and chill, changing the forest itself until the sky
became a paler shade of black.

The leader of the party made a sign to halt, and others carried the sign down the group in silence. Nyapetin came out of
his reverie to see that they were on the edge of the forest. Between the trees he could see the white lodges standing alone,
glowing with some kind of fire.

Hinacen walked like a ghost and whispered some words to
the leader. Nyapetin was surprised to see him. The old man
should not have run so far, so hard. He should be sitting at his
fire with someone to serve him cool water and breakfast.
Hinacen motioned to Nyapetin, and the younger hasute came
forward to where the trees broke.

"They have released the fire," Hinacen whispered.

Nyapetin stared at the stranger camp. It did not look any
different than it had when he had gone there with edonys.
Then he breathed deeply and sat down on the soft leaves of the
past year. He could feel the earth in him. Let snake brother
come now, he said silently.

There was something wrong around the camp, something
different. It felt like the world before the great noise and the
fire-from-the-sky came with the great rain. It prickled his skin

and made the little hairs stand on end. There was something here that reminded him of the Dead Hill, the feeling of fire running like water.

"This is for a young person," Hinacen whispered to him.

The b'hasute took a water bag from around his body and offered it to Nyapetin. The younger shook his head, but Hinacen was insistent.

"You will not see it clearly without edonys," the b'hasute said. "You know it is there, you can feel it, but if you cannot see it then you will not be able to do anything about it. The edonys will show you."

Nyapetin took the bag and noticed that it was very light, less than half full. He squeezed out only a few drops and rubbed them on his lips. Then he tasted the drug gingerly. Even the small amount he took burned and puckered his mouth.

The drug raced through him, heightening his senses, making everything unique, singular, and clear. Then he opened his eyes and looked on the enemy camp.

Very faintly against the grey light, he saw it, shimmering and moving like a reflection off the water. It danced like a warrior after victory, it shuddered like a prisoner bound to a staff. He reached out with the edonys self to touch it and then shrank back. It was hotter than fire, screaming, insane, a thing of the unseen chained where it should not be. It was the work of the Trickster, of that he was certain.

The drug burned through him once more and then was gone. He came back to himself and sat very still, recalling what he had learned of the thing that stood between them and the camp. Water put out fire, but sometimes a fire was too strong for River. This one was the strongest he had known. Sometimes a new fire would challenge the first, and they would battle until both died. This was a strong thing, and Nyapetin had seen it, but the invisible fire around the stranger camp was stronger than any fire he had known, and it would be victorious. Breath was often the friend of fire, and so she would not help. But fire is like man, he thought. It needs to breathe. So Rock could stop its breath, could make it suffocate.

Nyapetin opened his eyes for the third time and motioned to the leader. "Just in front of us there is a fire," he said softly. "I will open it just so far, as wide as between these two trees, and just so high that we can crawl through. I will open it there, just behind that large rock, so that people can hide before it is open and still give surprise. But let the lead one throw a small stone through first to make sure it is gone."

The leader nodded abruptly, and the raiding party formed behind the line of trees. One of the scouts ran low to the ground in position behind the rock. Even from this side, Nyapetin could barely see him.

Hinacen handed him the edonys bag again, and Nyapetin thought he could detect the hint of a smile on his teacher's face. Silently he drank the edonys down, three large mouthfuls. Not as much as he had had the first time he'd used the drug, but enough to leave his body feverish and shaking. It hit him harder, gripping him suddenly, overwhelming him. The dancing fire was very clear and beautiful, dazzling streams of color like sky, like sunset, moving too rapidly to comprehend. Yet, he could see the movement, follow the bits that ran against each other and collided, became larger as if with young, and then divided, giving birth. Something in him understood this thing, knew it intimately.

Then Nyapetin heard the sound of the flute, far off and teasing just at the edge of his hearing. He strained to listen to the music, but it eluded him. He followed, but it was always just out of reach, lower and lower. By the time he chanced to look back at the fire, it no longer tempted him.

It was not that its brightness had diminished, but that he was full of something else. Against the dancing rainbows, he felt the life-giving coolness of the soil and the nourishment it held for all things. He was part of its immense patience that had waited forever and would continue to wait, watching the generations of men and of standing people. Time lay there, all eternity bound up together and apart. The earth did not care that someone died. It was no matter that the great leafed ones of the forest burned and fell to ash, that the branched runner died of thirst one season and froze the next. It was all one, like the changing of the seasons, knowing that the green time will follow the white, and that the white will come again.

All this he knew as the rock knows it, as the mountain knows it. He knew it in a way older than the forest. Immense strength flowed through him slowly, seeping cautiously like mud. He became slow like the earth, so slow that the dancing fire did not touch him. It was a sparkle in time, the flicker of an insect's wing. He rose against the fire, pushing upward against it, changing it, making it slow. He brought all things around him into this no-time that had begun before existence and existed at the end of being. All of it was now.

He made the invisible flame slow, frozen and heavy. It dropped away from him, falling like stone, becoming stone in the first cycle of creation.

Tiny darts pierced him like stingers in summertime, and like the stingers he paid them no attention. Only the very foundation of being was worthy of attention.

He stretched out the eternity, opening himself to it and growing larger and larger, expanding across and through the dancing fire, absorbing it. It, too, was part of the foundation he had become.

And then, very clearly, came the sound of a flute. It was a single note, steady as the earth itself, strong and full and vibrating with him. He did not know if he had caused the vibration or if it had always been there. The single note grew larger than he was. It encompassed all the world. It encompassed all time. He strove, pleaded to join it. Then the note was all there was, and Nyapetin did not exist. And then there was nothing at all.

Nothing faded. Nyapetin found himself on a soft robe surrounded by sweet-smelling grass. Everyday sounds passed him, children squealing as someone made a point in a game, water sloshing into stew bags, and the low murmur of conversation. A hand rested on his shoulder, and he moved. The hand went away.

He opened his eyes slowly. It was very bright. Hinacen was sitting near him.

"So," Hinacen said, "you return."

Nyapetin tried to nod sharply, but his head was very heavy, and it was difficult to move. He remembered the greatness of being the earth and being the fire. Tears ran down his face, but they were not shameful. He remembered the note of the flute and wondered if it had been Hinacen playing. Without the flute, he would have stayed forever.

The old man did not look at Nyapetin at all. He gazed at the sky, at the single warrior-bird soaring in great circles above them. "You do not need my power," the old man said finally. "Yours alone is large enough. Maybe too big. When the spirit burns so strong, it can burn the wearer of it."

Hinacen rose and left him alone. The great bird dove, hurtling itself toward the camp. Nyapetin saw it coming for him as he lay against the earth, too weak even to move. Then the bird unfurled its wings and glided away.

So. Cahaute. Any day is a good day to die.

Dobrin sat at the scarred Board table trying to rein in his fury. Around him, the others were alternately raging or shocked silent. It took all his control not to pound his fist against the table. It simply was not possible.

"I think we should play the tape again now that everyone is here," YnSetti said smoothly.

"We've all heard that tape to four hells and back," Kaes snorted. "What we need to know is *how did they do it?* Yn-Tourne, your uncle spent more time on that infernal planet than anyone else. Did you ask him? Do we have any expert opinions at all?"

Kaes's face was so purple that Dobrin was afraid something would burst.

"Renan's theories would be of little practical value," he managed to say evenly. "He believes that they have some kind of supernatural power, if you will."

"At this point, that makes as much sense as anything else," YnOestal said in that lazy way that meant she was juggling at least three viable possibilities.

"The facts stand," Dobrin continued dryly, if a little too quickly. He was not about to let his moment pass. "The reactor wasn't up to full capacity. It is possible they slipped in during one of the checks. The power on base wasn't steady enough for us to assume that they actually got in through the barrier. What matters is that the natives are hostile, have proved their hostility even when not provoked."

YnOestal waved her hand gently. "It's very strange. They didn't kill anyone. They just stole some things. Not anything important, as I remember. Some shoes, one uniform, a set of coding chips."

"And what in four hells are they going to do with coding chips?" Kaes erupted.

"Haven't you noticed?" YnOestal looked almost surprised. "They're very pretty. Bright colors, sparkly, just the kind of thing you'd expect a primitive to want. No, it isn't what they took that makes me wonder, only that there was so little violence."

"And what do you expect them to do against power weapons?" YnSetti asked silkily.

"They wouldn't even know they were weapons," Dobrin said. He was disgusted with the rest of them. He knew what YnOestal was saying without saying it, in the way of the yellow. The more he thought of it, the more it affected him in the same way. Here they were, absolutely enraged because a tribe invaded a camp that wasn't fully protected and stole a few worthless items. It was that they had shown their power without needing to fight. It had shamed all of them.

It was an insult. It was the way people like Teazerin YnSetti played nerris. And it was the insult that riled them.

But how did the Cahaute know how to touch that nerve? That was what Dobrin wanted to know.

"Either we evacuate or we increase our presence there," Kaes said thoughtfully.

"Or we talk to them," YnOestal added as an afterthought.

"We can't talk to them," Kaes fumed again. "Only Renan speaks their language, and he's too drunk to say anything useful. To anyone."

"When the test, run in Adedri proves out, we could request that the Admiralty send Tanistin," Dobrin said. As the faces at the table turned to him, he knew he had them. It was the blue, pure and perfect. "It would increase our firepower greatly. After all, it was designed as a pirate runner carrying atmosphere-capable fighters. And my cousin Gaelian is aboard. She speaks Cahaute too, probably understands the people better than Renan does. So we can do both at once. That is, unless there is an overwhelming consensus that we should cut our losses."

"Brilliant, YnTourne," YnOestal smiled.

Dobrin knew he had won, knew it as surely as if there was a score flashing overhead in the wall. Whether it was the right thing or not wasn't nearly as important as that he had controlled the Board, if only momentarily.

The Admiralty had never defied the Board. Besides, until the operations were well underway, the mission on Cahaute, while primarily economic, came under their jurisdiction. And if the Board felt shamed, then the Admiralty should feel doubly so. Besides, why had Tanistin been built, if not to resolve inconveniences of this nature?

There was no need to vote. Kaes stated that he would make

the Board's decision known through the proper channels. Dobrin rose and took a slice of cheese from the platters laid out on the sideboard. He wasn't hungry, but he felt that he deserved it all the same—to show them that he was more than fully one of them now, one of the rulers of the Protectorate. And fully entitled in every way.

They had been underway for six days, and the excitement had worn off. Vi hadn't exaggerated their lack of duties, Gaelian thought, as she sat defiantly on her bunk in the tiny cabin she shared with Iesin again. Lowly ensigns didn't rate private quarters.

The senior pilots, those who had done the original test work on the systems and smaller antipirate craft, had all the interesting watches. They had already taken the APs out, run them near to max under all kinds of conditions, and tinkered with the insides. The four junior pilots, and she most junior of all, had done nothing yet.

Nothing but watch endless numbers march across a green screen, flat meaningless readings indicating that each machine in the hangar was functioning properly and that there was nothing out there at all except dust particles, a couple of meteorites, and a seriously complacent asteroid. There weren't even many other ships out to hail. Tanistin's course was far from the regular shipping lanes and patrol routes. After all, one didn't usually find pirates in well-traveled sectors. No, they were plodding through aeons of absolute emptiness. Pirates were probably a myth anyway, she thought in disgust. Or they were all on vacation.

"You've got the face of the blunt end of a stick," Iesin said as she entered the cabin.

"My, aren't we useful today," Gaelian groused. "I wonder when we get enough rank to stop being roommates. You'd think we were married or something."

Iesin made a face and shrugged. "At least we didn't get stuck with Vi. You want to put up with her this cruise, be my guest."

Gaelian started to say something and then thought better of it. She'd been complaining too much to Iesin lately, about the room, about her watches, about everything that wasn't important. And Iesin knew it. Sometimes she wished Ie would just come out and say something, about the festival or the raid on Cahaute or the fact that she never got a chance to see Golran. No, forget about Golran. Iesin didn't think that was very important.

Her soft-soled shoes didn't make a sound as she marched down the long corridors. It made her feel like a ghost, and then she remembered that Dinoreans didn't believe in ghosts. She stopped before the lift tube and shook her head, as if to dislodge an idea. There wasn't anyone around. They were on ship's night cycle, which was typical for junior watches.

Gaelian wondered if she were going insane. More and more now, she felt distanced from Ie who was her best friend, alien where she should have felt most at home. Something in her desired earth and wind and water that tasted of the ground it had come from. And yet, she had been on long cruises before and had never been affected in this way. She was even thinking in Cahaute more frequently, and the dreams had come back. Dark dreams, full of forests and burning and strange stories that twisted around in the back of her head. But she couldn't recall them.

She made her way unseeing to the console inside the hangar deck. Next week, or so the rotation read, she would be reporting to the control room. Which sounded more exciting on the screen and was meant to keep the youngsters out of the way in case there really was any action. She sighed heavily and signed in in the log. Then she saluted Sessov.

"YnTourne reporting to relieve the watch," she said mechanically.

"Turned and commendations of the day," Sessov replied with little enthusiasm. "Nothing, as usual," he informed her, now that the formalities were over. "I'll leave these if you want them. I've got another set or six somewhere."

She thanked him and took the flimsy fax chapbook. Smiling, he handed her a pencil to go with it and left.

The chapbook was one of a series of puzzles that Sessov had printed out before they left, with great foresight as it turned out. There were strict regs against using any of the consoles on the ship for anything so frivolous as entertainment. Not that puzzles and acrostics were enough to keep her alert during the watch, but they would at least help pass some of the time. Gaelian wished that someone would figure a way around the

device that registered unauthorized use of games, but she
wasn't engineer enough to attempt it. She assumed that was
what some of the others did during the long hours when they
monitored sector activities that consisted of a sudden, exciting
particle drift on rare occasions.

She was trying to think of a seven-letter word for a popular
Adedri fish when the monitor went crazy. Neat readouts
showing all systems normal, all conditions stable suddenly
halted, and new data flashed by so quickly she hardly caught
them before she realized that something was going on and
she'd better pay attention. One alarm sounded and then
another.

"It looks like something's going on out there," she commed
up to control.

"Indications of R-class vessel," a dry voice came through
her headset. "We're trying to raise them. Why don't you
stretch your legs and investigate?"

Before they identify themselves as some perfectly respect-
able merchant vessel already charted for this route anyway,
she added silently to herself. But even with that reminder, she
queued the hatch and hoisted herself into the pit of the nearest
AP craft. She waited, tensed, until the signal light indicated
that the airlock cycle was starting. The senior pilots would be
up and coming any second, and once they arrived she would
be relieved of even this minor duty. The light flashed on,
yellow, and the little AP rolled down the track, picking up
velocity at a startling rate as it was shoved by an increasingly
intense electromagnetic field. Faster than she could comprehend, she hurtled out of the hatch, her screen reporting
navigation locked on to the unidentified vessel.

"No ID yet," the rasping control-room voice informed her.
The things that had pushed at the edges of her mind for the
past fifteen days dropped away. Her hands were poised on
the controls, ready for action. Her bones vibrated with the
smooth rhythm of thrust. She was free.

"AP Seven to unidentified vessel, relay identification. If
you are in trouble, fire a flare," she said calmly. "Visual contact made," she said into the mitt clipped to her collar.

She drew closer and reduced speed. From this distance, it
was difficult to perceive anything other than the class and
design, but the readout in front of her told a different story.

Distressed condition, it flashed. Possible mechanical failure, she told herself. Or maybe a drifting derelict. At least that's what it seemed to be.

But something in her knew differently. Something sang in her veins, a Mikke raiding song she had often heard. She could feel the threat emanating from the drifting vessel.

More lights flashed on her control panel. Something about the configuration warned her even before the signals came through. The others were on their way.

Six years of Academy discipline made her hands stone. Not quite orders to turn back, only reassurance that help was coming, that the entire team was behind her. Nerris. They could not force her back, not now when she led. And then, in the grip of some impulse she didn't even note, she flared the power of the tiny craft.

The AP leapt at her command, and even with the instinct of danger, she knew delight. With her forearms strapped into position, every unconscious flicker of thought transmitted to her hands regulated the little fighter. She almost had only to think a move, and it was done.

The sound was off on the computer, and she had not thought to adjust it before. Now she was glad. "Pursue," she whispered. A red-lit pathway opened, between her and the R-class she was chasing, on the crystal screen. Even with its voice turned off, the computer heard and obeyed her spoken commands.

The old R-class was ahead, turning now from broadside to run. She could smell it, like fear in the prey. Like the runner after a black nistora, she would run them to exhaustion, run them, run them down.

But the unidentified vessel ran before her, pulling out the stops and pouring on speed. More speed than it should have, she knew. R-class wasn't capable, wasn't built for this.

Logic screamed protest. The runner ran, infuriated. The others, senior, stayed back as she took the court and played. The ball came faster, bounding off the walls, angles taunting her, pursuing and dancing away.

With an unvoiced howl, she opened up the AP's engines with the flick of a finger. The power thrilled her, velocity slaked her ravaging thirst for energy, and still the pirate danced in front of her, just beyond range. She ran and burned fuel close to the safety point. Desperate and personal, it taunted her out there. Far larger, it shouldn't have that maneuverability; older, it was incapable of its speed. Yet it stayed there, just barely outside her range, no matter how much she pushed this ultra-fast AP.

And then the pirate veered sharply in a way it shouldn't have been able to, in a manner that should strain its ancient hull to splitting. She matched the turn and then the next. Her mitt was silent. It was only the silence of Dinoreos itself, night out on the roof, darkness like the night when she had found Tembri on the tree, penetrated by the too-fresh smell of the time she had nearly lost control. When the rumors had said the Angel touch was gone. It was cutting around, and now she understood. That single, ungainly asteroid, it was going for the shadow.

Gaelian snorted. All animals went for cover. It was for the hunter to find them, to beat them out. It smelled like that, like the forest. Fresh and cool, too cool, like a warning, one she should remember.

A blast hit one of the AP's fins. Her head raged against it. She knew this danger, this danger was in here. It was not from outside. And rage was the last thing she knew as the crippled AP went into an accelerated spin, accumulated g-force pressing her back into the dark.

11

GAELIAN MOVED HER fingers experimentally. They worked. She felt something very soft against her skin, fabric probably. She moved her whole body and found that she wasn't restrained. No, the webbing she felt must be strained muscles and the burn of her harness.

Then there was a sound—soft and light, it lanced through her head like a siren. She couldn't identify it except as a hurting noise. It wouldn't go away. It was laughter.

She slept again. There was another awakening. This time she could sense light through her closed lids. The air around her face moved lazily. It was pleasant, not too warm, and fresh-smelling. It was the fresh smell that reminded her of danger.

"Gaelian?"

Reflex fluttered her eyes open at the sound of her name, and the light hurt. She fought the light, squinting to adjust. A figure in red sat just inside the scope of her vision.

"Are you hungry?" the presence asked.

She knew it was a person, but presence seemed a better word. Properly, as she thought about it, she should be in the hospital on Adedri Base. But none of the medical workers there wore red. That was a nerris color.

The figure came closer, and Gaelian could see it was a young woman. No, not quite, really just a girl, not even old enough for the Academy, if she were right. She wasn't good at ages. But there was something in the girl's hand that smelled good, hot and steamy. She realized that she was very hungry, but she was too tired to say so. It was too much of an effort to talk.

The girl must have known how weak she was. A straw was placed in her mouth, and she sipped on it, glad of the warm broth.

There were other periods of waking and sleeping, more of sleeping. The girl, or another like her, was always there with something to drink and finally solid food for her to chew.

After that she woke feeling stronger and refreshed. There was no one in the room this time, but a pile of red clothes had been laid where the girl usually sat. Gingerly, Gaelian left the bed and made her way to the corner.

They were not her clothes. The garment was unfamiliar, and Gaelian was too tired to struggle. She managed to wrap it around herself and tied it behind her neck. It didn't drape the way it had on the girl, and the additional length puddled around her feet, making it hard to move. But she was dressed, after a fashion.

She moved slowly to the door, shuffling so as not to trip over the extra fabric that wound itself around her ankles. The door was not locked, and she pushed it open carefully, only a finger crack at a time.

She peered through the crack and saw several red-robed people standing in front of another door, about halfway down the hall. She considered the wisdom of stepping out and demanding where she was and asking for something to read or such. And then she thought again and turned back to explore the space she had occupied for some unknown amount of time. It would be better to be prepared.

The place was quite empty. There was the bed and a chair without a back in the corner. She had never seen anything like it—the seat was slanted, and there was some kind of pad a little above the floor. She tried to perch on it, balancing her toes against the lower cushion while sitting on the upper one, but it was hopelessly uncomfortable. Yet the girl she had seen and the people standing outside seemed to be made as she was. The bed was certainly familiar enough.

The opposite wall was deeply shadowed, as if the only light panels were around the bed and in the corner. There was a door there that she had not seen before, and behind it was a completely uninteresting washroom. So much for exploration.

When she emerged from the washroom, its discovery being of little informational value but great practical use, the girl was there again. Gaelian was sure it was the same girl, and she did seem very young. Small, with a roundness to her face that made Gaelian regard her as childish, the young woman wore an expression Gaelian had seen frequently enough to place. It was the gentle firmness of a medical worker who was not about to permit a patient anything the medical authority did not deem therapeutic.

"It's good to see you out of bed," the medic said. "Nomis will want to see you tomorrow if you're up to it, and you can ask any questions then. But your little walk must have tired you after being in bed for four days. Not to mention not having had very much to eat. There will be a real dinner tonight, but I must insist that you rest now."

Gaelian was a pilot. All medics were the enemy. Also, they *always* won. This one might be underage, but Gaelian knew better than to argue. That just made the entire breed worse. But, as the young woman left and Gaelian sank into the bed, she realized something.

Nomis, the girl had said. She'd heard that name before. Nomis was the Priest of Adedri, or so she had heard.

She bolted upright, wide awake. The room had become dark, as if on some schedule with the rest of the building. The energy she had lacked from either the jostling in the AP or whatever they were doing to her suddenly filled her again. She slipped out of bed and draped the red garment around herself, partly because it was the only clothing there and partly because it seemed that was what everyone wore. Very courteous of them to provide her with camouflage.

The door was not locked when she tried it. This time she didn't open it carefully and slowly, but gently as she had seen the medic do.

The corridor was deserted. She walked purposefully down the hall, stopping first to try one of the other doors. It was open, and she checked quietly inside. It was much as her own, with a single bed and someone obviously in need of medical care lying there with some sort of tubing running into bandages. She didn't stay to look.

Near where the corridor turned was a door that looked different from the others. It was marked with writing, but Gaelian couldn't read it. It hadn't occurred to her before that she might be someplace where she couldn't communicate. If the writing wasn't Dinorean, this place had to be Adedri. Then what use would a terminal be if she couldn't access it, let alone read any of their newsfax? Or whatever else they had here.

She pushed the door open, stepped in boldly, without examining the area, and banged into a bucket. She had discovered a maintenance closet.

It struck her as odd that she had seen no sign of other medical workers around. To the best of her limited knowledge, there were always people on duty in hospitals. And it was not as if she were the only person there who was in need of attention. So that left mechanical monitoring. That led to another discrepancy. If there had been mechanical monitoring, she had seen no sign of it in her own room. Besides, why would that girl or woman or nurse or doctor, or whatever she was, be sitting there all the time? Unless something mechanical had given signals at the end of a sleep cycle. But Gaelian didn't know how anyone could monitor brainwaves without some sort of attachment to the head. Not that she'd ever seen it live, but she'd at least seen enough on the viddie to have some idea. After all, half the time all there ever were were doctor shows.

But if there were no monitors, why was the place so empty? What if one of the patients had a sudden seizure or something? It was definitely odd. But staying in a broom closet wasn't going to give her further information.

And then the very incongruity of a broom closet struck her. What did anyone want with one? After all, mechanicals could take care of basic cleaning chores. Oh, sure, some homes and places of business had human servants. Her grandmother had had Missili. But they were more for show, and for programming the housecleaner, and for making decisions that one would not really want to trust to a machine, like would everyone really prefer cold meat salad with hot spice, or did the mood run more toward an elegant creamed soup followed by a light assortment of cured fish. Missili wouldn't know how to use a broom or scrub brush. Gaelian could barely recognize the pieces only because she had seen them in a museum when her class in normal school was studying social history.

If there weren't even such minor aids as housecleaners, then there probably weren't sophisticated monitors. Which meant that there were bound to be people around. Maybe not in the corridor when she had been out, but soon at least.

Slowly, she pushed the door open and listened. There was no sound at all in the hall, and she decided to take her chances. She walked boldly, as if with a direction and purpose, to another marked door. She couldn't read the marking, but it was definitely longer than the first one and had more loops and swirls. She walked in as if she belonged there, not knowing quite where "there" was.

"Oh, yes, Gaelian, I've been expecting you," someone said.

She froze, searching for the speaker. The place was not well lit, but she could make out heavy pieces of furniture, the strange backless chairs she couldn't use, and piles of books. Not printouts, but old, old books, heavy and each at least as long as her forearm. Finally she spotted the speaker, an old man hunched over one of the massive tomes in the dim illumination.

"I am afraid we haven't been introduced," she said stiffly.

The man chuckled and rose. He led her to what seemed to be a seating arrangement, and she watched as he folded himself into one of the odd structures, half-kneeling against the lower part of the contraption. Gingerly, she tried it. It wasn't too bad.

"Forgive me," the old man said. "I am Nomis, not that it means anything to you. It's not that I'm exactly in charge of this facility, but if those idiot children could get it through their heads that they can function perfectly well without running to me for everything . . . Well, I'm sorry. I shouldn't ramble on about it. Not your concern at all. You should have something to eat. They've been giving you sick people food, that's my guess. Worse than honest starvation. Not that the regular food here is any good anyway, never been in any kind of facility where there's good food. But I manage to keep a private stock. I warn you though, you go telling those children that run this place about my little, shall we call it hospitality, well, then, no more. And you'll really have some cause to complain."

Gaelian watched him with amazement as he practically sprang up and opened a drawer in one of the three huge, cluttered desks. He pulled out some bread, cheese, and meat, then condiments, which he spread thickly over the whole, and handed half to her. The other he kept for himself and began to munch on.

"Now, ask away," he said genially.

"Where am I?" was the first thing that came to her. "And why haven't you handed me back to the authorities?"

"Oh, now, we can't do that. It would cause too many complications. Not at all," he said. "You see, we do know about you, Gaelian. I hope you don't mind me using that name. You see, we know you are a half-breed, which makes you more than doubly interesting. And it means that technically I shouldn't use YnTourne anyway. Although if it would make you more comfortable, I will. Anyway, here happens to be Adedri. The city of Adedri, that is, in the Temple complex. And, as to why we couldn't hand you over to the Navy, well, we had rather thought that you might enjoy a bit of a stay with us. We'd rather like to get to know you better, and vice versa, of course."

"Is this some kind of hospital?" Gaelian asked. She didn't really care about his answer. Obviously, this was not Nomis, not the real Nomis at least. This had to be some sort of madman being given humane treatment, incarcerated here for life.

"Oh, no, not at all. That is to say, we do do some medical work in emergencies and all that. Must be prepared, you know, and in our line of work, it does come to be necessary every so often. But that's not the major concern. Of course, what the major concern is, well, only those in the Temple here know. And we do run a rather strict security system, so there are only a few who have the whole picture. We'd be rather interested in you becoming one of those. That is, if it interests you."

"Am I a prisoner, then?" she demanded. "Can I go out if I want to? Call over to the Base?"

Nomis shook his head. "We'd of course prefer you to be our guest. Although, after a manner of speaking and according to the legal technicalities, yes, I suppose you might be considered kidnapped. Or something of that sort. But let's not let that mar what has started as a perfectly good friendship. Or rather, let's just say it was by way of invitation."

Gaelian shook her head as if to shake something loose. "And just how," she asked slowly, "do you plan to keep me confined?"

"Ah, and here we come to a delicate point," Nomis said. "We do not exactly plan to keep you confined, at least not in the traditional sense. But let me show you two things that I think might convince you to stay awhile."

He unfolded himself from the backless chair gracefully and waited while Gaelian untangled her feet from the struts and supports. Then he led her across the cluttered study and through a door that was semihidden in the shadows.

Obviously, she was in the heart of the installation, and installation was exactly the word for it. She could think of no other that would describe the almost military precision of the rows of cubicles, terminals, great wall screens, and red-robed people moving with a precision and concentration she had rarely seen among civilians.

"Nomis, we need you immediately for a consultation, if you have a few moments. There's been a development that we didn't expect, and with more than one wild ball around we've been worried about the situation."

The speaker was the girl who had sat with Gaelian. She didn't look so young under the bright lights, and Gaelian was surprised that the woman paid no attention to her presence here.

"Oh, yes," Nomis answered absently. "By the way, Gaelian, this is Ridra, who looked after you for awhile. She isn't entirely your nursemaid, of course, but you might find her helpful. Now, feel free to look around and ask questions while I talk to this team. Youngsters. Impatient."

He huffed out after Ridra, who seemed more than simply impatient.

Gaelian sat down at one of the unoccupied terminals, half enclosed by shoulder-high walls, and fiddled with the controls. The layout was completely unfamiliar, and she became frustrated as she realized that none of her skills was going to help her access the data she wanted. Nomis was obviously really Nomis and not some asylum inmate who thought he was the High Priest of Adedri. So this place was somehow connected to the Temple, which was connected to those festivals. And there were the people who disappeared during the festivals. Gaelian looked around her, searching for a Dinorean face or gesture, but the cubicle cut off her view of most of the workers. A blur of red passed by, and Gaelian found a pile of green fax in her lap. She looked up to see who had given her whatever it was, but the figure was already gone.

She picked up the pages and began to skim. It was Dinorean newsfax, useful but also not terribly revealing. She read through the first set of pages without interest, things about crime and some new legislation about immigration. Then, buried deep in the pile, she found a report of a raid on a Dinorean base on Cahaute. It was only a few brief paragraphs, and Gaelian shook with frustration. There had been no casualties, so the report went, and the field reactor wasn't up to full power yet. Engineers were trying to determine how the natives had breached the field, and it seemed most likely that there had been some sort of frequency waver, a common flaw in portapower packs.

Gaelian threw the green sheets down with disgust. There was no mention of where on the planet they were, what tribe had attacked, and what had gone before. No casualties. She knew that meant a raid of intent, insult. Somewhere, in the place that her mother had left, she was satisfied and pleased. The people had shown their strength.

She sighed and bent by habit to pick the pages up off the floor when a red circle attracted her attention. She studied the page, lifted it up, and read the circled article slowly. Then she read it again. It was an obituary. Her own.

According to the Dinorean news service, Gaelian YnTourne had gone after a pirate ship single-handedly in an experimental vehicle. Her AP was found abandoned, the hatch open and the life-support systems turned off. No trace of the body had been discovered. There had been some thought of kidnapping, but when no notice came from the supposed kidnappers, she was presumed dead. Her effects were being sent back to the YnTourne household.

"Oh, good, that was something I wanted to make sure you saw," Nomis said. How he had materialized leaning over the half-wall of her cubicle, she couldn't say. She hadn't heard anything.

"Yes," he continued, "we did set it up rather neatly. Of course, we can't provide a body. That would be very bad manners and not exactly moral besides. But wouldn't it look just the slightest bit strange if you turned up now? Of course, you are almost free to do so, if you can find your way out. Which is not to be taken as a hint or a challenge, I'm afraid. We are prepared to share a very large amount of knowledge with you, but not that. At least, not just yet. On the other hand, wouldn't you like to know what we're doing? Doesn't that interest you just the tiniest bit?"

Gaelian slumped. She had forgotten how to get out of one

of these stupid chairs, and she didn't want to think about being dead. When she was very young, she had thought about what would happen if she died. Now she was going to see it.

Nomis studied her very closely. "You should get some sleep," he said finally. "It's late, and this really is your first day up. Quite a bit of excitement, too, I should say. Ridra will show you back. You'll learn your way around soon. Ridra will help."

He practically shoved the young woman at Gaelian. Ridra shrugged helplessly and glanced once at Nomis. Then she held out her hand.

"Nomis can be a lot of trouble," she sighed. "He always makes you work twice as hard, and you've got to put everything together yourself. Then, if you've got it right, he only mumbles something about how long it took. But, believe me, you won't get everything you need tonight. The morning will be soon enough, and I've got to get some sleep too. Besides, tomorrow I'll show you how to put a copali on properly, so you aren't tripping over everything."

Gaelian managed to get out of the chair again, this time remembering to pull the extra fabric of the garment she wore away from the kneepad, and followed Ridra. They didn't go back through the study, but out another door and down a short corridor. The door they emerged from was next to her own room.

Ridra left down the hidden hallway, and Gaelian didn't try to follow her. It would not be particularly useful at this point. She had about as much information as she could use.

The lights were at about half illumination, from what she could measure. She shrugged the copali off and climbed under the covers. There was something small and dark on the white expanse. At first she ignored it, took it for a shadow. But as she pulled up the covers, it moved like no shadow ought to.

She reached out very slowly and then snatched it. It was soft and made of leather. Her medicine bag, that had once had quill work on it that had all rubbed off now. Inside, she could feel through the worn leather, was the nistora necklace. Four tiers high made with every single claw and tooth and most of the smaller bones, nothing left out, nothing stinted. Cahaute.

She took it out and looked at it. In the half-light, the polished claws glistened softly, like fine-combed fabric. It fit nicely on her neck, the collar of dangling foreclaws hanging

across her shoulders in a decorative style. It felt good and
warm and alive.

She took it off and replaced it in the bag. Then it hit her.
How had they gotten it? The fax article had said that her effects were being sent to the household.

Suddenly, a kind of excited curiosity replaced her anger and
frustration. Nomis was right. He had caught her quite surely,
but she wasn't angry. There was just enough here—and now
the necklace—to make her wonder. The pirate ship had been
too fast, the necklace too sudden, for it to have been anything
other than very carefully planned.

Dobrin YnTourne, Head of the household, poured the
brandy slowly. The other two were silent, Kaes YnArretl and
the head of the YnOestal. Both of them wore green scarves
draped formally, showing respect for the mourning of the
household. Only Dobrin wore no green to mark Gaelian's
death.

"You see," he said softly as he brought glasses to his two
guests, "she isn't dead. At least, I don't think so. It isn't delu-
sion, it's simply based on the facts and having played nerris
with her."

YnOestal merely nodded. It made Dobrin uneasy, as if they
thought that grief had warped his judgment. Not that many
people would give him credit for any grief over his cousin's
demise, although he knew that they were closer in the end than
he had ever believed possible. That he felt no grief now was a
clear sign to him that she was still alive. Besides, knowing
Gaelian, he wouldn't believe her dead unless he saw the body
himself. But that didn't convince these representatives of the
Board.

"Then why publish the obituary?" Kaes demanded. "And
why the memorial service and the legal proceedings to declare
her dead?"

It was Esrin YnOestal, master of the yellow, who answered
before Dobrin could even open his mouth. "I should think the
move obvious," she said. "After all, should she appear alive
and sane, it would take less than five minutes to restore her
position and possessions. And such an action, properly reported in the newsfax, might bring her out of hiding more
quickly. But I am quite sure that is rather a simplistic mask for
the reality."

"What reality?" YnArretl growled, standing and staring directly at Dobrin. "I want to know exactly what is going on. We are, after all, representing the Board in this."

YnOestal chuckled.

"It cannot be proved that Gaelian is alive," Dobrin said steadily. "Gaelian is going to be the root of the campaign. Something is going on on Adedri. We've been calling it piracy for a long time, but none of us are children. It isn't simply piracy, certainly not with the ability to corner one of the experimental APs like that. I've suspected that the Adedri are up to something more than they've ever let on since I served on Adedri Base."

"Dung-eaters, Adedri," YnArretl muttered. "Couldn't touch us if they wanted to."

"You never served on Adedri," YnOestal reminded him gently. "You have never seen their festivals or observed how they treat their Temple and their priests. Actually, from old records of the Board, there was a good bit of speculation that they'd be rather well assimilated by now."

"Well, aren't they?" YnArretl protested. "They wear proper clothes, speak Dinorean, act like civilized people. They seem pretty well assimilated to me."

Dobrin took a sip of the brandy. It burned his tongue pleasantly, grounding his thoughts. Privately, he thought Kaes Yn-Arretl a fool.

Dobrin hesitated, wondering if he should spell out exactly what he and YnOestal had planned or if he should simply keep Kaes in the dark. He was not such a moron that he didn't understand the power represented in this room. The YnOestal, the YnTourne, and the YnSetti controlled the entirety of off-planet trade in the Protectorate. The massive YnArretl holdings in refineries and fabrication could be closed down in a matter of two or three years by these major families, a fact that Kaes knew perfectly well.

"Very simply this, then," Dobrin began, knowing the risk. "There is a good deal about Adedri that we don't know, and this piracy of theirs is only the smallest part of it. In fact, none of their pirate craft has ever been captured, and as president of the Craft Company, I know something about design. I have reason to believe they either have their own or have adapted our technology in such a way that we would not recognize it. In other words, they are hiding an entire underground culture

that is a direct threat to us. We are not dealing with a few
malcontents and a couple of free-market entrepreneurs. We're
dealing with a highly organized conspiracy, completely analo-
gous to the top level of Adedri authority. And that authority
lies in the Temple.''

YnOestal rose and went over to the table. As she opened the
decanter to pour herself another glass, she smiled secretively at
Dobrin.

"Yes," she agreed. "And Gaelian's death gives us just the
opening we need to get the support we need to commit resources to going in and uncovering whatever is going on on
Adedri.''

They sipped in tense silence. Dobrin closed his eyes for a
moment as his mind raced. He had no idea why he was sure
Gaelian was not dead, but he was equally sure she would be
delighted with the use put to her supposed demise. Besides,
there was something that even YnOestal didn't know. He *had*
to throw it on the Adedri. Tanistin was a prototype that had
cost billions in development. The final order and contracts for
six more vessels were contingent on her performance on this
cruise. Without that contract, the Craft Company was in serious trouble.

It was no question of preferences anymore, he thought. It
was survival. The YnTourne's, and the Protectorate's. Dinoreos would survive. It was nerris that had taught them, and
they had been found worthy.

Gaelian waited until she was decently dressed and had
breakfasted before she started interrogating Ridra. The other
had come early and showed her how to drape, twist, and tuck
the copali into a proper garment and had brought her outside
to the courtyard for food.

The small garden itself was a curiosity to Gaelian. It had
neither the carefully planned and pruned formality of a
Dinorean household's garden nor the wildness of the forests
of Cahaute. Around the walls grew a hedge that bloomed with
palm-sized flowers, the scent naggingly familiar. As Gaelian
approached, she was struck by it.

"What are the festivals?" she asked Ridra cautiously.
"What is the Festival of Anoni, really?"

"Did you like it?" Ridra countered, laughing.

Gaelian shot her a look of disgust, but Ridra merely shrugged.

"What is nerris?" Ridra asked.

"It's a game, but it's more than a game," Gaelian said quietly, wondering just what words could make this Adedri woman understand. "Maybe you could call it a miniature. Of everything. Of how everything works. Like a model. To practice with."

The Adedri lowered her eyes momentarily. "The festivals each have their own purpose. The people of Adedri are really not much different from the majority of your Dinoreans. How many of them know about nerris? I mean really know, use it, work with it the way you say it should be worked with? I would guess not many. The festivals are on the same order, but they aren't models, and they're not for practice. It's a way of teaching people. Only, not everyone can be taught. Like some people can't play music or paint no matter how many lessons they have. They just can't. And even more people can't think."

Gaelian looked at her suddenly. She felt as if she were being attacked and didn't quite know why. People who can't think. That was a contradiction in terms. Oh, sure, some were slower than others, and some had particular abilities, but not to be able to think at all? Even animals could think.

"What in four hells are you, anyway? I thought you were a bunch of priests or something," Gaelian exploded.

"We are priests," Ridra said softly. "But you don't quite understand our religion. There aren't any gods. There never were. This Temple is actually more of a university. Who is Anoni, anyway? And what about your Cahaute gods, like Breath and Rock and the others? Yenhica? Who was she?"

"They're names for basic types of forces," Gaelian said. "Useful labels for something people know and can use. It doesn't matter what you call a thing, as long as you can use it."

"And Anoni? Do you want to really know who and what Anoni was?" Ridra's voice was cutting, her face a sneering mask. "Or are you afraid to know?"

Gaelian smiled. It wasn't a pretty smile, but the answer to a challenge.

Ridra took her back into the building. This time they didn't bother with the installation but went directly to the study where Gaelian had met Nomis. Ridra pointed to one of the slanted backless chairs, and Gaelian settled herself in front of the desk. The Adedri priestess pulled several large books out and laid them in front of Gaelian.

"I won't tell you," Ridra said softly. "You'll have to read it all for yourself. You still might not believe it or understand it, but take a look. And don't bother trying to tell anyone outside of the Temple. No one will ever believe you. If you ever leave the Temple. But we aren't worried about that. At least not yet."

Ridra left, and Gaelian stared at the volumes in front of her. Her legs ached from the strange position, and she longed to lean back and rest her shoulders, but it seemed as if none of the Adedri had ever thought of that. If she never left the Temple, she thought suddenly, she might never sit down comfortably again in her whole life. It amazed her to think that that idea scared her far more than the loss of her liberty, or her household, or anything else. Even condemned criminals were permitted to sit in furniture with backs, where they didn't have to strain their knees against a slanted seat for balance.

She picked the top book off the stack, untangled herself once again, and lay down on the floor. She found a title printed on the third page, *Proceedings of the Eight Hundred Seventy-second Convention on Genetic Manipulation and Bioengineering*. It looked hideously dull. But as she skimmed the table of contents, a name caught her eye.

She sprang up and leafed through the other books in the stack Ridra had left. Yes, names and other things.

Then a sense of wonder overcame her. How could she even read this? She couldn't make out Adedri script at all, but this was in the writing form of Dinoreos. But the language wasn't Dinorean. It was the names she understood, and their placement on the page. And if she sounded out the words, said them aloud, although they were not written at all that way . . .

She had an impulse to run into the installation, find Ridra, and demand a translation at that moment. Demand another explanation. But Ridra wasn't completely forthcoming.

She went back to the title page. Yes, the title was not written in Dinorean, but the words were familiar enough that she could read it easily.

Returning to the stack of books on the desk, she found the

one she needed and smiled. Ridra had provided. There was a dictionary. But the name of this new language was not Dinorean, nor Adedri, nor Cahaute. As a matter of fact, it was the name of no place Gaelian had ever heard of.

That was not so important as the other part. In the *Proceedings* book, which she now saw had been bound after it had been issued, she returned to the table of contents. There was no mistaking that name in the place where the authors of articles usually were, at least in the publications she was familiar with. *Vitembri Anoni, Poltenacra.*

She looked up "poltenacra" in the dictionary. The definition ran, "*1.* member of the political/intellectual ruling body, usually retired from research/arts *2.* division heads of government departments *3.* heads of university departments at the four 'ruling' universities."

She closed the books and rolled over on her back, breathing deeply. The entire universe swam around her. Everything that was neat and sensible, that fit into the order of things and worked, all these were gone. Shattered. She wanted very much for it not to be true. She wanted to cry, only on Cahaute children learned not to cry before they learned to walk.

On Cahaute only one gift was *recognized*. Only one gift had any value. Only the flute, the gift of the True and the Real, was needed by the people. All other things were simply things.

Bracing herself with a deep breath, Gaelian turned over and opened to the article written by Anoni the Trickster, member of the ruling Board somewhere she could not identify.

12

IT WAS THE season of the black nistora and of the branched runners. It was the season of the great hunt before the white time, when the people of all the tribes would gather meat and dry it in the sun. Or they would pound it and seal it in nistora fat for the hungry times.

It was a time of work. New hides were needed now, too, to cover the thin places of the lodges. It was a time to prepare for the cold season that came; the smell of the cold was already in the air, the sky already becoming clear and brilliant at night.

The season of raiding was over. The time of laughing and playing with all the people, of marriages and the births of children and runners for the herd, the time of sitting up at night and listening to the grandfathers' stories, these times were ending. Now the people must make provisions for the white season, so the tribes could come together laughing when the first green began to show. Laughing, not weeping or mourning or starving.

Nyapetin sat at the fire with Hinacen. In front of them lay six lances, symbols of authority from the hunting associations. Now it was not the warriors but the hunters who led the tribe.

He was content. Since he had found his true power in the raid, he had been Hinacen's associate, no longer simply a student. Although Hinacen still taught him—he was now learning from him how to put power into the hunt. There was a difference, though, not only with Hinacen but with all the people.

Some even called him b'hasute, although he took no notice of it. But none of them were takka to him, as many were to each other.

Still, he was takka to Hinacen, and that was enough. To find more than two who were takka in a single life, that was a very great thing.

Hinacen looked at him and coughed. Nyapetin blinked and returned to the lances. Hinacen was right. He shouldn't let his mind wander. This was his place in preserving the people through the hard season.

When he had finished, Hinacen called in the six leaders of the various associations and gave each of them symbols of the hunter's power. To one he gave the thigh bone of a runner, and to another he gave the jaw of a nistora. To the others he gave the skull of a hopper and a winged one, the claws of the small, fierce eats-nistora and, finally, the bundle of lances. Nyapetin watched each react to the part of the hunt his association had. The one with the nistora jaw, who would lead the hunt, tried very hard not to smile, and the one who had received the claws, and thus would be responsible for keeping order among all the hunters, seemed to puff with pride. The one who had received the lances, though, and gave them to the others, this one looked worried and sad. Nyapetin made note of this, for he had been given a high honor and great responsibility. It was this association that would make sure all the people ate. Of every two beasts they killed, one was for their use alone and the other to be distributed among those who had no one to hunt for them.

The association leaders left to prepare for their tasks. Nyapetin remained in the lodge with Hinacen.

"Will you go?" Hinacen asked.

Nyapetin shrugged. He hadn't thought about it. Most of his time had been spent in the b'hasute's lodge, not on chatoya, the great branched runners that carried people swiftly on the hunt.

Hinacen looked at him very carefully. "You should go. You are not a healer like Tyakral, never to make death. Now you can be just yourself with all the tribe."

Nyapetin's heart leapt at this. Of course, Hinacen himself had gone raiding and hunting before he was too old. Nyapetin knew this. Usually young hasute were not expected to spend so much time with a teacher.

"Besides, you will need robes to make a lodge," Hinacen said.

Nyapetin nodded and left to return to his mother's lodge. There were things he had to do if he were to join the hunt, things he had not done for many seasons. He would have to chip stone for the arrow tips and straighten the shafts and put feathers in them so they flew straight. And he needed to make a new string for his bow. Or perhaps his father had an extra that he could use.

The thought of these tasks made him happy. It had been a very long time since he had straightened arrow shafts over the fire. Of course, those with many robes could trade with Amese for straight arrow shafts, but Nyapetin didn't have one robe of his own. And he wouldn't trade any he would gain on this hunt. He would need many robes to cover a lodge fine enough for a woman to consider it her home.

It was pleasant to be home with his family, sharing the things they did. He sat at the fire and chipped flint, one of the things he did well, as his younger brother straightened shafts. His father had lent him a chatoya for the hunt.

"You are b'hasute," his father had said. "You should not run behind children because you have no chatoya of your own." And the runner his father had chosen was Bright Water, a three branch that had won many races.

On the morning of the hunt, he awoke to a scratching at the lodge flap. It was one of the group who had the ordering of the hunt, rousing everyone early so that they would be ready to ride at a good hour. Nyapetin bundled up his arrows and his bow with the new string, two pairs of shoes and a water skin. He found Bright Water in the herd and mounted, pleased to feel the speed of the animal and her high spirits on this day. He was happy as he had not been happy in a very long time, thinking of the meat and the robes he would bring home. Many robes that his mother would tan and stretch and he would paint with pictures of the white time and runners and nistora. And then he would offer them to a person in the tribe, a sitting food woman who could always find things to eat even in the cold season.

The sun was bright, and the sky was brilliant. The light made the trees stand out clearly, the rocks throwing sharp shadows against the ground. The hunters rode in an orderly line, those charged with the hunt supervising gently but with authority. They passed through the tree-places easily and then emerged onto the great land behind the high cliffs. Here was the good pasture where the nistora gathered at the end of summer, spotted by the scouts who had run ahead days ago in their tall sees-from-high feathers.

And then Nyapetin felt the power move in him, turning over and protesting.

There was nothing he could see that was wrong. The nistora land was clear and bright, the high grass that they loved waving softly in the breeze. He could not see the tall feathers of the scouts but knew that they must be somewhere in the high cliffs or hidden in the grass. But as much as he looked, he knew that something was wrong, something was missing.

Perhaps it was that the earth itself was not heavy, not shaking so very slightly as it did when the great herds moved. Perhaps it was that quietness beneath him, or the shrill cries of the black-wingeds that dotted the sky.

The hunting moiety, their faces painted red and black so that they would be easily identified, moved back through the line, halting people. There was a kind of stillness. Mautahin, who led the hunt, sat on his chatoya like a stone, his hand raised to show they went no further. Even from this distance, Nyapetin could see the expression on Mautahin's face, the flaring nostrils as he tried to catch a message from the wind, the stillness of the runner as he tried to feel down into the earth, feel the movement of the herds.

A figure came over the hill running. At first Nyapetin saw only movement, but as it came closer he recognized the scout's tall brown feather. Mautahin kicked his four branch, and it showed a racer's speed as it galloped forward to meet the scout.

All those who had come watched in silence. They looked at each other, flickering eyes over those nearest, and then returned their gaze to the two meeting on the grass. One mounted, one standing, one painted red and black, the other painted brown and yellow. Above, the black ones wheeled and screeched, dove and pitched, and plummeted to the earth behind the rise.

Mautahin raised his hand sharply. The red and black moiety quickly reformed the lines of the march, of the hunt itself. They did not speak but gestured with their clubs of authority that the line ride forward, that they follow Mautahin.

They rode slowly. Nyapetin could feel Bright Water resisting, not wanting to put one foot before the other. She shied and nickered, but he held her firmly. She walked only with great reluctance. He saw that others, even his father and brothers who were far better riders than he, were having the same problem.

It was late, judging from the sun, and his stomach protested. He had beaten meat covered with fat in his bag, but the thought of it made him sick. Even the idea of water was not good. No one else ate or drank either, although it was long past the time they usually did. He wondered if the others had the same dread, the same stomach sickness that told him something terrible was ahead. Not terrible for himself alone, but for all the people.

The whole group gathered together and rode over the rise as one, a line stretched out across the ridge like a surprise raiding party.

It was the line of hills that had kept the smell from them on the downwind approach, but now it came up and hit them full in the face. A cry went up, a howl, rage and agony all in one.

Scattered across the grass lay the nistora. Tens of tens of nistora, large and shaggy, their coats heavy and black, loomed like rocks. The nistora did not move. The black-wingeds swooped low and pecked at them.

Nyapetin accompanied several hunters down onto the field. The kill was fresh, and there was a light smell of cooking meat —as if there had been fire, but there were no signs of fire. As they came closer, Nyapetin could see that other ground dwellers were feasting along with the wingeds. They could not carry this back to the people, not like the grubs and the carrion eaters.

There was no doubt that this was the work of men, but it was a work that made him wonder, that tightened his stomach and brought bile to his mouth. What men killed so much more than they needed, what men butchered animals and then left their meat and their hides for ground dwellers and wingeds?

And he knew who had done this. He knew who used Flame and not the lance or arrow. There were no arrows on the ground, in the hides. There was nothing but the smell that engulfed them.

"This is war," Mautahin said.

They agreed, with voices piercing the sky. Revenge was only

a part, revenge for those who would starve in the coming cold season. There would be no more raids, no more insults to the strangers. They had broken the balance of the land, and that alone was enough. But it was Mountain and Rock who were injured, their creatures who had been slaughtered, and their power would lend strength to the revenge.

Nyapetin looked at the dead herd, and his being grew cold. He knew that he was Roneedee, b'hasute of the tribe, and he wore the robe of Mountain's power. It was his place to right the balance again. For now there was no longer cahaute.

"Now, I don't suppose you were able to get more than the basic idea," Nomis said, "although I suppose at this stage it's really quite enough. On the other hand, you are rather something of an important and exciting specimen."

Gaelian glared at the old man and then judged the distance to the large book and how hard she could heave it. She could probably break his skull at this distance.

"Oh, no, please," he said, waving a hand. "I don't mean to say that we think of you as you might view something caged in a lab, so to speak. No, not at all. We have every respect for your humanity. The thing is, you might well have rather more of it than any of the rest of us, a blending of several different strains and traits that Anoni was working with. I don't suppose you read that far, though. It's difficult in a different language."

"I did not read that far," she said coldly. "And now that I know what you're doing, you would be well advised to release me at once. I have absolutely no interest in being 'not a lab animal' as I think you put it."

Then, years of training overrode the anger. Use the ball, play yellow, subtle, feint with one player while the other scores. Sacrifice one, win. Always define the goal and work from there.

"Gaelian," he was saying softly, comfortingly, "we don't want to do anything of the kind. We only want to run a few tests, very minor, ask you some questions, that's all. And in return, we'll teach you about the experiment, and you'll be treated like royalty here."

Gaelian raised an eyebrow. "I'll be free after you're finished?" she asked.

Nomis nodded vigorously.

She paced the length of the room, stopping to study titles along the shelves, trying to gain time. "How long do you think these . . . sessions . . . will last?" she asked nonchalantly.

"Perhaps only a year, maybe a little more," Nomis answered brightly.

She kept turned away, knowing that she had to hide her face. Maybe he could read her feelings from her carriage, but then the Academy had ingrained bearing. No. She had to make her opportunities and get something besides. She would need a certain amount of freedom on the grounds. Among other things.

"While I am here," she said, not turning to look at him, "I want to have complete freedom in the Temple area. I am not used to being in a cage. And I want to know more, not only about the experiment, but about your technology. It looks different from ours, and the Dinoreans know very little about your capabilities. I would like to. I will promise that the information won't reach unfriendly hands. Also, you know I'm a pilot. I want free access to at least a simulator of your design. I don't want to slow down while I'm here."

She turned and watched him try to decide. His face jumped like a mask, his tongue flickered over his white moustache, his brow knit. "That's hardly fair," he said finally.

"Kidnapping me was hardly fair, was it?" Gaelian said in the soft voice of rage. "Having me declared legally dead was hardly fair. You went and took my life from me, and then you say it isn't fair that I want something besides room and board in return?"

Looking at him, Gaelian knew that she could kill him. She didn't need the books she had wanted to heave or any of the other tools that were so conveniently strewn around the cluttered study. The outrage of him, them, breaking cahaute, the circle, was sufficient. Even here, in this place among strangers far from the open sky and warm dirt, even here she could feel the outrage in the Power Clan around her. It coursed through her, and she could see it, moving and interwoven through itself, the structures glistening like strings waiting to be plucked. She could touch it now, and the whole flow of energy would alter to suit her design.

Nomis saw it in her. She knew that as he looked, knew that she could see and use lines and currents of power that he couldn't even sense. Like flying, it was something she was made for, to see and arrange the flow, direct it. And she could direct it at him and his Temple, and the whole thing would crumble. She could see his fear written clearly.

"Perhaps we can work something out," he said at last.

Gaelian smiled without humor. She did not look back at him as she left the room and went out, not into the corridor leading back to her own room, but to the installation. Something was growing in her, and she needed to find Ridra. There were certain things she needed to know if the half-swirling mist in her head were to solidify and show her a course of action. It was the way of nerris. It was cahaute.

As she wound through the corridors searching for the courtyard and Ridra, she went over the things she had demanded. Use of their simulators was important; if she could find some sort of craft to steal she would be able to operate it. Surely they knew, Nomis knew, she would try. It was just a matter of which one of them would win.

Ridra was seated in the center of the courtyard, stacks of paper spread out around her. In one hand she held a marker, in the other a three-quarters eaten piece of fruit. She was engaged in some fascinating conversation with two others also dressed in red robes, also eating and making marks as fast as they could. Gaelian approached and looked over her shoulder for a moment. When Ridra turned and saw her, the Adedri's face fell. Gaelian sighed.

One of the men she had been talking with said something in Adedri and began gathering up the papers. Ridra shrugged and turned back to Gaelian.

"I have work to do," Ridra said carefully. "I'm involved in a project right now . . . not that that would matter to you."

"So why were you assigned to me?" Gaelian asked.

Ridra made a face as if the fruit had suddenly gone bitter. "Why does Nomis ever make decisions? You think any of us know? I guess part of it has to do with my work in linguistics and part because he thought we would be compatible. At least, that's the best anyone's come up with so far."

"Linguistics?" Gaelian asked vaguely. Any educated Adedri would speak excellent Dinorean. It wasn't simply a matter of communication.

"Oh, that should be obvious. Or would be if you were used to working for Nomis," Ridra replied. "I'm interested in Cahaute. Well, everyone here is, naturally, the same as anyplace else, but I have done some work with the language, and I guess Nomis thought that you would be able to help. Give me some more words, meanings, nuances, that sort of thing. It would have been fine, only now he's also dumped another whole load of analysis on my team and wants answers in fifteen days. So I've got you, and I've got this work to do, and I only bet that by the time I've got any time to get into language, he'll suddenly switch keepers on you and then bawl me out for not taking advantage of my opportunities."

"Does he do this sort of thing often?" Gaelian asked.

"All the time," Ridra moaned. "It seems to be one of the rites of passage. No one ever had it easy writing their first real contrib. Everyone gets dumped on. You know, I used to think that all I wanted was to get into the Temple. And once I got in and found out about the competition, all I wanted was to be accepted as an advanced student in one of the Faculties. Now I wonder why I do it, and when it's my turn, I'll probably be as horrible to anyone in my underteam."

Gaelian sat for several moments searching Ridra's face. Then words came out of her. "Give me the equipment, and I'll record everything you'll need for your studies. And I can probably help with whatever else it is you're doing—at least some of the statistics, if nothing else. Just get me a computer manual in a language I can read and give me the translations formats."

Once she got into their computer, she could find out what she needed to know. There would have to be some sort of map of the Temple in there, along with schedules and such. And Ridra would be able to give her the access codes. It didn't look like there was much security around here, and Gaelian suspected that, with some understanding of their system, things would be relatively easy to find.

For the first time, Ridra smiled. "Yes, of course, that would be perfect. Although I can't see why you would want to."

"I'm going to be bored to tears if I don't have anything to do," Gaelian pointed out. "Why don't you get the stuff and meet me back here or in my room or something?"

"In your room," Ridra replied and rose to leave.

Gaelian waited for a moment and then followed. Her head was racing. Already she had obtained enough clues to know that, once she made a break, there would be little trouble. They weren't used to the idea of holding anyone and so weren't doing very much about it. Getting out should not be the primary difficulty. The thing was, she reasoned, she should stay just long enough to realize exactly what was going on here and to find the location of the pirate bases if she could. With that, she could return to Dinoreos, to the Board, and present it to them. That would be a session. Her career would be assured.

Or would it? The Board might not be content with having her come back to life. Things were moving on Cahaute, balances coming undone and shifts in the clans. Shifts in Dinoreos, too.

Then she thought about her own capture. The Adedri also seemed to know too much. How had they managed to pull her so far, how had they managed to get her necklace? They must have far more information than anyone ever gave them credit for. And that was the key. Yes, she would find out exactly what was going on on both Cahaute and Dinoreos and then decide just how to come back. And where. And carrying what.

Tanistin seemed to be made only of silence and shadows, Golran thought. No one was in the wardroom watching the viddie or snacking on leftovers from last night's dessert, no one in the gym for the required daily hour of exercise. He had checked both places. Even on the long central corridor between the living quarters and the AP hangar, he had passed only two crew members.

He would have preferred to be on duty now. He hated these off times when the entire ship was aggressively silent and menacing. At least when there was work, he could focus his mind away from Gaelian's death and the problems with the AP.

Something was very wrong, he knew. He knew those specs better than he knew his own name, and there was nothing that could outrun those tiny fighters. Nothing. And he knew them all.

He hesitated a moment before entering the assignments room just off the hangar. He didn't know if he wanted to talk to whomever was on duty there, didn't want anyone to watch him watching the bevy of engineers who were, it seemed, intent on taking apart Gaelian's AP molecule by molecule. And then he couldn't wait any longer and moved so the door would check his security and pass him in.

The first thing he saw was the giant assignments board, taking up nearly a full wall of the room. Whoever had this shift had turned off the color code on the plasma display so it showed only dull orange. It took him a minute to adjust, to find his own name and assignment for the next shift. Then he understood why it had been reset. Gaelian's name was missing. It was harder to notice without colors. The board looked strange with that brilliant red gone.

"You know a six-letter word for an Adedri flower?" Sessov muttered.

Golran shook his head.

"Hells," Sessov grumbled by habit. "What do you want?"

Golran said nothing for a moment. Then he gestured over to the window that looked out into the hangar. "They got it broken down yet?" he asked.

"Didn't find anything," Sessov replied. "No failures. Nothing at all. Only the recorder, and that was erased. Not broken, not shut off, erased. Deliberately."

And then, slowly, Sessov met Golran's eyes. Golran understood. It was most clear with the lower nobility, those who were the closest to him. Gaelian's death was an Ot-tan matter. Sessov's eyes slid to the green band around his belt. Golran held himself from flinching. They were all wearing it, all the junior pilots who had known the Angel. But to Sessov, it was now impudence from a commoner. Carefully, Golran backed out of the assignment room. Sessov's eyes followed him until the door slid shut.

He went back to his cabin, the cabin he had alone—not because he rated the privacy, but because no one wanted to room with a commoner and there was enough space on the ship. He thought about going by the galley and getting something to eat, but Sessov's look haunted him. He didn't want to run into any of the other officers who might look at him in the same way, nor did he want to see any of the enlisted personnel who ignored him. He understood that, too, had encountered it everywhere he had served for any length of time. They didn't like to give respect to someone who was no better than they.

So, still a little hungry, Golran entered his private cabin and flopped on the bed without removing his shoes. They would return to Adedri Base the next day, and he was just as glad. He could get lost there, away from this failure that was Tanistin.

No, Tanistin wasn't a failure. It did exactly what it was supposed to do. Only, no one had ever encountered anything like what Gaelian had chased. There had never been pirates who could run that fast. Unless . . . maybe the Adedri always could and had held back, knowing the capabilities of Dinorean ships. Maybe the Adedri were hiding more than what was in that Temple with those sick festivals of theirs.

He tried to sleep as he had tried every night for the five days since Gaelian's disappearance. The others didn't want him around. Playing with the puzzles made him think of Sessov, and Sessov was the last person he wanted to think about. So was Gaelian.

He had tried to stop, had tried to tell himself it was better for him. Better not to see her, better not to have any hopes. Now, in the dark privacy that Tanistin condemned him to, he let himself see. It was not her class but his own pride that had kept him away from her. Only now did he know that Gaelian had always seen them as equals and all the barriers between them had been of his own making.

Tanistin was not the failure, he acknowledged. Golran Vontreidi was.

"I really can't expect you to be able to read it all," Ridra said, half smiling. They had taken their trays into the smaller courtyard where there would be different flowers during this time of year. It had been Ridra's suggestion after a long session on the different parts of the hunt on Cahaute.

Gaelian listened, hoping that the other woman would go on. She tried to tear the spongy bread the way the Adedri did, entirely with one hand, and found herself with a mess. Unobtrusively, she brought her other hand around and pulled off a piece, which they used as tableware to scoop up the stewed meat and vegetables. Her grandmother would be shocked.

Ridra finished a bite and swallowed. "The experiment, Anoni's experiment that is, is really quite simple. Only, it's larger than anything else undertaken, and the time frame is longer than any done before. In short, and quite simply then, there were two major factions on Salakris at the time. It seemed that there was a group that had developed particular psionic abilities, very carefully tested and charted, you understand. At this point, we believe it has to do with the E_8. With the string equations, that is. Since we know the E_8 exists and is a part of the real universe, it stands to reason that it can be manipulated. Of course, not everyone agrees with the string theory of quanta, but without it we can't explain anything at all. The other group showed a marked ability for tinkering, building, organization. But a few generations before Anoni, a scientist named Arlin Henica had done some genetic engineering to isolate these particular traits and then kept them in an isolated breeding pool.

"There were some questions about the humanity of this. The experimental populations were generally drawn from prisoners, usually selected for high intelligence. They received a life sentence in one of the experimental communities, which was considered far less severe than other punishments of the time. The experimental communities were quite normal towns with the exception of the genetic tinkering.

"Anyway, it had been going on for about a generation when Anoni stepped in. There was a good bit of debate over the second generation, since, while they were the immediate products of the experimentees, they had no reason to stay in the communities. And why should people be punished who had done no wrong, isolated from the culture in general, from opportunities for advancement, for higher education, and restricted in their choice of mates? It was considered immoral.

"On the other hand, a lot had been invested. It seemed that whatever traits had been engineered in were recessive in the extreme. If the experimental groups interbred with the general population, there was every chance they would be practically obliterated.

"It was volunteers only, mind you. Three planets had been identified as habitable and were to be set aside as isolated. Groups could choose exactly what kind of society they wanted to create, would be given support for a specified period of time until they were viable communities, and then would be left to develop in isolation.

"Of course, someone would keep track of their development."

Gaelian only stared. Her mind was a complete blank, overwhelmed. Anger coursed through her and then curiosity mixed in with it. "Why?" she finally managed to ask.

Ridra looked at the ground. She twisted a blade of grass in her fingers, playing with it, avoiding Gaelian's eyes. "Really, I've told you all I know," she said softly. "Only Nomis would know why. He's the coordinator in this generation."

"What about these other people?" Gaelian asked hesitantly. "Where are they? Do they ever break their isolation? Does Nomis report to them? What is going on here?"

"I don't know," Ridra replied helplessly. "There are some things that none of us know. Only Nomis. And that's why you're so important, you understand. You're a mix of the two strains at their height. You've got the abilities of both. And so far as we know, you're the only one."

"And what about you Adedri?" Gaelian asked bitterly. "What are you?"

Ridra shook her head. "Don't you remember anything about lab? We're the control. Only here, there are far fewer of us than either Dinoreans or Cahaute. It seems as if you engineered types are a whole lot better adapted than we are."

Gaelian mopped up a few vegetables with a chunk of the tasteless bread and then threw the whole thing down on her plate. She wasn't hungry. She lay down on the grass and closed her eyes, trying to let the new knowledge wash through her, to assimilate it and see.

Of course. Even she had argued that she couldn't exist, a crossbreed between two species. But they weren't different species at all. And there were other clues, too. The four sacred colors, the same for nerris and Cahaute.

And the legend. The tribes that had broken and the gifts they were given. She had always thought it a story, a superstition, and yet with what Ridra said it was a true reporting of the facts. The gifts were the things they had been given genetically. And who were the children of Anoni? Always she had thought, in an allegorical way, that it was the Dinoreans. But that clearly was not true. It was the Adedri, through the Temple of Anoni, who had run the experiment for how many generations now? The Adedri were the children of Anoni the Trickster, Anoni the Wicked One. Vitembri Anoni, the man who had set up three worlds, was the Trickster indeed.

Then the Power Ones weren't real. Or were they? But the abilities that went with them, that was no superstition, that was no primitive belief. That was real, as real as the craft she'd flown, as real as Cahaute and the Navy and all the rest of it. Although there was a slightly poetic point in calling whatever it was the Power Clan rather than the E_8/string theory.

Gaelian picked up her tray and dumped it down the chute near the door. Ridra did not try to follow. She walked down the hall, not noticing the red-clad people who passed her. She returned to her room, featureless as it was, and flopped on the bed in preference to the awful excuse for a chair.

Really, on reflection, she knew nothing about the Adedri. Inside the Temple it was so different from the festivals that they held. She hadn't been to one, hadn't heard whisper of one, since she had been imprisoned here. The areas she had seen—her own room, the installation center and work areas, Nomis's office, and the cafeteria—were all featureless. The walls were uniformly tan, the floors were a little darker, there was little evidence of mechanicals to keep the place clean, although she had once seen someone rubbing the floor with a wet cloth. Only what Ridra told her was of any importance, and this she didn't know how to explain.

How would the Board react? Would they level Adedri? Surely not; the Dinoreans were civilized and that was not a civilized thing to do. Or try to find this mother-planet, wherever it might be? Or would they simply decide that she had been brainwashed, deluded, manipulated?

Gaelian breathed deeply, trying to quiet herself. She knew. It was clear. If she brought this story back to Dinoreos, they would lock her away in some crazy house for the rest of her life. Medical discharge, most likely. The end. Oh, the Adedri had played the yellow, all right, played it all too well. She was their prisoner, or guest, as they chose. But try to escape and where could she go? Not back, to pick up her old life, to fly again.

That, more than anything else, infuriated her. Tears rolled down her face, and she wiped them away with the back of her hand. She had given up so much, so very much, and now it was all gone. So carefully built, so meticulously maintained, now the whole edifice of her existence no longer existed. Poof! Gone!

There was a knock at the door and then a shuffling sound. Gaelian turned to look without response. There, under the door (why didn't they use normal doors that slid on tracks?) lay a few sheets of green faxpaper. Gaelian had an urge to take them and tear them up, run out and kick whoever had delivered them. But that would do no good at all. She turned her face away to stare at the blank wall and continued to mourn her former existence.

•   •   •

•

She must have slept, she reasoned, because somehow the conversation in the garden and the rest seemed distanced. Sluggishly, she washed her face, and returning to the main room, she noticed the sheets under the door. Sleep had dulled the anger only slightly, but the anger didn't carry over to the innocent fax that lay there.

She gathered them up and brightened the light enough to be able to read. It was just the Dinorean news. Someone always made sure she got it. She skimmed without interest until a single word caught her eye. Cahaute.

The report was brief. There had been another raid on Cahaute base, this time resulting in two fatalities, several wounded. Why the tribes attacked was not clear. The one fact the article repeated several times was the ability of the tribespeople to get through the barrier. It was now fully operational, and repeated examinations revealed no malfunction. Only, there had to be a malfunction.

Gaelian smiled grimly. Primitives. Magic. She knew that magic, that feeling, the subtle understanding of currents of force. There were even times she had manipulated them, flying, feeling the Power Clan around her. There were Power Ones, of course—how stupid she had been. Perhaps they didn't have names like Breath and Fire and Mountain, but they were basic energies all the same. And it was no longer primitivism but engineered psionics, according to Ridra, that the tribes had developed, with a good bit of symbol and story on the side.

Energy. The hasute manipulated energy. She knew that when she was seven. She had done it herself. So. Some great b'hasute had managed the barrier. Good. Very good. She was pleased.

Suddenly she laughed out loud, hard and fierce the way the warriors did before a raid. The laughter shook her so hard that she fell backward onto the bed. Without thinking, her hand reached under the pillow and brought out the medicine bag. Slowly, gently, she pulled out the nistora necklace and fastened it around her throat. It fit perfectly.

She went into the washroom and unpinned her hair. It had grown some since her graduation, long enough to wear up in regulation style as opposed to cut short to regulation length. Unthinkingly, she had kept it pinned up the whole time she had been here. Now she let her hair down, parted it, and started to braid it at the sides. She remembered that, how the women always wore their hair.

The braids were uneven, lumpy, not made by practiced hands. But reflected in the mirror, she saw herself. The slightly strange features, the just-too-dark skin now fit perfectly. She was Cahaute. Of the tribes, of the people she remembered only vaguely. There was one more option, now that others had been closed, one she could only assume the Adedri hadn't considered. Or perhaps had and discarded. Staring back in the glass was someone who belonged in the winter lodges, telling stories, out following the hunt in the summer, laughing and dancing with the Fire Ones.

There would be none of the things she had once dreamed of, but at least she would be free. The Adedri, being civilized like the Dinoreans, reasoned like Dinoreans. They were blind to the unthinkable options. And those were the options that were at times the most useful.

Golran sat in front of the screen unmoving. It took all his concentration not to splinter the glass in front of him. Tomorrow was gone, a blank place in his mind. All the tomorrows.

Last night he had signed onto base. Tanistin had finished this cruise, finished without the glory they had hoped for. Gaelian was gone, dead according to the reports. He had tried not to think about her, tried and failed, as he had failed when he had left the Academy. It had done no good. But there had still been the ship, the intricacies of testing it, and the fury at the pirates who had killed Gaelian. It would have been enough. He could have easily let that be enough, to go on and fly and fight. Perhaps one day to command, although never anything of Tanistin's class. Hints of it had come through, like Vi saying he would be the first commoner to hold real rank. He'd heard enough.

And now this. Pulled from Tanistin, ordered off to the backwater. In one word, all his hopes were dashed, his career stuck on hold with the double curse of being unable to forget her and unable to take revenge on the pirates who had killed her. Cahaute. They were sending him to that minor base being built on Cahaute.

Perhaps things weren't good yesterday, but they weren't over yet. He had a few days of shore leave and had intended to use them for his own pleasure and then ship back out. This time, it would be a long assignment, long enough to keep him occupied and away from the Admiralty until he was forgotten.

Feeling ambition, the one thing that drove him. He knew it, kept it secret from the others, but they read it as if he wore it on his forehead.

Now, everything was gone. If he had been of one of the households, he might demand an explanation. If he had been a little less civilized, or less ambitious, there would have been trouble. Even now, it seemed a reasonable prospect, though he didn't think anyone would understand. His family didn't know the difference between one assignment and another, and to his colleagues, well, he was still a commoner. One with enormous ambitions, true, but a commoner nonetheless who should have been more than content to be an officer without that fierce need to advance.

Right now, suicide was very appealing, but in the back of his mind the drive burned in him. He would manage somehow and one day return. In victory, the way he had before. When so very few could compete in the Academy, he had done it, and he had gotten Tanistin to boot. He could not accept the idea that he was being locked away, taken out of the line, and left to rot in a trivial assignment. Even there, there would be some way to distinguish himself, and then he could return to Dinoreos, to the best ships, to command one day. He resolved it would be so.

In a way, it was almost funny. Cahaute. He was going to Cahaute, where Gaelian had come from, a place that had once interested him. Only now he was going as a member of the security forces to keep the new base safe from primitives who used chipped stone projectiles and bone knives. For the life of him he could not imagine why they needed additional personnel against the natives. And he couldn't understand why they couldn't get the security shield working and keep the natives out.

Raids. Tribal raids, and he was ordered there to fight against people who were almost unarmed. It made him angry.

He got up to walk to the lake. No one would be there now; no one was ever there. It was dry and dusty, the walks hazy under a thin film of grey dirt. Even the best military precision and shine couldn't keep it away for long.

He passed the gate without a second look and turned past the row of dusty trees (some strange, alien sort, he had never learned their name) and to the small lake beyond. It was almost dry, only the faintest reminder of the deep swimming place he had known earlier. It was a dry time. He kicked off his sandals and waded into the shallow water. It was warm and cloying and reminded him of blood. Even the lake was an enemy now, part of that one thing that oppressed him. One thing, all of them, the entire structure of his universe bore down on him. Even the lake betrayed him, once large and full, now reduced to a hot puddle. All of Adedri was drying up with the season, and the season dried him as well.

He left the lake and headed into the city of Adedri, to the poorest of the three business districts and the dirtiest. He found a cafe and sat in the back on a stool, one of the three or four that had in better times been intended for enlisted personnel from the base. None of them were in use. He ordered a carafe of the local wine and tipped the waiter generously. Getting drunk was fine, and the cheap, bitter wine suited his mood. A holo display droned on in the back, pictures of the countryside and people talking. He didn't try follow it.

When it became dark, he ordered one of the specialties of the region, a cheese that was too sharp with a fruit compote that was sticky and too sweet. Together they made a pleasing combination, but he barely noticed the flavor. It had been the only thing he recognized on the menu. After a second carafe of wine to erase the aftertaste, he stumbled out into the narrow streets.

In two blocks, he found what he wanted. The door of the place was old and splintered, and the sign that had once been painted in gaudy colors was now faded. He couldn't read Adedri, but what remained of the picture explained things clearly enough. When the mistress of the establishment let him in, he could see that the curtains, which had once had pretensions, were now faded and mottled. On the edge of the stairs, the carpet had been entirely worn away. But everything was clean, at least as clean as could be expected.

Sitting neatly in a way that looked as if they were half kneeling were several women, a very young girl, and two boys. One of the women looked familiar somehow, but he couldn't place her. He had drunk too much at the cafe. Her skin was a little darker, a little warmer than the others in the vaguely yellow light. He pointed to her, and she rose. He followed her up the stairs, grabbing hold of the bannister with both hands to keep from tumbling down. When they got upstairs, she led him into a room that had at one time been attractive. The light here was better, and he could see her more clearly. A name came to him thickly, and then he shook his head. Gaelian was dead. The Adedri woman regarded him with boredom and then began to remove her clothes with the disinterest of a professional.

Golran Vontreidi reported back to Adedri Base three days later after dark. He walked close to the buildings as if avoiding the light until he came to Temp Quarters. There he turned in sharply and made his way quickly to the room he had left. No one had seen him, not that what he did on leave was anyone's business.

He flicked on the screen and saw that a number of messages had piled up. He flicked it off, and the blue light vanished. He didn't want to read any of them. Instead he took a long shower, as if trying to wash the alcohol and the Adedri woman off. He was disgusted and didn't know why he had gone there. He had money, and as an officer, he would have more naturally gone into the better parts of the city, to better places.

When he had dried off, he erased all the messages that had been left, all except the official one that gave him the time and number of his transport in the morning.

13

A COPALI, GAELIAN had to admit, was a very useful garment. True, without any fastenings except three ties and two holes for hands, it was difficult to get into and out of. But it was voluminous and had big pockets that reached almost to her knees. It was impossible to tell if anyone was carrying anything. Gaelian wondered if there had been much general problem with theft.

Probably not. Most of the people of Adedri wore Dinorean garments. The copali was the outward symbol of the Temple. Ridra told her that it was taken from the formal university garb of Salakris and reached back somewhere into the far nether regions of Salakris's history.

Ridra had even approved of her taking packaged high-protein snacks "for late nights." In the past three days, at least as Adedri counted days, she had stored up quite a reasonable cache.

Now she resolved to take care of another detail. It took no small amount of courage to walk up to the door of Nomis's study.

"Oh, come in, come in," he said. "So good to see you, although you understand we've been rather busy lately. You can't get those children to do anything right. Just this morning, again, they came to me with this." He swatted a large pile of printout onto the floor. "Trash, all of it. Why, you ask? The sample areas weren't well chosen, and so there's bias written across the thing in letters you could see from here to the next millennium. Well, but that's not your problem. So. Sit down, don't stand on ceremony please."

Gaelian settled herself on the slanted stool, carefully balancing her knees on the padded rest. If they had all been part of the same culture once, she wondered where the Adedri had gotten their strange idea of furniture.

"Now," Nomis said, without waiting for Gaelian to start, "Ridra told me that she told you everything. Without any of the fine points, of course, but the general outline. Now I suppose you have questions. Like why and on and on. They all ask. All of you. Impatient."

"Well," Gaelian started, trying to keep her breathing steady. "I want to know. But that isn't why I came. The thing is, you didn't explain to me that I am somewhat more than a prisoner here. If I should try to go home and I told them what I've learned, they'd think I was crazy."

Nomis practically glowed. "It's so nice to talk to an intelligent young person sometimes. No doubt you'll turn out to be a bit impatient, like all the rest, but it is a rare pleasure all the same. There are some secrets that can be shouted from the rooftops, and they're still secrets because nobody will ever believe them. Which leads me to a question. Why do you believe us?"

Gaelian was glad that her training helped her to conceal her shock at that question. "First of all, because you'd ask a thing like that," she replied after a long pause. "And because I saw Anoni's name in that volume. And all the things that are a little too close to parallel, the legends, the colors, the games, even the fact that I can exist, are reasonable evidence."

"Yes, yes," Nomis mused. "That's the key. Nobody lives in more than one culture. Nobody ever sees more than one. Oh, the Dinoreans come here to Adedri, but they don't really see us. They see our festivals and never understand it's our version of your nerris. It's only when one can compare that the unnatural closeness becomes obvious. Like Anoni, for one." He chuckled broadly. "And now, seeing what you see and knowing just how your family might take your resurrection, would you stay as our guest? And I do mean that term quite honestly."

"I might not have to tell them the truth," Gaelian countered. The thought only now occurred to her. The lie was a thing of Anoni, and Anoni's priests were the ones to bear it, not a Dinorean officer, not a person of Cahaute.''

"And what would you tell them?" Nomis demanded, amusement plain on his face. "That you were held captive? You're far too well fed and much too brown from the sun. Did we keep you inside? Or did we keep you caged outside? Then, of course, you'd show the classical symptoms of exposure. And if not a prisoner, why didn't you just walk out, back to your base? I should think there would be a lot of very sticky questions you wouldn't want to answer. But, of course, as an officer, you would have no other choice.''

She thought about that. There was no question that she couldn't return—she had made a decision and become accustomed to it. Nomis might be half crazy or not, but he was no fool, she realized. He was right. There would be too many questions. She nodded miserably.

"Oh, wonderful, very good," Nomis exclaimed. "Let's have a drink to your new status. Free and invited guest, and perhaps student. Well, I shouldn't rush things. Not everyone wants to be a student. Even most of the students don't want to be, but they don't have much choice about it now, do they?''

He pulled out a dusty bottle from a drawer and poured from it into two none-too-clean glasses. The liquid was pale amber and would have looked lovely without the film on the glass, but when he handed it to Gaelian she recoiled. The stuff smelled like nothing she had ever drunk and nothing she wanted to try.

"Oh, yes, the smell does that sometimes," Nomis agreed cheerfully. "But the taste's the thing, and I think you'll rather enjoy this. It's one of those specialties that we Adedri don't give out to anyone.''

Gaelian sipped carefully. No wonder the Adedri didn't give out this particular recipe. They couldn't pay a Dinorean to drink it. It was vile.

Nomis sipped and smiled broadly, raising his glass to Gaelian. She merely looked at him wonderingly knowing there was more than she saw.

Nomis chuckled again. "Not saying anything, young guest? And thinking like lightning. I would assume, anyway. What a pleasant change, not too impatient for once. That deserves a reward.''

Gaelian tried not to wince as he poured more of the hideous stuff into her glass.

• • •

In the dark, she felt movement. It was not the gross movement of something physical, or the sudden change in energy levels that a storm created. No, it was more and less, a subtle turning, a shift. It was a thing of Rock, father of Mountain, deep in the ground, a kind of violent shudder. She rose and made her way out of the room, through the semidark to the installation.

There she paused momentarily, hearing the undervoice of the machines at work, the soft steps of the students unfortunate enough to have drawn the night watch. Then she went on, following a tremor of energy so slight that only her deepest concentration could pinpoint the path it made.

No one stopped or challenged her as she went past the courtyards and through the doors that only days ago had been locked against her. The conversation with Nomis had worked as she had anticipated. There were few restrictions now.

Still, she had never been in this part of the enclosure before. The heavy double doors swung apart and then closed behind her, leaving her alone in a narrowing corridor. Here the walls were polished steel, and behind them she could hear machinery operating. What work was going on she did not know but felt certain she could guess with fair accuracy.

The hallways dead-ended into a bank of elevators, and she selected one at random and pushed the lowest button. It was a long way down. When she emerged from the lift, she was not surprised at what she found. But there was still something shocking about seeing it with her own eyes, large and moving and almost unreal.

The pit was huge. Probably the entire Temple complex could fit into it with room to spare. Atmosphere-capable craft rested lightly in the center of the cavity, clusters of Adedri surrounding them like some insect ballet. Carts and floats whisked themselves by on prearranged schedules that she could not perceive, and she pressed her back against the wall. Some of the carts were empty, others full of boxes and packing materials.

All the packing cases had the markings of the Dinorean Navy. The Temple was the Adedri pirate base.

Gaelian had exactly the information she wanted. Keeping a smile from her face, she returned to the elevators. No one noticed her. The copali she had thrown on kept her indis-

tinguishable. They ignored her, if anyone had seen her at all.
They didn't like student-priest-experimenters interfering with
operations, she guessed. Pleased with her new information,
she returned to the experimental station and went back to
sleep.

Golran Vontreidi reported to transport sixty with his kit and
was promptly taken up, transferred to a cruiser, and assigned
temporary duties aboard. They had really stretched things,
trying to find something for him to do that would suit his taste
and training and not give him too much authority. For the
twenty-three slow days of the trip to Cahaute, he stayed in the
Engineering section, taking third shifts on watch and speaking
to no one. It suited him. He was dead, felt dead. The complete
isolation on the ship permitted him the luxury of not confront-
ing anyone. Like cargo, he went down to Cahaute.

In truth, he thought, he must be dead. If anything could
make him alive and feeling again, this place should. The
breeze was soft on his skin and scented with green things. The
base sat out in the middle of a plain. Clean white buildings and
several different kinds of craft and equipment were neatly laid
out in elegant geometric configurations on a broad swath of
grassland. The reactor dome looked like a large egg perched
over a miniature town, with carefully kept walks and well-
tended landing strips. Only two strips, he noted to himself,
vaguely disappointed.

He waited for only a moment with the cargo and supplies
that had been dropped. Several officers in immaculate uniforms came to greet him, one of whom he recognized. They
saluted crisply, and he returned the gesture with precision and
without thought.

"Lieutenant Vontreidi, we are happy to have you here,"
someone said. Golran forced himself to pay attention. The
speaker was the one he recognized, Ensign Teazerin YnSetti.
He'd never liked YnSetti and assumed it was because Gaelian
had to marry him. The idea of working with him was close to
intolerable.

"I'll take you to your quarters so you can get settled in, and
then I'll show you our setup. I believe you've been apprised of
our situation," YnSetti continued.

Golran shouldered his kit and nodded. He recognized something in the ensign's voice, a hint of contempt, a sharpness

that reminded him of the nerris stick. Then he remembered how this officer had played nerris as a midshipman, and he felt the coldness through the isolation he had built around himself.

He was a commoner, not a nerris player in the true sense of the word. And yet there would be no choice with YnSetti. He was about to play in truth for the first time, he could read it in the other's eyes. He had seen them like this before, those who made nerris of all the universe. Well enough. Nerris was at least an honorable way to die.

He followed YnSetti to one of the neat buildings and found his quarters, although not luxurious, certainly acceptable. YnSetti smiled unpleasantly and left. Another man stayed, enlisted by his uniform.

"Excuse me, sir, I'm Kaesoma AnAserin," the stranger said.

Golran nodded, acknowledging him. It would be like them, he reflected, to send a commoner to him. It was not the first time.

AnAserin did not begin to unpack or behave as an orderly. Instead, he stood quietly and held Golran's eyes. After a moment, he drew out an envelope, small enough to be concealed in the pockets of a heavy work uniform. "These came for you, sir. Top priority." AnAserin retained his blank look, pivoted, and disappeared through the door.

The envelope had a heavy seal and a thinner strip of magnetic tape around the edge. Gingerly, Golran touched the ID band of his disk to the tape, and it released. He broke the heavy seal and began to read. It was not something generated by the computer.

As he read, he could feel the blood stirring in him. Near laughing, he cursed his own stiff-necked pride, the pride that had made him wipe out every unofficial message before he left Adedri. A smile grew over his face, and becoming aware of it, he tried to compose himself. It would never do for them to find him like this.

He had not been demoted to souped-up policeman, had not been sent into exile to be forgotten as his classmates forged ahead. Instead, he would report directly to the Admiralty on the troubles with the natives.

He read the contents of the packet three times, carefully, before throwing the whole down the disposal. Then he dressed

in his best uniform and waited for YnSetti to return for his
tour of security facilities. Golran put the time to good use. He
practiced looking as blank as he had felt that morning.

"I don't like it," the YnOestal said, delicately sipping her
brandy in the YnTourne library.

"Do you wish for a recall?" Dobrin asked solicitously.

She shook her head. "Things have gone too far. And I have
certain, well, reservations we might say, about the situation."

Dobrin YnTourne, the YnTourne, regarded the YnOestal
carefully. Her support was one of the crucial elements in this
plan, and he could not afford her lack of cooperation now
that things had been initiated.

"No," she said, looking up from the topaz liquid, "it's not
the operation." Her words were slow, thoughtful, each one
heavily weighed. "It's the fact that this is the first time we've
used someone, how shall I say it, not completely familiar with
our methods."

"Iesin's recommendation," Dobrin reminded her quietly.

It was not so much that Iesin was her daughter, he thought.
Iesin had proved her intuitive gift often enough, an uncanny
perception of the way people and events worked together.

The YnOestal nodded carefully, and Dobrin knew she was
merely going over the facts, not ready to oppose. It was the
way of the yellow, careful consideration, masks and paint to
cover the truth.

"We know two things," the YnOestal said precisely. "First,
there is the fact that the tribes have been able to penetrate our
barriers. And, more important, we know that they must have
some reason. Exactly what the reason is we can only speculate
on now. We need the information. With piracy up in the
Adedri system and Tanistin being something less than the success we anticipated, we don't have the people or the funds to
commit to a full-scale uprising on Cahaute."

"So what are your objections?" Dobrin asked.

"We already have AnAserin in place," she replied. "There
is always a risk in bringing in someone new. And someone
who has no experience with this kind of thing as well . . ."

"We needed an officer," Dobrin reminded her sharply.
"And Vontreidi is perfect. Because he's a commoner, he is less
likely to be suspect. We discussed this earlier. He also worked
with my cousin on the language. Only a little, of course, but

even a little is better than nothing."

"It's YnSetti I'm worried about," the YnOestal said softly. "Not Teazerin, but the YnSetti. The household. If he ever hears any hint of what we're doing . . ."

Dobrin smiled carefully and set his glass on the edge of a table. The opening was over, and now he wondered what the next round would be. It was classic yellow play, sections folded carefully into one another. As he played the blue, fluid and yielding but wearing down the opposition, dancing away. She knew he played blue, just as they all knew each others' colors. It made life simpler but no less watchful for all of that.

"What exactly do you want?" he asked slowly.

She regarded him for a moment, the heavy liquid in her glass so steady that he thought it might have turned to stone.

"Golran Vontreidi is to take no steps against Teazerin Yn-Setti," the YnOestal said. "He is there only to see and report, to us alone. And after this job, I want him eliminated."

Dobrin tried to search her face. He'd never heard the Yn-Oestal ask for that before. He composed the question before he asked, making sure that there could be no misunderstanding, that he asked with all respect.

"Because," she answered heavily, "he will know too much. Too many people who are in key positions. And he's not one of us and never will be."

Dobrin thought about her objection dispassionately. He hated to waste anything, raw materials, talent. If he had known of her objections in advance, he might have chosen someone who was part of their network. Or someone without other talents. Someone easily expendable. On the other hand, she was right.

Besides, no matter how talented, it simply was not possible to permit a commoner to publically humiliate one of the Ot-tan class. It had been a consideration all along, of course, but Vontreidi was so perfectly suited to the situation, and no one else had quite the qualifications. . . . "Done," he said quietly.

"And one more thing," the YnOestal said. "You are young and still single. Unusual for a Head of household. It's rather irregular for me to approach you directly, but I can't see any other person I might ask. Iesin is not engaged and is of suitable class and age. And, if only for your cousin's sake, she would see to the interests of the YnTourne."

And your own, he thought. Yours, and Intelligence's, and your Adedri clients'. Dobrin said nothing. He didn't need to, not yet. She would give him time to think about it, and perhaps she wasn't entirely wrong. The more Dobrin turned it over in his mind, the more he could see other advantages. It would be good to know who was keeping an eye on him, and for whom. And Iesin was intelligent and capable. He would definitely think about it.

They sat in silence for a few moments until Missili appeared from a shadow. "Dinner is ready at your pleasure," the Adedri servant said.

They both rose, Dobrin following the YnOestal, who was senior. He thought it had been a reasonable afternoon's work. Not great perhaps, but reasonable.

14

IT WAS SUPPER time. Very little was sacred in the Temple of Adedri, Gaelian had learned, but supper was one of those very few things. There were people in the installation and probably down in the shuttle pit, but it was a skeleton crew at most, and even then they were most likely concentrated in groups snacking on protein bars and griping about having to miss the main meal.

Gaelian sat in her usual place in the courtyard with Ridra and two other members of Ridra's team, or class, as Gaelian thought of it. She had taken very small helpings, but still it had been difficult to finish, although tonight's was one of the best dinners.

She rose slowly and gathered her tray. "I'm going back for seconds on shabish. Anyone want anything?"

The three on the ground looked thoughtful for a moment. "Not if you're not going to the dessert line," Ridra said finally.

Gaelian shrugged, took her tray, and headed back inside. If she moved a bit briskly, they would only conclude that she wanted to get seconds before the shabish was all gone and something that looked vaguely like last night's dinner was laid out on the serving lines.

Once inside, Gaelian glanced through the large windows and noted with satisfaction that Ridra and her classmates were in deep discussion. They were probably pleased to have a moment's privacy. She deposited the tray and turned, not to the left toward the cafeteria, but to the right.

It took all her concentration to keep her back relaxed, to move at an even pace. The copali did not move easily; it was weighted down with ten days' worth of protein bars. The pockets swung and hit her knees with every step.

There was no one in the corridor. She took the elevator down to the pit, and when the doors slid open, she casually crossed the expanse of floor to where several Adedri in work clothes sat.

Gaelian smiled as pleasantly as she could. In the three weeks since she had been a "guest" at the Temple, she had been down to the pit on several occasions and had gotten to know at least two of the techs now eating their makeshift dinner.

"Don't bother getting up," she said quickly, addressing an older woman she had met more than once. "It's just that I've got a few hours free now, and, well, do you think I could take out one of those?" She pointed to the larger craft, an old-style shuttle that was both atmosphere- and deep-space-capable.

"What's a red dress like you want with a shuttle?" asked a tech she didn't know.

The woman she had addressed previously smiled. Gaelian tried to match her expression and shrugged. "You know, from before. I was an in-system hauler." She patted the folds of the red copali.

The annoyed man huffed a bit, but the techs who knew Gaelian quieted him. "Seventeen sixty-one is fueled and ready. Is anyone going along on this joyride?" the older woman asked.

"Well, you know, I just thought I'd like to go alone. Just to keep my hand in. I mean, I've been upstairs studying and working, and I haven't gotten a chance to do anything . . ."

The tech grinned. "I know just what you mean," she said cheerfully. "Well, the ignition code's in the computer, no problem."

Gaelian sauntered to the oversized shuttle, hauled herself in easily, and waved. They ought to be able to see from her ease that she was comfortable with the craft. She set the wheel sequence, and the bulky shuttle started to glide down one of the several long slipways that connected the outside to the pit. Her knuckles were white on the controls as she held the ignition code open.

Smoothly, exactly on cue, the diaphragm swirled open. It

was dark out now. She entered the ignition code, and the shuttle trembled slightly, gathering thrust to itself before it surged through the lock.

She was free and clear so far. Good. She hadn't expected any trouble at this stage, anyway. She turned her mind to the trouble she *was* expecting and had spent the better part of the week figuring out how to avoid. The Adedri would be chasing her for stealing one of their craft, albeit an old-type clunker. And the Navy would run her down if she crossed any of their patrols, since the Adedri pirate craft carried no authorization beam.

Sighing with concentration, she fed data into the keyboard controls. Working in the installation had given her the freedom to find what she wanted, and the information had been erased immediately. Now it was only a matter of setting up the right sequences and hoping that Yenhica would protect her.

She had one advantage the Adedri didn't have when they made their pirating runs. She knew the patrol schedule and routes. There was little chance that they had changed in the time she had been in the Temple. That had been three weeks, and the new schedule had just become effective when she was captured. A patrol route usually remained constant for about six weeks or more until it was changed, another thing the Adedri didn't know.

Always keep something moving between you and them, she remembered from a tactics class. The bigger the better, and the more solid the more safe. She programmed a pattern that would weave her between the Navy patrol lines and hide her behind two moons and a few smaller chunks of rock on the way.

She had a few hours before the Adedri would suspect. She had a habit of disappearing after supper. Ridra would most likely think that she had found someone else to talk to. And the Adedri down in the pit wouldn't suspect for awhile, and if they were relieved by another shift, which was common around dinner hour, it might be a good while longer.

As long as luck was with her she was fine. If that failed, then it would be all over. If they discovered her gone, and the craft with her, Ridra and Nomis would know. And they would know where to look for her. But if her luck held, she could outrun them. It wasn't this old, beat-up junk heap that would barely get her through, but the Power Ones who were singing in her blood. She had it again, that intimate connection with the craft itself and with the cold that surrounded it. All had come together and filled her in the new way nothing else ever had or could. It was the act itself, apart from the necessity, that gave her the power. She had ignored that ability, that gift. Now, free from Dinoreos, from the Navy, from her own life, she let it fill her, burn her. It didn't matter if she were consumed, she was dead anyway.

The safe hours had ended, and still there were no signs of pursuit on her screens. She reached out tentatively with her being and could feel nothing surrounding her. Nothing but the cold vacuum, the harsh moon rocks, and the glitter of light aeons away.

Carefully, as if savoring something very special, very much her own, she set her course to Cahaute. The coordinates were burned in her mind. Only action existed. Only the goal mattered, the first step.

Alone, Gaelian laughed out loud. She took the nistora necklace out of the bag and fastened it around her neck. It looked strange with the copali, but the smoothness of the bone and claws felt good against her skin. She laughed again, hard, because she had always been an outlaw, and she was now free.

"Now tell me, Ridra, what exactly were your speculations, your final analysis, and your findings?" Nomis demanded.

Ridra stood before him as he sat composed. She clasped her hands in front of her, her long, thick hair half hiding her face. "You will find all the data there," she said, gesturing with her face at the neatly bound report that lay on the desk.

"No, no, sum it up," Nomis said impatiently, his eyes snapping at her.

"We have a Weberian cycle of interactive components, each one of which is vital," she began in her most precise manner. "Personalities are almost impossible to predict, and yet it seems necessary for convergence at a place in time in order to effect events and insure proper culmination. Otherwise there are several possible alternate scenarios . . ."

"Get to the point," Nomis snapped, quite uncharacteristically. "By which I mean, if one truly understands a problem, then recitation of three mountains' worth of academic jargon isn't necessary. In other words, is our subject on course? Were we correct in our evaluations?"

Ridra let out a long sigh. "Yes, Nomis, we were correct. I didn't know it would be so soon. I thought she'd at least try to get the why of it out of you. Although I did warn her it was useless. I hadn't expected it yet. But Gaelian has taken the route we predicted at the beginning. She should arrive on Cahaute in approximately two weeks, our time."

Nomis grunted. Then he broke into a smile. "I've read your team report, by the way. I thought you would at least figure that much out. And you have passed. That *was* intended as your final student presentation, wasn't it? I surely do hope so."

Ridra smiled widely. "So I'm not a student anymore? I'm a team leader in fact, not just in function?"

Nomis snorted again and shook his head. "You're the one who charted and predicted her movements. You should have been able to figure that out, once we decided to go along with your experiment. Children! Stupid and impatient."

Ridra sighed and closed her eyes. It had been close, she thought. Weberian personalities rarely followed patterns that could be understood before they were complete. On the other hand, the simulations of transmissions in E_8 showed distinct possibilities of interconnected action in that dimension that they still knew so little about. But the simulations and all the rest had been completely theoretical.

"Theory," Nomis said pedantically, "is often all we have to go on. The basis of original research is the ability to take risks. Intellectual risks, of course, which are then confirmed or not confirmed by practical experimentation. You took the risk, Ridra, and so you get the reward. Very good. Things are going nicely, exactly as they should."

Ridra shook her head. "I know what I did in this experiment. But I still don't know why, or what the larger implications are."

"Impatience!" Nomis bellowed. "None of you, not one, can wait. If you knew everything, it would prejudice your research." Then he leaned over and patted her hand. "But I think I can at least give you some of the background that you don't know. After all, where we go from here is our own decision. Essentially, Ridra, Anoni was looking for survivors, to make sure our race could withstand being transplanted. The interest was not a purely theoretical one. And it is necessary

now to make sure the strains don't adapt to the point of speci-
ation, which means reintegrating the gene pool.

"But we should celebrate," Nomis said, pointing to one of
the stools. "You have successfully completed your project.
You are no longer a student here, Ridra. As of today, you are
an investigator."

As Ridra settled herself comfortably, Nomis got up and
poured out some deep amber liquid into two very dirty glasses.
There was a thin film of dust on the outside, and there was a
sticky dark residue on the inside.

Ridra didn't seem bothered by it. Instead, she took a single
sip and closed her eyes in delight.

*Raids have been minor but consistent. Casualties are low, as
indicated in official reports. The major factor that has kept us
from trying to approach the tribes and negotiate has been
Teazerin YnSetti. Although he only holds the rank of ensign,
the importance of his household on the Board has given him
somewhat more authority than that rank should denote.*

Golran listened to the lines twice and wondered what he had
omitted. He hadn't mentioned the fact that Tembri Linassi,
the commanding officer, had been very careful about the
Ot-tan under him. Linassi was a fine officer but, like most
Dinoreans, a little in awe of the Ot-tan, especially those like
Teazerin who came from important Board households.

Nor had he said anything about the constant checks of the
reactor and the shield. Every test checked out perfectly. They
performed in every situation and simulation they could devise.
And somehow, the natives were still getting through.

It made everyone on the base nervous, Golran admitted to
himself. They were shaky, never sure if there really was something wrong with the reactor.

Was it worth it for mineral rights? Golran wondered. And
then he stopped himself, amazed. Through all he had done, he
had never questioned the main assumptions of Dinoreos. As
he fed the report in the sealed recorder into the code transmitter, he let himself explore the possibility.

The matter of Cahaute lay with its mineral resources. Why
should they use the word "rights"? he thought. Perhaps the
tribes didn't need the minerals now, as primitives, and perhaps
they never would. On the other hand, wasn't Dinoreos primitive once? He let the thoughts cycle along with the code mit

until the soft bell told him that the message had been sent and the original destroyed.

"And who are we sending coded transmissions to?" a voice came from behind.

Golran whipped around to face Teazerin YnSetti, leaning lightly against the open doorway. Golran could have sworn that he had shut the door after him.

"Aren't you going to answer my question, Vontreidi?" Teazerin hissed.

"I think you'd better return to your post, *ensign*," Golran responded dryly.

Teazerin looked down at the transmitter and back to Golran. "I'll be watching you," he said. "I know about the festivals on Adedri. Espionage is a capital offense, although I can't understand why any Dinorean, even a commoner, would do anything for the Temple."

"This has nothing to do with Adedri," Golran said evenly. "I suggest that you stay out of it."

YnSetti smiled and raised his eyebrows and then left. There was something in that smile that made Golran cold, some kind of threat that he couldn't identify or counter. Only the word "espionage" stuck in his mind.

He had thought of himself as a source of information for the Admiralty. Still, it was YnSetti they had wanted information on, the only Ot-tan of a Board family. And his information was sent only to Metten YnOestal, the third YnOestal brother in the Admiralty. Golran knew nothing of Board politics, but suddenly he wondered that he was set by one Board family member at the Admiralty to watch another. It did not bode well. He wondered if he had gotten into something deeper than he could handle.

Gaelian pounded the board again, and again it gave no result. Luck and planning were one thing, and a certain amount could be expected. But this was suspicious. It had been eight days, and she was well out of the immediate vicinity of Adedri, yet she had seen no pursuit.

Her fingers sped over the keys again, trying to locate a possible ambush point in the journey ahead. The screen blinked negative each time, each combination she tried.

There was nothing untoward in the area, hadn't been since she'd left. It was her own knowledge that permitted her to avoid the Navy, and the lack of Adedri pursuit had to mean only one of two things. Or maybe three. First, clicking off the possibilities, there was the chance that the craft itself was sabotaged. She had gone over it thoroughly four days ago when no Adedri appeared. It had taken two days to check every system, every board. She wasn't entirely sure of all aspects of the design on the old shuttle, and there were indications of Adedri repairs, boards somewhat different than the original Dinorean type. But she had found no signs of recent tampering. That led to possibility two, that there was an ambush waiting ahead. It would have been easier for them to try to find her earlier, though. The longer she was gone, the greater the radius of possible action, and even if they were sure of her final goal, there was more than one course. If they had been planning to take the ship back, they would have done so earlier. Which left her with a more frightening conclusion, one she did not want to think about.

Nomis had wanted her to go. He was secure enough in his own analysis that he had figured her most likely destination and had some reason of his own for permitting her to leave.

The more she thought about it, the more it made sense to her, but she couldn't figure out why. That was the trouble.

Why would Nomis let her go? Perhaps his whole manner, the entire situation on Adedri, had been a setup. Maybe she could quite easily have walked out the doors and back to the Base. Perhaps even the fax they had brought her were inaccurate. It wouldn't take much to fake an obituary.

Gaelian pounded her fist into her palm. None of this had occurred to her earlier. The long days spent in isolation had brought their own twisted logic.

Or so she told herself day after day of the journey, every second bringing her that much closer to Cahaute, to a home that was no home. Maybe it was only the protein bars, day after day of them, chewy and tasteless and slightly tainted by the wrappers. There was little other food on board, and what there was she didn't trust.

Her attention began to waver as the time went by. Games with the computer didn't help, nor did routine maintenance. She knew it was boredom, rampant and threatening, assisted by constant low-grade hunger brought on by strict rationing of food. For long hours she lay in the acceleration couch and fantasized about food, about bread most of all, and cheese and meat. Sometimes she thought of the great feasts in the Yn-Tourne household when some other Ot-tan came to visit, the seven formal courses, the cream soup, the cold peppered fish, the meat that had been marinated in oil and spices for three days and then grilled over an open fire.

The hunger only made what she did have to eat more unpalatable, and she grew to detest the rations that were available. On rare occasions, she wanted to eat them all at once to still the constant, nagging awareness in her stomach. She was even tempted to eat the three meals that were stored in the shuttle. The very idea of something to taste again, different flavors, some bulk to fill her, was enticing.

Perhaps this was what Nomis had in mind. She considered it. And then she realized that she was only making the situation worse. There were tapes in the ship's computer, but they were all in Adedri and she didn't know the language. She was even considering learning it, just for something to keep her mind off food, when the nav comp blew a whistle.

Her first thought was that something was wrong, and she began to run checks again by rote. Then Gaelian laughed. She was entering the Cahaute system, closing in on her goal. Now there was more than enough to do; she didn't have any Navy schedules for this area, and from all reports there had been some activity lately.

She swept the area with passive surveillance. Two small craft, Navy make, old, were taking the usual patrol routes. It was easy to avoid them. Play yellow. She kept herself hidden behind large chunks of rock and other debris, on low energy. With enough distance, the emissions would scatter, and they wouldn't be able to pinpoint her position.

It was like stalking the runners through the grassland, she thought. Run and hide, keeping always downwind. Stay silent, stay motionless for long periods of time, until you blend in with the rocks, the trees, the grass. Then dodge, swerve, never in a straight line, and come to rest behind some other bit of cover. Blend in and always keep downwind.

There could be no impatience on the hunt, no sudden movements. And she remembered that she had been hungry before, too, in the winter lodge waiting for the white time to end.

With great thought, she dodged from one bit of cover to the next, always aware of the position of both Navy craft, trying to keep her concentration. Trying to remember that, although she had spotted two, there could well be others.

The moon of Cahaute served her well. She was sorry there was only one to use in hiding, but it simply made things more exciting. With patrol flights, she dared not try to orbit and find the right place to land.

There was only one place to land. It was the place that had been made for landing and taking off, the rock smooth and fused along the top surface, the place sacred to the people. She took in segments of the surface as they came into view without the patrol cover, swept down like a warrior-bird, and surveyed the terrain. A hunter, she swooped, surveyed, analyzed.

Gaelian was surprised. She hadn't known Cahaute was so large, so old, so much of it water. The computer spit out more information than she could comprehend. Old, very old, large masses broken and broken again with worn-down mountains and open crevasses that had once been the scenes of great volcanic activity. No wonder the place was so perfect for mining. They barely had to scratch the topsoil, and minerals were there for the taking. No wonder the tribes had always had fine obsidian for knives and tanners, for projectile points, and for ornament. Huge outcroppings of green jasper rose up along the ledge of one of the two large land masses left, jasper that was ground into the death paint that was so valuable.

It was this land mass that interested her, and she knew it. She couldn't say why, particularly, but piece by piece, section by section, the survey showed the arid regions and the grasslands and the fringe where the grasslands met the wooded hills. The infrared even picked out the vast herds of nistora on the plain, and she knew she was home. Or not home—a place remembered from a life before, so far distant that it might have simply been the imagination of childhood were it not for the language she carried in her head and the necklace she wore.

Her sweeps went lower, penetrating the layers of atmosphere, low enough to see the land itself. Then she saw it, surrounded by the matte-green forest, a brilliant reflection, a beacon positioned to catch the light and announce its presence.

Gaelian drew in her breath. There was no question that this was the Dead Hill, a place made for landings. She had not realized that it had been so carefully fused, that the position had been so accurately calculated to signal its presence to the whole sky.

Gently, she brought the craft closer to the brilliant beacon. She could feel the soft breath around her, coaxing her to play on the high wind with the sky friends.

The Dead Hill drew her on. She didn't need a mineral breakdown to know this place, to feel it moving in her, in a place lost from some other time that now became fully alive. Gently, softly, she approached the light, and it resolved into a large, flat, polished mound. Like the whisper of a petal falling on the earth, she brought the shuttle to rest on the Dead Hill.

As she powered the ship down, Gaelian felt a strange emptiness. Something was missing, something she knew very well. What exactly was gone nagged at her as she opened the door and set foot on Cahaute for the first time since she was seven. She was lightheaded and had to pause, resting against the shimmering hull of the battered, ancient craft. The bright sunlight flooded her eyes, and she blinked rapidly. The world reeled, took on new shape, and then reformed. She steadied herself against the warm hull and carefully slipped down until she sat on the sun-baked black rock.

Then she remembered what was missing. Her dit. The Angel always landed on a dit. Here there was no one to put it down for her.

Funny, she thought. The Angel always did that, and she had not. By an exercise in logic, she was no longer the Angel. The Angel, the Navy pilot, the YnTourne, was gone. Sadness touched her, and Gaelian had the sudden urge to paint herself green and mourn for all her former selves, who had died and vanished without acknowledgement.

The past, the many different pasts, were gone. They were dead, as surely as the person she had been was dead. As she sat in the sunlight on the Dead Hill, she could feel each of them drift off into the breeze, into the smell of the green things, into the rock itself. She was nothing, a person newly born, and she had nothing but a nistora necklace. The necklace of a hasute, which she had not earned. But she must have, because the white nistora, like the hoppers, came to those they chose and to none other. They gave where they chose, and they could see into the hearts of people and into their futures, because to the animals there is no future and no past, but only the infinite now. Gaelian was animal with them, without past or future, with only a moment. There was no reason, no sense to anything at all, just the pure experience of being.

Then, very faintly, she heard the music of a flute. The voice of the people called to her softly, the flute that was the gift of the Power Clan, the gift of some other people in a distant place. There was no difference. Only the music was real, weaving around her, covering the forever of the now. The music called to her, beckoning, and she did not resist.

She circled the top of the Hill as best she could and began to climb down on the side where the music seemed the loudest. It was not a difficult climb, and she thanked the flute itself for choosing the easy side of the hill. The copali she wore was not made for climbing.

At the bottom of the Dead Hill, she turned toward the music. In front of her stood a person who looked like no person she had seen. Even memory of the time she had been of the tribes did not serve her. The man before her was tall with skin the color of copper and hair as black as obsidian, which fell below his shoulders. He was lean and strong-looking in the manner of a person who has run down prey on the grasslands and climbed often in the hills for the feathers of warrior-birds. The thing that made him different from the people she remembered was the necklace he wore, one like her own with four layers of bone and claws making a collar, the mark of a hasute. And on the waist-string of his leggings hung a small white pelt with brown spots.

"I have waited here many days for my friend to return. The edonys dream showed me that she was coming," he said in the slightly inflected language that had been her mother tongue. "I remember a friend who gave me a hopper," he said, touching the pelt that had drawn her eyes.

The phrases came back to her haltingly, not so much the words but ways in which the people of the tribes spoke, the meaning they wove. "What name does my friend wear now?" she asked hesitantly, afraid of the language itself and of the warm eyes that regarded her so closely.

"For this time I am called Nyapetin," he said. "Is my friend wearing the name I knew? Or has her vision given her a new one?"

She didn't know the answer. There were many things he could call her—Gaelian, the Angel, YnTourne, she had been all of them. But for now, Gaelian was the most familiar, the least associated with any of the things she had been. She merely nodded.

He turned and began to walk through the trees on a path that she could barely discern. She followed carefully, holding the copali up over her shins with both hands. Twigs caught at the fine fabric, and she found the walking difficult.

They stopped at a clearing with a small spring. Gaelian noticed a travel lodge of few hides pitched beside a stone firepit. Nyapetin had made himself comfortable, she thought, in the way of the winter travelers who spread news and stories among the white camps. She was breathing hard and sat in front of the firepit, not realizing, or not remembering, what it meant. Or perhaps, she thought, she did and hadn't realized her hunger. It was still with her but had grown more usual so that she didn't notice it so much with her stomach. And her reeling head could be as much from the events or the sun as lack of food.

Nyapetin looked at her and at the dead fire, and his eyes clouded. He disappeared into the small lodge and returned with a length of meat, beaten and coated with fat. She accepted it and began to chew, her gums growing sore with the work required to soften the barklike food.

They sat in silence. Gaelian knew there were things she wanted to ask, wanted to know, but it was not the way of the people to speak without cause. Her grandfather had said it was not good to fill the air with chatter, like the stupid-birds.

Nyapetin moved noiselessly, sitting up and pulling the lodge flap aside. "You will need a good rest before we join the tribe," he told her.

Silently she entered the small lodge. There were only three robes on the ground, although they were thick and looked comfortable. An unfamiliar shyness came over her as she tried to lay down without taking up too much space. Then, from without, she heard the flute again and sighed, relaxing deep into the black fur.

Scratching on the hide woke her, and she pulled back the flap. Already it was bright, time for walking in the forest before the people moved again. Nyapetin did not enter the ledge but squatted outside until she emerged. Then he went in and found more of the stiff meat and began bundling the whole lodge together. The cover came off and the heavy robes she had slept on were folded into the cover. The long sticks that had been supports were made into two large bundles, and Nyapetin lashed the hides between them. The three bags, bow, and lances she had noticed were hung from the poles, although he kept the flute tucked into the rawhide drawstring of his leggings.

Without a word, she picked up one end of the travois while Nyapetin took the other. He must have taken it alone when he came, but she could help him bring it back. She had, after all, slept in the lodge herself.

It was hard work, and although the path here was well defined and easy to walk, the drag was heavy and would catch on rocks or twigs. Her shoulders and back ached, and she was breathing hard. Nyapetin looked perfectly at ease, as if the travois were no strain and did not slow him in the least.

When it caught again, he said, "It would be easier if I took it in front. Then, if it catches on anything, you can remove that thing. This will be faster."

She nodded, her cheeks burning. When she had been only six, she had taken a child's sledge with no trouble at all, could walk and run all day without fatigue. She felt shame when he had been so careful not to shame her, to act as if her task would make it easier for him as well. She remembered how people would shame her when she was small and how her grandparents in the tribe would make little excuses like this, so her face would not burn.

She remembered all that, how she had gone with another young girl of a different clan to pick the sitting food for dinner. They had been far from the camp when she had felt it running through her, a raid of some kind, something terrible. She would have cried, but her parents had taught her never to cry. It made a person easy to find. She had gestured to her friend, and both of them had hidden in the underbrush.

She remembered the long legs of the chatoyas going by them, the frightening paint and high plumes of the Kills-Many tribe, their enemies. They had waited a long time, until the last chatoya disappeared, until she could no longer hear anything in the ground, before returning to camp. And then she saw. Her mother and grandparents were dead. Her mother's lodge was gone, burned. Many lodges were burned, and many people were crying, howling in fury as much as pain. Some of the people had memory sticks sunk into the flesh of their elbows and legs.

She hadn't looked at anyone, hadn't noticed who was there and who was gone. Her mother and her grandparents were dead, that she knew. And her father was off hunting with another clan. They were all gone. She had barely noticed when Tyakral had come and led her away to a nice, clean hasute lodge, had given her food and told her to sleep. Tyakral did that on many nights. Then, Gaelian had thought that Tyakral was very old; she was a grownup, and all grownups were old.

Suddenly, with a shock, Gaelian realized that Tyakral, the hasute of the Mikke, had probably been a good bit younger than she herself was now. And Tyakral had been as her mother for almost a year, until they found her father and she had returned to him and him to their other people.

Thinking occupied her as they walked. It was warm, and the heavy cloth that seemed to cling to her legs was moist. Her side hurt, and her breathing was ragged. When she looked up, she could see that the slant of the light was different than it had been and the colors had turned more golden. They had come a long way and had not stopped to eat. It was far past the time she was used to eating.

She did not even see the camp when they arrived. She should have heard the low murmur of talk and the shouts of playing children, smelled the good meat cooking over firepits, seen the clearing and the lodge tops festooned with feathers and brightly dyed runners' tails. She had noticed none of it, only her bleeding feet and sore legs.

Nyapetin turned and smiled at her warmly. He didn't seem to notice how tired she was, or perhaps he pretended not to notice so as not to shame her. "You will use my lodge," he said. "I will stay with Hinacen or my mother. You might want to set up over there, near the Mikke." He pointed with his chin to an area where the lodges had bright red paint, the fish pattern she remembered from her time with Tyakral.

She simply sat down. She was too tired to go any farther, and the jumble of sticks and hides was too confusing for her to think of setting up the lodge. Nyapetin turned to her, and she saw a slight sadness in his look. She didn't know why he was sad, only that he was. Perhaps for bringing a weakling back to the people, for having hoped that she could be one of them, could live up to her hasute necklace, when all she could do was sit.

He returned and sat next to her, his eyes on the ground. "I

know it isn't a very fine lodge," he said slowly. "I don't have one made from twenty robes, and I don't have a chatoya. Not one, not even one branch. I was stupid, I am sorry."

He took the drag and pulled it over to an empty space in the camp, a smallish space, and began to set up the little lodge. It was almost laughable, like a newborn child next to grownups. Gaelian heaved herself from the ground and went over to him, watching him start to cover the shelter. She would have to learn again, but that could come later.

"No," she said and tapped him on the shoulder. As he turned, she looked at the ground. "No," she repeated. "It is I who am ashamed. I have not set poles and coverings for many seasons, and I have traveled for more than two hands of days. I am honored that my friend offers." There was more that she wanted to say, more that she needed to explain, but talking was not the way of the people. She had already said too much.

Nyapetin looked at her for a moment, studied her face, and then turned back to work. Hurt, she began to move away.

"Gaelian?" she heard a woman's voice say.

She looked at the speaker, and her eyes grew wide. Under the strain, the look of age, Gaelian recognized this woman. For all Tyakral had aged and despite the fact that her thick hair was now streaked with grey and there were lines around her mouth, Gaelian could see the ghost of the beautiful healer who had been her takka mother.

She went to Tyakral's lodge, a large one with seven robes on the ground. Tyakral had married a great hunter who had brought her more robes and hides than she could use. She even had five gowns, all of them trimmed with beautiful quill work or bone beads and claws, and one had three shells, which must have meant many fine horns in trade.

Tyakral was entranced by the scarlet copali, and Gaelian immediately offered the cloth to her. Tyakral would make it into lovely trims, and Gaelian knew that her foster mother would trade a gown for it, a gown of the people made of sturdy nistora hide that didn't drag on the ground. Tyakral smiled and chuckled and braided Gaelian's hair with dyed feathers and bands of beaded rawhide. Then Tyakral laid her hands on Gaelian's head and said some words and gave her hot water with some sour and bitter sitting foods in it. She suddenly felt fit and strong again. She belonged to the tribe once more.

She spent that night and several more with Tyakral and her family, remembering lost skills and learning new ones—how to prepare and tan hides, how to heat stones and throw them into cooking pouches, how to make fine, soft shoes and dye quills and feathers.

"The herds are dead," Tyakral told her sadly. "Many will starve in the white time that is coming."

So she went out with the other women and gathered the sitting foods and the sweet grass and dug in the ground for the hiding foods that had no flavor but would fill someone. She gathered seeds, bleached them in the sun, and dried them. For all the work, though, Gaelian felt something missing, something she could not quite place.

She had not seen Nyapetin for eight days, since she had returned to the people. Her back was sore from bending down and digging; her legs were sore from carrying wood and water and from walking over trails to the stream and into the woods. Her hands were raw from the work and from the many small cuts from obsidian scrapers as she worked to rid hides of hair and clinging fat.

On the tenth day, there was a storm. Gaelian was walking back from the woodpile when the sky darkened suddenly. It was like flying, she thought with amazement, as the change in pressure made her skin tingle and her muscles tense. Others around her ran to their lodges, tied chatoyas to stakes in the ground, and made sure that lodge poles were secure. Gaelian simply dropped her bundle and stood, arms outstretched, waiting.

The wind came in first, whipping through the high grass with darkness in its soul. She raised herself on tiptoe, trying to catch the might of the wind, letting the power rip through and past her. In her head, she thought about the change in ionization, about the electrical charges that were changing around her. The electricity poured through her, laughing and sparkling in her body, commanding her and yet an extension of herself.

The sky cried out, screaming and open, as great drops of water splashed downward. Gaelian danced, danced to the movement of the water, of the clouds, of the great noise above her. It was her storm as nothing had been hers since she had woken in the Adedri Temple, in another life. She called, not pleading but with authority, to the fire-in-the-sky, and it came at her beckoning. She danced. She lifted her heels high and arched her back, extending herself into the power of the sky, and it answered. Before the flash, she could feel the energy gathering, and with an act that was part will and part glory, she directed the burning flash to this tree and then to that.

It obeyed her as nothing had obeyed her before. Even the memories of flight were not as pure, as directed, as this feeding and riding the storm. Surely she rode it, flying on the black clouds, reining them in and directing them as she had small craft. Only this time, there was nothing between her and the energy. There was no skin, no inside or outside. She was the mind that directed, and the great bolts of lightning fed her more surely than meat.

Gaelian danced the storm. Without thinking, she leapt and danced down the path to the river, away from the camp of the people. There was no conscious direction, only the wish to be alone with this storm that was a gift to her alone. Weariness left her, and there was only the dance.

She danced until she was exhausted, until her legs trembled and wouldn't hold her weight, until the clouds trembled and had no more power to give and the storm dissolved into a gentle rain.

It was Nyapetin who found her lying on the ground, in a place the swollen river had left untouched. He bent and touched the necklace he had made for her when they were children, and Gaelian smiled. He held out his hand and pulled her to her feet, and she followed him back to his small lodge where she fell asleep in the deep warmth of nistora fur.

15

WHEN HE WOKE her, it was moonlight. Nyapetin was a form, a shadow, moving silently over the heavy furs on the ground, the curve of his smile touched by the thinnest strand of cold light.

They left the lodge together. The camp was asleep, the sounds now sounds of night. Even the evening birds were resting, and there was only the gentle hum of insects, the whisper of a remnant of the breeze through the broad leaves. The sky hid layers of color in darkness, colors that she could see only with the aid of the shimmering moon.

Nyapetin took her hand and led her down to the river. His hand was warm, the skin calloused and the tendons hard, but his touch was gentle.

The river appeared before them like a swath of obsidian, dark and glittering, cutting through the terrain. Even the laughing sounds it made were subdued, merging into the night.

Nyapetin unbound her hair and ran his fingers through it. Then he stepped out of his shoes, dropped the painted robe from his shoulders, and waded into the water. Gaelian followed him, leaving her gown in the shadows on the bank.

His body was warm after the cool autumn river. In the shadow play, there was a fine sprinkle of magic, as if this night were not real. And because the night was not real, she let it enter her and moved within it as in a dream, her silent partner solid only to her hands, ephemeral to her sight.

Nyapetin drew the robe around both of them and touched her face. "Tomorrow we make war on the sky people," he said smiling. "And because it will be after this night, it will be a good day to die."

Golran Vontreidi hesitated over the microrecorder in the palm of his hand. Since his arrival on Cahaute, the reactor had been working perfectly, and the screens hadn't wavered once. Perhaps now that they were operating smoothly, there would be no more raids.

But hints of other things, things not quite wrong in and of themselves, made him uneasy. The matter of the nistora still haunted him.

"We had to eradicate them," YnSetti had told him breezily. "That particular herd was a little too close to the mining stake, and could you imagine what would happen if they stampeded the workers? Or the machinery? To say nothing of the weight, once we've gotten into the ground a ways."

Golran could see the sense behind that. It was the way the others agreed with Teazerin, jumping in a little too fast, grasping for other reasons why the animals had to be destroyed. It wasn't, Golran told himself for the hundredth time that day, that he was concerned about some animals. But there was a subtle unease when people talked about it, as if they worried about being overheard by ghosts.

There was a second undercurrent as well, an indistinct disruption in how the entire base worked. Teazerin YnSetti spoke about things easily, the others not at all. And often, if he asked a question, he was directed to YnSetti for the answer.

Golran closed his hand on the recorder, thought for a moment, and then slipped it into a pocket. He had not sent anything to the Admiralty since YnSetti had seen him at the code transmitter.

He stretched and left the small room to step out into the evening. A sudden afternoon storm had curtailed several scheduled activities, but now the air was clear and fragrant. A fresh sense of order had sprung up since the storm had washed them, and Golran wondered if his musings simply arose from overcaution.

He nodded absently to the canteen workers as he picked up a dinner and brought it back to his own quarters. He would get the report done tonight, he had promised himself. But something in him rebelled, something that told him he was being used in some deft play of the Board that he wanted no part of. So he drifted, not quite sure what everything meant and where it was heading, drifted into and out of half sleep as night came.

Screams woke him. Red flickered on the back wall, and he jumped out of semiconsciousness into full awareness.

He threw open the door and stood, watching painted people with torches charging through the base. The red he had seen was not the dawn, which had dyed a portion of the sky. It was fire, burning supplies and nonpermanent tents, now skeletons blackening against the grass. Without thought he hurried to a group, mixed workers, enlisted people, and officers, who were handling a long hose, aiming a jet of water at the rapidly spreading conflagration. The grass was burning wildly around the supply shed, reaching hungrily toward the living quarters.

Heat assailed his face, and he turned away. There were raiders running for the perimeter pursued by officers with low-charge sidearms.

At any moment, they would reach the energy fence and fry, Golran thought with satisfaction. He tracked them, waiting. The painted figures dived low into the grass and continued running at a crouch farther and farther until they reached the line of trees.

Their pursuers were not so lucky. Near the point where the raiders had dived, the first man after them continued to run and was suddenly outlined in brilliant electric blue. The others stopped dead.

Golran forgot the hose, the fire, and the heat. He dashed to the perimeter, to where the single Dinorean had run into the energy fence.

He was not Dinorean but Adedri, Golran saw as he approached. Even the crisping of the fire couldn't hide all the differences in detail, in his uniform, in his madness. Now he lay twitching on the ground, already dead, the muscles thrashing in death throes, individually responding to the massive shock.

Someone thrust a shovel in Golran's hand and screamed an obscenity. He ran to where the dim roar of flame still engulfed a good portion of the base and began to dig, clearing ground.

"We're lucky for that rain," someone said near him. He hadn't thought about that. The grass wasn't quite dry enough for the fire to spread as rapidly as it might have.

He dug fire ditches for the rest of the morning and well into the afternoon, until the muscles in his back felt as if they were being torn open, until the light had changed from clear to gold. He didn't notice the time, the changes, or his own lack of breakfast and later lunch. There was only the fire, and the dirt and the pit that would keep them safe. When Golran finally allowed himself to collapse on the ground, the fire was burning low, consuming the last flammable material and feebly licking the edges of the pit.

"Vontreidi, is it true that you know the native language here?"

Golran opened his eyes, squinting in the glare. Teazerin YnSetti stood over him, clean and precise, not a speck on his white pants or perfectly tailored grey jacket. He couldn't remember seeing YnSetti on the fire lines earlier, although that meant nothing. There had been confusion, and a shower and clean clothes could have taken care of the rest. Golran swore to himself that he was not going to make rash judgments.

He heaved himself up on his elbows and nodded slowly.

"Then would you please report to the security office as soon as possible?" Teazerin asked, his tone just hinting at condescension. "After you've had a chance to clean up, of course."

Weighted by sheer exhaustion, Golran got to his feet and made his way back to quarters. He was aware of the fact that he smelled like smoke and was covered in filth, of the fact that he was hungry and could use a few hours' sleep more than a meal. He didn't have that luxury. He washed and changed mechanically, as he did when there was an early flight call, all the time wondering why YnSetti needed his very inadequate language abilities.

The security office was a single concrete shack, windowless and dark for all the jury-rigged lights. A scarred metal table surrounded by derelict chairs stood in the center. The table had been full of neatly piled folders and fax, now all cleared haphazardly to one side. At the other end sat a single prisoner, tied to a chair.

Teazerin stood over the native stiffly, not quite concealing a sneer. He whipped around when Golran entered the office.

"While you were off so valiantly fighting the fire," YnSetti began, "I had the perimeter shield lowered. We found this . . . person . . . behind a rock. He was in no condition to run, so I had him tranqued and brought back here. Unfortunately, it isn't quite possible for us to ascertain how he managed to breach the power fence, since we can't talk to him. If you would be so good . . . ?''

Golran gestured to YnSetti with his eyes, and the ensign moved into a shadowy corner. Golran took a seat next to the prisoner and studied him. Behind the pain, he could tell the man was young, although no child, and the prisoner's eyes snapped with challenge. Golran touched the necklace he wore, of bone and claws, which covered most of his throat and little else. The rest of his upper body was bare, and Golran rather doubted that this was some form of armor.

The prisoner watched him guardedly, and when Golran touched the necklace, the Cahaute said, ''Hasute.''

Golran blinked. Gaelian had told him about that once. He placed his hands on the table making a fence, wiggling his fingers rapidly to mime the energy. ''How?'' he asked, one of the words he still remembered. He didn't think he would understand the answer.

''Hasute,'' the man replied firmly, and then uttered a long string of sounds that Golran couldn't quite make out.

''Well?'' Teazerin asked.

''He says he's some kind of magician and opened the shield with magic,'' Golran said.

Teazerin came out of his corner and faced Golran directly. ''You may outrank me, commoner,'' he said. ''But I want this matter cleared up. You figure out how they're doing it.''

There was threat implicit in the words. Golran heard him as if he had never heard Teazerin before. ''Good,'' he replied evenly. ''Leave me alone here. And send in some food, will you. I think we're all hungry.''

Teazerin left, slamming the door, and Golran sighed with relief. There was no way he could communicate with the prisoner's hands tied. With the thin laser knife he usually carried, Golran freed the Cahaute's hands, although he left his legs bound to the chair.

First, Golran pointed to himself and said his name. The prisoner repeated it and then pointed to himself and said, ''Nyapetin.''

Golran nodded. They understood each other, at least this far. And this person, Nyapetin, was willing to try to communicate. They used hand signals, the few Cahaute words that

Golran knew, and when those weren't enough, the backs of
flimsy green fax and the orange security markers that had been
left in the shack.

Golran pointed to the necklace again and asked, "Hasute?"

Nyapetin nodded sharply and then looked around the shack
carefully, looked most closely at his still-bound legs. Then,
deliberately, he met Golran's eyes and held his gaze. Nyapetin
made a sharp chopping motion with the edge of his hand to his
neck and said something that Golran couldn't follow.

It didn't matter that he didn't understand the words. The
gesture and the defiance in the prisoner's face was enough.
Something about it stung him deeply, and he leaned back in
the chair and closed his eyes. He knew. Nyapetin didn't care
for their rules, had no interest in the Dinorean ideas of education or the benefits of the Protectorate. There were only the
dead nistora and those who would starve in the coming winter.
That, he had communicated clearly with line drawings and
pantomime. Nyapetin saw only invaders.

And Golran saw it too. For the first time, he felt completely
disoriented. Even this assignment, to report on the activities
here on Cahaute secretly, he had suspected. Now he knew,
clearly and precisely, that he was being used. The Board used
them all, Dinorean, Adedri, and now Cahaute.

All the assumptions that Golran's life was based on crum-
bled. They had no right to shun him because of his family
background, no right to shunt him aside and keep him from
the work he had earned through ability and determination.
Just as they had no right to kill the nistora, to starve the tribes
of Cahaute simply to make things easier for the Protectorate.

It was not the Protectorate altogether. It was only a few, the
Board, people like Teazerin YnSetti. Golran could sense a
larger force at work, an entire historical epoch opening, but he
couldn't see what had to be done or how it would come about.
He was a commoner, had only lived to fly and to make the
best place possible for himself. Suddenly, there was very much
more.

When he opened his eyes, he found Nyapetin gazing at him
with some deeper understanding, as if the other knew the
realization he had come to and the new comprehension in him.
Nyapetin held his expression steady and gestured between the
two of them. "Hasute," the tribesman said by way of explanation.

Well, thought Golran, if they could get through the shield by magic, this magician could certainly see the change in him. With gestures alone, Golran tried to explain his idea to the Cahaute. The other only smiled and nodded, and Golran was not sure he had understood correctly.

He didn't know how long it had been that he had been talking to Nyapetin. Without windows, it still felt like the middle of the night, and he had forgotten to put on his chronometer in his rush to change. His stomach was growling now, and his throat was dry. He used the WC, a primitive arrangement attached to the single office, and scooped the water in his hands to drink. There was nothing to put it in. Then he freed Nyapetin, keeping the laser knife ready in case the other didn't understand, and brought him to the facilities. The native didn't seem to know what to make of the plumbing arrangements, but when Golran showed him, Nyapetin expressed no surprise. The Cahaute even seemed at ease, calmly resuming his seat when he emerged.

Golran rapped sharply on the door. "Vontreidi here. I have the information now."

"Sorry, sir. Ensign YnSetti's orders are that I let no one out."

"What?" Golran screamed, rage tinged with shock. "This is Lieutenant Vontreidi, and I'm ordering you to open up *now*."

There was no response. Golran counted to fifteen, thinking that they had to get the key, that someone of higher rank would validate his order. He reached one hundred, and there was still nothing.

He rapped again. "Get the Commander," he barked through the thin metal.

"The Commander is not to be disturbed, sir. He has every confidence in Ensign YnSetti."

The Cahaute had not moved. The hasute's face showed sad comprehension, almost as if he had known from the first. It was all very, very simple. He went over to Nyapetin and clasped the other's hand firmly. Then he reached down for the laser knife, and his fingers brushed something hard.

The recorder, sealed to the Admiralty. He had not transferred his chronometer, but this thing, new to him, he had taken as if it were part of him. Slowly he smiled. They might accuse him of many things, but cowardice was not one of them. Now there would be no trouble in making the report.

"To the Admiralty department of Protectorate Development, Intelligence office, Lieutenant Vontreidi reporting. Situation nearing critical. Locals have some traditional magic that can be used to breach energy shield. Raiding is constant. Today, three quarters of supplies and approximately one quarter of the general area of this base destroyed by fire set in native raid.

"Reason for increased raiding is local Dinorean policy toward the natives, threatening their survival. This is in direct opposition to the Board and Admiralty position on the treatment of new Protected populations.

"Ensign Teazerin YnSetti is effectively in charge of this base. He is independently responsible for destroying a large herd of the beasts that comprise the major source of food for the locals. He is also holding me prisoner in the security office at this time.

"Recommend that YnSetti be immediately recalled and interrogated for practices here pending court martial. End. Vontreidi."

Golran tossed the recorder onto the table in plain sight. There was no way, short of Intelligence, that anyone was going to get that report. YnSetti should be smart enough to know that the recorder would alert Intelligence should it be destroyed and had a homing beam so that it couldn't be lost or hidden.

He pulled out the laser knife and gestured at Nyapetin. The other smiled at him broadly and gestured quickly. Golran shook his head, and Nyapetin began again, more slowly, making each movement very clear. Golran shook his head, barely able to believe his luck. As far as he could understand, Nyapetin was inviting him back to the tribe. Good enough. YnSetti was a more powerful enemy than he had given credit for, and there was little chance he would survive for long if he remained on the base.

One last time he knocked on the door. "Hey, can you at least tell me what time it is, or if it's morning or night or what?" he yelled, trying to sound upset.

"Second hour of the morning," the reply came. "No one will be up for hours. Why don't you go to sleep?"

The voice sounded tired as well. Golran thought he detected a hint of a yawn. He motioned to Nyapetin to be quiet, and he himself settled down. He would have to time this carefully. It would take awhile for the guard outside to go back to sleep, and there was no question but that their escape would wake him. Then he would have to get to the generator and close down the force shield.

As he thought about it, it didn't seem so difficult. It was the middle of the night, and most of the base would be asleep. The guard would be groggy, and it would be easy to knock him out with minimal noise. There should be a few people in the camp itself, but most of those awake should be around the perimeter. Of course, there would be someone on duty at the reactor, but one or even two should not be much trouble for Nyapetin and himself, especially with the element of surprise.

Or perhaps Nyapetin could open the field again. Golran grinned, thinking that he would like to see that. But Nyapetin had indicated that keeping the area open for so long, for all his people to enter and then leave again, had been what had drained him so completely. Otherwise, Golran thought to himself, he was not the kind of person who would normally be taken.

If he were caught with Nyapetin outside the security office, he was simply escorting the prisoner to a more secure area. He could hardly imagine that YnSetti would be so stupid as to announce to the entire base that he was under arrest.

It was only fear of Teazerin, Golran suspected, that kept most of them in line. As he waited, he remembered watching YnSetti play nerris at the homecoming game. There was something strange about him, about the fact that he was unscarred and untouched. That was rare in a nerris player. And about how he had smiled on winning, playing not for the team, but for himself alone. It seemed, as Golran reflected, that he had enjoyed the blood, enjoyed inflicting pain.

Golran winced at the memory. They were Dinorean, they were civilized. Teazerin YnSetti, for all he could trace his family through the generations, was some kind of aberration.

Golran heard a slight shift outside, tapped Nyapetin on the shoulder, and took out the laser knife. It was small and had a limited range, but it was enough to cut through the thin metal of the door. As long as no one saw him, as long as the guard stayed asleep long enough, he should be able to cut around the bolt and get them free. Sparks flew around the lock and landed on the concrete floor. The smell was nauseating.

"Hey, what . . ." came from the other side of the door.

Golran muttered a quick curse and kicked, barely hoping. It was enough. The door was thin enough, and he had cut enough. It swung violently open.

Nyapetin, who came out just behind him, jumped the guard from behind. Even without a weapon, the Cahaute landed heavy enough blows that the single sentry doubled over and then slumped to the ground after a strike to the back of his head.

Golran motioned to Nyapetin, straightened up, and took the thin chain that had been around Nyapetin's wrists. He looped the chain so that the Cahaute would appear bound, then took the long trailing end himself. He did this quickly in the dark, but even so he could see the Cahaute's smile for a brief second. Nyapetin understood and was willing to play along.

He led Nyapetin in the direction of the reactor, hoping to shut off the fence. Much as he wanted to run, he kept both his pace and his breathing steady. This had to look like a prisoner transfer, like it was fully authorized and no one need question them.

"Just where do you think you're going?" a silky voice asked from behind.

"Transferring the prisoner," Golran replied evenly, turning to see who had asked. He tried to move as if unconcerned, not too hurried, not afraid.

"I don't remember giving any such order."

Golran faced the speaker. In the drizzle of moonlight stood Teazerin YnSetti, a powerful laser gun resting lightly at ready in his hands.

"I think you're helping the prisoner to escape, commoner," YnSetti said, tapping the barrel of the gun gently against his palm. "That's treason, Vontreidi. I'd be perfectly within regs to fry both of you."

He flashed Nyapetin a look, so quickly that he hoped the Cahaute had caught it in the dark. Then the two separated, running to opposite sides.

Golran saw the movement of YnSetti's hands, the blazing violet light, smelled flesh as Nyapetin was cut almost nearly in two. He was aware of laughter and then the pain.

As Golran Vontreidi crumpled in the dark, the last thing he knew was astonishment that it was all going to end like this.

• • •

It was near evening when the raiders returned to the lodges of the people. Gaelian stood with the rest, hooting cries of victory as the first warriors appeared, dancing into the center of the camp. One by one, painted and whooping, they danced the dodging through the shield, the fire, and their escape.

At first Gaelian was pleased. But as she watched them dance, counting each on his return, she knew one was missing, knew who it was by the paint, by the absence of his face. According to the traditions of the people, her escape into the night with Nyapetin, their bathing in the river, made her a wife. Someone would tell her.

Tyakral came over and stood at her side, not touching. "If he were dead," her foster mother said in an undertone, "they would not be dancing."

One came to stand in front of her. By the paint he wore and the lance he carried, tipped with a green jasper point and festooned with brilliant feathers, she knew he had been the leader of this raid.

"Nyapetin was weak from walking with the spirits. He told us to leave him in a particular grove, a spirit place, to rest with the power. It will make him strong, to speak to snake and Mountain. We left one of the water boys to fetch and carry for him, but do not be concerned. The child understands that the b'hasute must not be disturbed."

It was wrong, she thought. There was something essential that was missing, somewhere lost, a wholeness that was not made by the balance of the two, Dinorean and Cahaute. They were of the same circle, family lost and found again, the same and opposite. Of the same circle, but where was the center, which should be everywhere? Where was the center?

With a stick, she drew the circle and point in the ashes of the dead fire. She stared at it and then closed her eyes. In the earth itself, she could feel no wholeness, as if she were missing a part, the part that she needed to make the whole thing clear.

Ridra had said it. They were one people, all of them, a single whole. It was Ridra, those who were children of Anoni, who were the center. But that was not enough.

Lost in her thoughts, Gaelian had not noticed that the noise of the celebration had stopped. There was a scratch at the lodge flap, and she sprang up to open it. The person who waited for her was only a small boy.

"Hasute," he began hesitantly. "I was told to wait with Nyapetin while he rested after the raid. I know nothing of the raid, since I stayed with the other boys near the chatoya to keep them and get water. After the raid, I stayed in the glade with the b'hasute. He told me to go and get water. He told me that he needed to speak to his snake brother, and so I should stay away from him. I got water from the stream, and when I came back I stayed in the brush near the clearing.

"The b'hasute lay very still. If I did not know he was speaking to the snake brother, I would have thought that he was dead. So I knew to stay away and hold the water until he had finished and wanted me.

"While he was walking the spirit world, two of the short-hairs came and carried off his body. I do not know if his spirit knew, since he did not return. I hid and waited, and when they were gone I came to tell the elders. They told me to come and tell you myself what my own eyes saw."

The boy could not be more than nine or ten, Gaelian thought, but he sat quietly with the dignity of one far older. She knew he was waiting to be dismissed, not because she was his elder but because she was hasute and he *recognized* her.

Keeping her mind off the information for the moment, she rummaged through the travel bags for some gift. There was very little. She found Nyapetin's arrows and gave the boy the entire quiver. "Thank you for bringing me this news," she said.

He accepted the gift and left without another word. Then it hit her. They had captured Nyapetin, taken him to the Din-orean base. She sat on the robe again and moaned low in her throat, rocking back and forth. There was nothing she could do for him, no way to reach him, to help him. And then she remembered the hasute necklace.

She was hasute. In dancing the storm, she had learned that she was one in truth and not just honor. But there was one hasute step she had not taken, one that would release the power and perhaps give some indication of how she could free Nyapetin. She was frightened. To taste edonys was the final step, the final opening to what she was born to be. Gaelian thought about Iesin, about her time in the Academy, about Dobrin. And she thought about flying, how she had merged perfectly with the machine and the very physicality of the power had saved her. It was not that she had flown, no, it was that she had manipulated atmosphere and space and the power of the thing itself. With edonys, she would no longer simply manipulate it, she would *be* it, her skin no longer confining her being. And it would change her forever.

Then she looked down at her hands, at the leather gown that covered her lap. She had already been changed forever.

Cautiously, walking behind the lodges, Gaelian went to Tyakral's place. She scratched lightly on the flap, and Tyakral appeared. Her foster mother did not seem surprised.

"What can I do for you?" Tyakral asked.

"Edonys," Gaelian said before she knew the word had been spoken.

Tyakral nodded and disappeared into the lodge. Gaelian waited outside, shivering slightly from no cool breath of air. She remembered when Tyakral had taken edonys, when Gaelian was very young. Tyakral had looked dead, and then she had spoken in a voice too low for a woman, too broad for a man. It was a spirit voice, a thing made by the power in the woman herself, in the very pattern of her genes, if Ridra was right. And now Gaelian had no question about that.

Tyakral appeared at the flap of her lodge again, a bowl in her hands. She raised the bowl and handed it to Gaelian without words, with reverence. Gaelian took the bowl in both hands and lowered it before her. In the darkness, the liquid had a solid aspect, reflecting darkness, reminding her of the river the night before.

She returned to the empty lodge that was now her own. It was an act of courage to drink the viscous drug, to force herself to take the whole bowl, to open the secure doors to the other parts of her mind that knew things she was afraid to know. The taste was bitter and made her gag slightly. When every drop had been drained, she dropped back against the robe on the ground and let the drug, which was a door within herself, take her.

It was not a place or a thing she knew at first, but a far distant sound, the melody of a flute as she had heard Nyapetin play on her return to the people. The music wove around her, penetrating deep within her. She could only permit it. One did not fight edonys.

There was a shattering, and knowledge flooded her. Not

visions, but abstract proofs, elegant and clear like blades of ice, like fragments of a broken mirror merging and becoming whole again.

Ridra had been right, but Ridra had not known all of it. Gaelian was amazed that she could think so clearly, as if the drug had torn away all resistance and thought flowed free and abandoned like River, solid like Mountain, through her. Nomis had known the answers, had let her go free. They were all parts to the whole. As in nerris, the mimic of the universe, perfect in every aspect, she saw the players of the game.

Nerris. Four players. Three places she knew, and one was veiled in the past. That fourth place, and the why of the experiment, was perfectly simple. They were no more. Anoni must have known, must have set up the experiment as a veil, a way to keep the species alive without threatening those who did not believe. And he had made sure that those who did survive had what they needed, abilities that would permit them to rebuild the people, stronger and greater than they had been before. Now, there was no experiment anymore. The black wall, the source of all, was opaque.

So Nomis had let her go, with full knowledge that she was the first of what would follow—that she would somehow have to make the whole, cahaute, the circle complete. The skills of Dinoreos guided by the power channels of Cahaute together as a single entity would be invincible. And Nomis knew.

It was for the people to survive.

Then, within the edonys vision, she saw Golran and Nya-petin, sitting opposite each other across a metal table in a dark room. She was surprised. She had thought that Golran was still in Adedri. And then she shook the emotion from her and observed them together, talking with their hands as the people of the tribes sometimes did. It was slow, but she could see the understanding flowing like a bright silver stream between the two of them. Then, as she watched further, she saw Golran rise. He said something, but within the edonys vision she could not hear it. He shook the door. Both, then, were prisoners.

The vision faded. Suddenly, everything was very easy. Gaelian felt calm, sure, and relaxed. There was something she had to do, something that Nomis had sent her to do. And it wasn't difficult, as long as she permitted both of her selves to come together. It was keeping them apart for so long that had been trouble. Now the two, the Dinorean and the Cahaute, merged with the knowledge, like Golran and Nyapetin with the silver mist flowing between them.

When she rose from the edonys trance, it was midmorning. She went from her lodge to the place of the elders and to the place where the warrior and hunter moieties had their leaders. They must hear her, *recognize* her. She had become b'hasute, one who knew, who kept the circle and saw the center.

"We must go to the short-hair camp and raid again," she said simply. "But we will not raid as before. We will take captives, as from the other tribes. Then we must control part of their camp and call their elders. I saw it in the edonys."

"And revenge?" one of the leaders of a warrior society asked her. "Don't they deserve revenge, those who will die during the white time, which is coming upon us? For the nistora?"

There were shouts of agreement. Gaelian stood with her eyes on the ground. Then, as the group became quiet, she raised her eyes and looked at them. And they *recognized* her. They saw what she was, saw the edonys in her. She was the one who walked with the Power Clan.

"That will be resolved," she said softly. "For now, the first thing is to talk to their elders. Today, I will go and look at this place. I will find the b'hasute who can open their fire shield. Tonight I will return, and you will know."

She turned and left without looking back. There was no reason to do so. They would come and tell her their decision.

She bundled together the things she would need, a water bag, an obsidian knife, the last strip of hard, fat-preserved meat. Then she walked boldly through the center of the camp and down the first part of the trail.

They came after her. She could hear them, not with her ears but with her breath, with the warmth that prickled the skin on her back. Many followed, and they were armed, but they didn't want her to know. She was b'hasute, as Nyapetin had known a very long time in the past.

She walked easily, briskly, pleased at the feel of movement in the daylight. There were armed men behind her, and there were enemies ahead, but she felt no fear. She only knew that she must do one thing, and it would not be difficult. Nyapetin would help her, and there would be others. There would be Dinoreans who would understand, Iesin and Golran, the Yn-Oestal and Dobrin. So it was a good walk. She had water and strong shoes, made from two thicknesses of nistora hide, one that had been boiled for strength.

She had started in the morning, and it was near evening when she approached the area of the Dinorean base. The edonys vision had not been an allegory, had not been something drawn from her own mind to teach her. It had been fact. Fear ran through her. She turned back up the path and moved carefully, crouched so that the low branches would cover her. Cautiously, she crept forward until she could see the Dinorean base across the expanse of grass.

The energy shield caused a slight distortion at first, until she became used to it. Then she peered more carefully. Mostly, it was like she remembered things of Dinoreos. The white concrete, the heavy dome of the reactor set well aside, the heart of the compound, and the seared places that were the only marks of the most recent raid. That she had expected.

There were too many people, though, all walking around as if without purpose, not looking out to the trees. They came and stared and moved away, and another group moved forward.

Gaelian looked where they looked. It was something she had never seen in a Dinorean enclave before. There were two large poles set apart, carried by people in enlisted uniforms. They carried the poles around, through the ruler-straight grass streets between the buildings, and then brought them forward, as if bringing them directly to her. Just inside the energy fence, the poles were planted facing outward. There was something on the tops.

Gaelian motioned with her hand, to let those who followed know that she was aware of their presence and that they should remain concealed. Then she stepped out from her cover and walked slowly over the grass, her arms spread from her sides, her eyes on the poles.

As she came closer, her sight became more clear. And then she saw, and she howled, the long ululating cry of the tribes. On the poles were heads, and even behind the greyness and sagging of death she recognized Golran Vontreidi and Nya-petin.

Fury ruled her. There was no longer any recognition, no place for pain. Anger ripped through the sky, through the land, and as she was angry, so were they, responding to her call.

Gaelian began to dance. The movement was only the mimic of other movements, gathering around, waiting, her army greater than any she had known—the forces of being that responded to her anger, energy that responded to the direction of something that organized itself. She danced. In her there was only a place for destruction, for revenge. She wanted only to raze those who had done this thing.

The evening grew suddenly dark, and a chilly wind whipped the long grass on the plain. Power grew around her as she embraced the forces that came to her summoning. It was something in her; she had done this before; her very being was made for this one dance. And so she danced.

She felt the rumble above her, tense and awaiting the command to strike. She stood still then, looking over the Dinorean base, and smiled slowly, without humor.

The power she must use, the storm itself, had to find the key place, the weak link. The reactor. Plasma fields were unstable when influenced by enough electromagnetic energy. And what else was the fire-from-the-sky, the lightning she directed? They were shielded deeply but only against what was reasonable. The direction of that much lightning at a single time was not reasonable. It was barely within the realm of possibility. And so, she became the clouds and rode them. The lightning that was in her, that was the anger of her being, that was all the years and her grandmother and Dobrin, that was Golran and Nyapetin and the Academy and Teazerin, all of it came together. Bolt after bolt, so rapid that there was barely a pause, hit the white dome.

She was of it, with it, waiting for the tremor of reaction. There was none. And then there was a sudden absence, and she felt it in the energy that surrounded her far more than in her sight. The screens were down. The lights on the Dinorean base no longer functioned.

Arrows went by. Still, and again, she unleashed the storm, and still there was nothing, only the heavy drops of rain like drumbeats pounding the earth. She was only Gaelian again.

Before her was a tangled melee, Cahaute and Dinorean entwined. The Dinorean weapons, laser guns and knives, had greater range than arrows or lances, spears or clubs. But they had to be aimed, and the first volley of arrows had struck many of the defenders. She ran through the thick of it, heading to the reactor to see what had gone wrong.

The place was unlocked. At the controls sat Teazerin Yn-Setti, panting, his fingers trembling as he raised his hands from the control keys. She knew he had shut down the reactor. All the boards were black. Opaque. Black was no longer in the game.

The obsidian knife was in her hand, and without a sound she moved forward and quickly pulled back his head and pressed the sharp, chipped edge against his throat.

"This time, I've got the sharp end of the stick," she said softly in Dinorean. She cut him lightly, just enough to make the blood run. She released his head and went for the gun he wore at his side.

She was Cahaute, she was quicker than he had ever given her credit for. She knew that, as she knew he had never really understood how she played nerris. She had learned more of him on that court than he of her.

With the laser gun, she was in a better position than with the knife. She held it on him.

"Now, go out there and order your troops to surrender," she told him. "And then we, you and I, will send a transmission to the Admiralty. There are a few people who ought to be here as quickly as possible."

"You're insane," he said. "Give me the gun." He began to move toward her slowly.

Gaelian fired at his knee, and he fell howling onto the concrete floor.

"I know you've got auxiliary power here somewhere," she said, her hands searching over the varicolored buttons, dismissing the majority of them. "Now you will give the order. And you'll inform Iesin YnOestal that I need her, and Nomis and Ridra from the Temple of Adedri, and my cousin Dobrin as well for the Board. That should be about right."

He looked up at her miserably and nodded. Keeping the gun trained on him, she dragged him over to the seat and watched as he brought up the old-style generator and began to talk. She kept the gun aimed at his head while he ordered the Dinoreans to surrender. From behind him, Gaelian clipped out phrases in Cahaute, telling the tribe they had won.

She could hear the noise outside abate, but she did not move from her guard of Teazerin. Gazing down the stub barrel of the sidearm, she wondered if she should simply kill him now, the same way he had killed Golran and Nyapetin.

"You don't want to kill me, Gaelian," YnSetti said, his tone tinged with arrogance even now. "You're civilized. Civilized people don't kill unarmed prisoners."

She didn't lower the weapon. Civilized? What was civilized? Only one thing was sure. If she simply executed Teazerin Yn-Setti, she would be eliminating a nuisance as she would an insect that annoyed her, and there were better uses for him.

No Dinorean Ot-tan had ever been tried and convicted of a major crime against non-Dinoreans, Gaelian remembered. If she could find strong enough evidence, Teazerin YnSetti would be the first. He was not civilized, but most of Dinoreos was. Genocide by destroying a major food source and the cold-blooded murders of a fellow officer and an unarmed prisoner were each capital offenses. To let Dinoreos deal with him, though, to force their own civilized standards on them, that would be an historical lesson.

She called two leaders of the war moieties to tie Teazerin up and guard him and explained that his own elders would judge him. Neither spoke to her, and she left them with their prisoner.

Alone, Gaelian walked through the base. Her hair was dripping with the rain and, for some reason she could not name, the small shack on the edge of the work area seemed familiar. She entered it and recoiled. It was the place she'd seen in the edonys dream, the battered table, the chair with some links of chain still attached to the leg, the gloom. Slowly she went and sat facing the door, put her elbows on the table, and rested her head in her hands. She felt overwhelmed by what had happened, and there was still more to do. She blinked as her eyes became accustomed to the dark.

Then she saw the recorder on the table. She reached for it, and as she closed her fingers around it, she realized it was heavier than regulation issue. Curious, she looked more carefully, trying to switch on whatever had been left inside. It was frozen. Only Intelligence used things like that, she thought, and it made her wonder. Golran and Nyapetin had been the last people in this shack, she was certain of it. The edonys vision had been no image drawn from her subconscious mind. It had been true. She wondered who had left the recorder there, if it had been Teazerin or Golran or some other person.

It became darker as a figure filled the doorway, blocking the light. "Please let me have that," he said in broken Cahaute.

Her hand was immediately on the gun she had taken from
YnSetti, but she kept it under the table. "Who are you, and
why do you ask?" she asked harshly in Dinorean. She could
not see his reaction to her use of the language because of the
back lighting. "Come here and sit down," she ordered, Ot-tan
and officer emerging without conscious direction. "Information."

"There were two of us assigned here," AnAserin began
slowly, his eyes shifting from the table to the wall beyond her
to his feet. "One of them is dead. He left that recorder. I just
wanted to pick it up, send it where it's supposed to go."

"Why were you assigned, and who was the other?" Gaelian
demanded.

"The other was Golran Vontreidi," AnAserin said. "And
why? I don't know. Only that we were supposed to observe
and report. Perhaps Lieutenant Vontreidi knew more. He was
Dinorean."

Gaelian thought about this. The recorder had been left by
Golran, then. Perhaps it contained evidence that would be
useful in convicting YnSetti.

Gaelian smiled a little in the dark. For the kind of public
court martial she wanted, she would need an Ot-tan ready to
testify. She asked AnAserin casually if there were any Ot-tan
who had disagreed with YnSetti, and she was pleased that he
told her about Abs YnLodri. YnLodri was perfect, an impec-
cable source and yet of a family not quite important enough
for him to stand up to YnSetti alone. Abs would be punished
only lightly for his inability to stop Teazerin, if at all.

"I think I'll keep this," Gaelian said, tossing the recorder
lightly in her hand. "I'll turn it over to the authorities, who
are on their way here. This base is being controlled by the
tribes, by the way. Knowing them, as long as you don't touch
anything that might be a weapon and behave yourself, there
shouldn't be any trouble." She waved her hand, dismissing
him.

It was not a terribly long walk back to the camp. No one
talked to her on the base or the path, and she was just as glad.
She was too tired to engage in any conversation. For a moment, she was tempted just to lie down under a tree and sleep,
but it would be better to return home.

It was well after dark when she arrived. In the firelight, she
made her way to Tyakral's lodge. Around her there were

people, those who were not members of the warrior moieties who had stayed to secure the base. But they did not turn to speak to her, to offer her some stew from their fires. She found Tyakral's lodge and scratched on the flap.

Tyakral opened the lodge flap. When she saw Gaelian, she turned away and let the flap drop without saying a word. Gaelian had no strength to move. She huddled up outside the lodge and began to sob softly. She didn't know why Tyakral wouldn't say a word to her, wouldn't invite her in. Then she heard some words inside the lodge.

"There is a spirit walker outside," she heard Tyakral's voice. "Go and put this bowl of stew outside the flap. But don't speak to a spirit walker, even if it looks like a person you know. Or you will become part of the spirit world, and we will not be able to see you again."

Gaelian moved deep into the shadows and watched as a child put out a bowl of stew. She understood now. She had been hasute, one who walked both worlds. Now she had danced the great fire. She had become one with Fire and with Yenhica, she belonged only to the Power Clan, not to the people any longer. She had become sacred, too close to power things that day, and so she was now taboo. To see her was to see the spirit world, to talk to her was to talk to the Power Clan. Even a b'hasute would not do that in the flesh. And so, among the tribe no one would see her or speak to her. To them she had gone wholly into the realm of spirit.

She took the bowl of stew and made her way slowly to Nya-petin's lodge. There she sat alone, cut off from the people forever. Now there was nothing but silence, interrupted only by the gentle splash of rain.

"The case against Teazerin is airtight," Iesin said. "Abs YnLodri was about ready to pay his own way to the Judge Advocate's office just for the chance to testify."

Gaelian just nodded. She was glad to know that, but it seemed very distant just now. Iesin, Dobrin, the Adedri, and several lower-ranking officials had been on Cahaute for only two days. Yesterday, with the court martial promised and negotiated for Teazerin YnSetti, he had been turned over to the Dinoreans. Gaelian thought back to that meeting, to Ridra interpreting the terms between Dobrin and Hinacen. Her cousin spoke for the Board, and she was not surprised that

Hinacen had been chosen to speak for the people.

She had tried to greet Hinacen, thinking that the old b'hasute at least would see her. He had acted as if she weren't there.

She and Iesin walked across the blackened patches of seared grass. They reached the admin center early, but Dobrin was already there. He stopped them both and then accompanied them into the meeting room.

"Gaelian," Dobrin began softly, "this isn't a formal meeting yet. But I speak for the Board alone. They've given me the power in this situation. Let's work it out between the two of us, with Ie telling us what's realistic." Dobrin looked at her carefully and then down. His face was relaxed and steady. "I've always treated you honorably, Gae. There are some things I can do and some I can't."

He was right, she thought. He had always treated her honorably, and even well. There was something she trusted about him, as there was about Iesin. "You've talked to Nomis, I take it," she said.

Dobrin nodded. "They're sending a few of the original papers to Dinoreos. The Board isn't going to like this, but I think I can manage. With Teazerin's court martial, the Yn-Setti's influence will be wiped out. And we've got Kaes Yn-Arretl as well as the YnOestal, even though Kaes is going along more because he knows where the power lies than because he's ever thought about anything in his life. The Yn-Lodri aren't on the Board, but they have media shares, and with Abs involved they'll make sure the story is spread. Nomis said it's necessary for us to reintegrate the entire population soon. That's going to be difficult."

"It has to be done," Gaelian said softly. "Ask my father. He's always known. Look at both peoples. The Ot-tan have the greatest concentration of the Dinorean engineered skills, the hasute the greatest of the Cahaute. With a mix of the two, there would be no end to the things we could do. And while the Adedri weren't engineered, they were chosen as the experimenters. They were all originally scholars, and even we know that the few Adedri students who go to our universities are invariably the best. If we all go on looking out for only our own interests, we'll destroy each other. Look at this base. Dinorean weapons against Cahaute hasute, who don't carry laser guns because they don't need them. It's a stalemate, every time. We don't have a choice."

"It will take time," Dobrin said slowly. "I'll do the best I can, and the Board will back it. That's all I can promise."

"That's all I can ask," Gaelian said.

"But what about you, Gae?" Iesin asked, concerned. "You're the symbol of this whole thing, you're the one who was first, who's lived it. What are you going to do?"

"Do you really think I can go back?" Gaelian asked. "I'd be confined to the household with only you or Dobrin to talk to, a celebrity trotted out on public occasions. In a generation or two, there'll be a place for people like me, but right now there's no place I can go. I've done all that I can do. It's up to you and Dobrin now. If I returned to Dinoreos, I'd be as much taboo as I am among the tribes."

"You've played well," Iesin said.

"But the game is over," Gaelian replied. "And it is a good day to die."

She got up and left the admin center, left Iesin and Dobrin waiting for the Adedri and the Cahaute and all their aides and assistants to make her vision a reality. She left the Dinorean base and walked down the path. This time she did not need a knife or water. This time no one followed her. No one would dare.

She walked for several days without quite knowing where she had to go. She had not thought of a goal, only that she wanted to be away, for everything to stop. There were few sitting foods, but she was not aware of hunger. River and a few small springs served for water as she made her way from the grasslands and into the hills. The forest became thicker, and the ground started to slope upward.

Then she saw the Dead Hill. She had made no conscious decision to go there. It arose as if it had a will of its own, as if it had come for her.

She looked to the top. The shuttle she had left still sat there, patient, waiting. She smiled. It was right. All things came to center.

There was a faint melody resting lightly on the breeze, a melody she remembered from some other time. She climbed the steep hill, going from ledge to handhold freely, abandoning herself to the place that had called her.

The top of the hill was crowded with the flying thing sitting there. She knew what it was, that it had been hers at one time.

Now it puzzled her. She got inside, her body remembering easy movements when she was not sure what drove her. She looked at the gauges. Imperceptibly, she nodded. She had been brought here for a reason she could understand. There was almost no fuel left. That was not important. She didn't need much fuel to reach her destination.

Under her guiding fingers, the shuttle coughed and heaved itself, protesting, skyward. She smiled as she turned the small craft into the glare of the sun, away from the hill. She was pleased when the shuttle cleared the hill and when the fuel gauge dropped suddenly because even the fumes were gone.

The hill was no different than it had ever been. The polished black rock was without a sign or scar. The melody of the flute wrapped around her, free. Light, free, she climbed once again.

The light was exceptionally clear and fine now. She looked across the hill, and now there was a difference. On the far edge sat two figures. One looked at her and beckoned with his hand. She recognized them, but they were not as they had been. Currents shimmered unseen under the snake-painted skin of one, under the carefully cut uniform with the polished starbursts of the other. She went and sat with them, no longer of the people but of the spirit world and the place of the gods. For if Anoni could become a god, why couldn't they?

Nyapetin smiled and laid the flute aside, but the music did not stop. The music was him, was the being that wore his shape.

Golran stood and smiled down at her. Then he arched his back and the russet of his jacket and hair shimmered as he dropped over the ledge.

Gaelian felt the music enter her, and she reached out with it to a great, russet warrior-bird, a god spirit that dove and rose and wheeled on the thermals.

IESIN YNOESTAL LEANED back in the library of the YnTourne house and closed her eyes. It had been a long day, but a good one. She and Dobrin had worked together for it for fifty-seven years now, and she felt every day of it. But today had been the final victory. Her place and Dobrin's had been assured in the history texts, he as the major mover on the Board and she as the Admiralty Coordinator and Prime Negotiator. Now it was done.

This morning, Ridra, High Priestess of the Temple of Adedri, and four Cahaute elders had taken their seats on the Board, the final change. It was a different Board than the one her mother had sat on. Not only were there Ot-tan of the important industrial households, but Li-tan, Sonna-tan, and even two commoner-client representatives. All of them, including the Cahaute elders and Ridra, had votes.

After the meeting, the first with the entire Protectorate represented, there had been a formal reception. Her granddaughter, eldest of the eldest of the YnTourne, had managed to come down from the Academy on personal leave. After all, her Dinorean grandparents were celebrating the installation of her Cahaute grandparents. Iesin was pleased.

After that, there had been a game of nerris. It was not like the nerris she remembered from her own school days. The sharp end of the stick was slightly blunted now. There was no blood in nerris anymore. After all, they were civilized.

219